A Family of Their Own

ALSO BY MALCOLM O. VARNER

Looking Beyond the Storm: Selections of Poetry

Creating Positive Ripples: 100 Messages of Encouragement

Looking Beyond the Storm: Now the Rainbow is Out

Cotton Candy Coated Chocolate Kisses: Black Gay Love Poems

A Family of Their Own

Malcolm O. Varner

A Family of Their Own

Book cover design by Mark Wilson.
ISBN 9781702753746

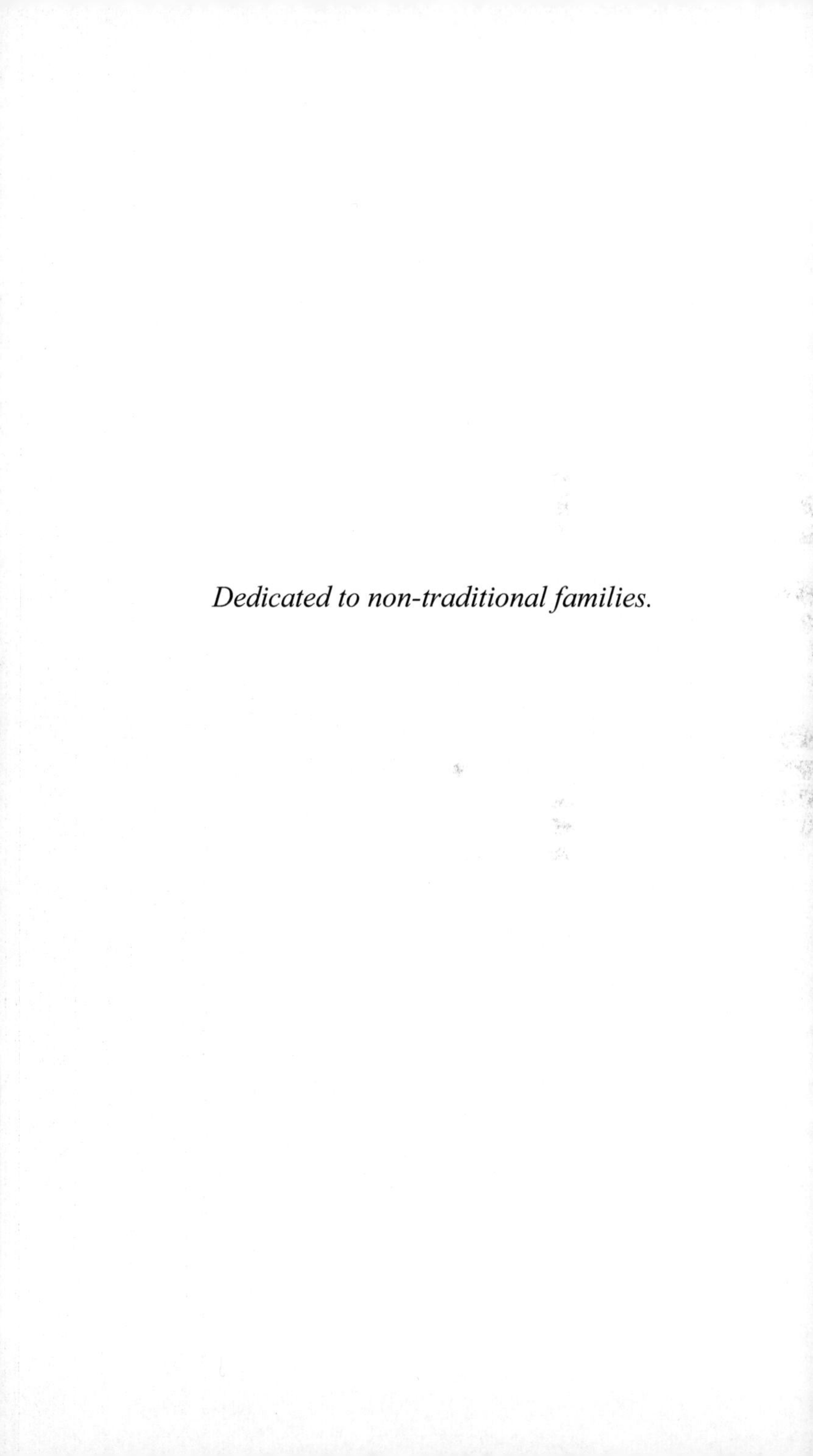

Dedicated to non-traditional families.

ACKNOWLEDGMENTS

To God, who has consistently opened seemingly impossible doors, I'm forever grateful for so many continued blessings. I appreciate the artistic voice buried within me, which I'm continually learning to unleash through the power of words. May this first novel be the tip of the iceberg.

Where would any of us be without family – immediate, extended, blood, or the family we build for ourselves by virtue of friendship? Without mine, I would surely be lost. This book was written in honor of my departed grandma, Ellen Varner, who taught me how to fight and never give up. She made all my achievements in life possible. I miss her dearly. As for my Aunt Donna, what a beautiful butterfly she's become since emerging from her cocoon! Our phone conversations over this past year, to use a popular idiom, have *given me life*. Credit is also due to my Uncle Man, who, through his music and self-defense work, has shown me what it means to pursue one's dreams. He's made me one proud nephew through his own example of walking in his purpose.

And then there's John and Eunice Ravenna…What more can I ask for? As friends, mentors, and family, they've had my back unconditionally since I was a fifteen-year-old high school student whose purview of the world was limited to my inner-city neighborhood, Over-the-

Rhine. It's such an honor to have people like them in my life, and for that I'm immensely blessed.

Next, there's something special about surrounding yourself with like-minded individuals who share similar experiences, aspirations, and feelings. Serving in this capacity, the Grove City Writers' Group has been a central and steadfast motivating source for me in the progression of this book. I appreciate all my exceptional peers from this body of scribes for welcoming me into the fold. On a related note, I'm deeply grateful to my editors, Diane Kinser and Jake Magnum, for their tremendous input in helping me shape and bring this work to life. Their engagement in the latter stages was priceless!

I owe a special thanks to five gentlemen who have never given up on me: Michael Sering, Jae Denson, Dwayne Steward, Sidney Brown, and Steven Knight. Each of them, in his own unique way, has shown unwavering belief in my potential and gifts. Their undying support has encouraged me to keep my eyes fixed on the prize, as church folk would say, rather than my own fears and doubt.

Finally, I started this book back in 2016; however, it wasn't until the first half of 2019 that I decided to complete the second chapter and resume this undertaking. Without my husband, Anthony Brown, by my side, this book might not have been completed. I'm profoundly thankful for his support.

A Family of Their Own

Chapter 1

It was 2:18 a.m. on Monday morning, and Max Webber couldn't sleep. He lay in bed shirtless on this humid August morning thinking about the circumstances that both he and Brian faced. In less than six hours he would be starting his new role as dean of arts and sciences at Greater Cleveland Community College. Max reached for the two plush pillows on his partner's side of the bed and wrapped his arms around them as he wished that Brian was there next to him. The scent of teakwood lotion was the closest Max would be to him over the next week, given that Brian had left the previous evening for a conference in San Francisco. Inhaling the unmistakable trace of Brian's body lotion, Max decided to give him a call. He picked up his cell phone and dialed his husband. There was no answer. Not wanting to worry Brian in case he had already called it an early night, Max decided against leaving a voicemail message.

Fifteen minutes later the pillows Max held tightly were beginning to lose the cool sensation they provided when he initially clutched them. As his thoughts drifted to his new position and increased responsibilities, his phone beeped. Max picked up his cell again from his nightstand and read the incoming text message: "Hey, baby. Just got out of the shower. What's up?"

Max smiled to himself and replied, “Thanks for the mental image of you standing in your towel. Anyway, I can’t seem to sleep.”

Within seconds Max’s phone started ringing. It was Brian. “What’s going on, Max?”

“Ever since I got into bed a few hours ago, my mind’s been racing. There’s been so much going on lately, from Mom’s passing to this new job. Maybe the weight of everything is starting to sink in.”

“Yeah, a lot has happened in our lives over the past few months,” admitted Brian. “Is there anything that you need to talk about? I may be in San Francisco, but I can still listen.” Max carefully thought about his question for a little while before replying.

“No,” he said. “I guess I just wanted to hear your voice more than anything. Everything will be all right.”

“Yes, it will, baby. You know she’s proud of you, right?” Brian asked. Max smiled to himself and thought about his mother, to whom Brian was referring.

“Yes, I know that she’s proud of all of us. It hurts that I can’t just pick up the phone to give her a call.”

“That must be tough since you two talked nearly every day,” said Brian. “You were blessed to have such a close relationship with her. Just know that you have me, your sister, and our friends to support you. We're here for you."

"Thanks, babe. I really do love you."

"And I love you, too."

"Okay," continued Max. "I hope the conference goes well tomorrow. I can't wait to hear about your first day and presentation on Thursday."

Brian, who was in California to attend a national LGBTQ conference focused on people of color and mental health, gave a hearty laugh over the phone. "Please don't remind me, but thanks, Max. You should try to get some sleep and know that everything's going to work out in your new role. President Nelson wouldn't have chosen you for the position if he doubted your capability."

"You're right, babe. I'll talk to you tomorrow. Have a good night."

"Sweet dreams, Max."

Max returned his phone to the nightstand next to him. He thought about how fortunate he was to have found Brian, especially in northeast Ohio. Very few cities in the Midwest were gay-friendly, and Cleveland was no exception. Nevertheless, he and Brian had built a comfortable life together over the past five years that neither of them had previously believed was possible. During their five years together, they had weathered Brian completing his PhD courses, career transitions, the loss of a mutual friend to AIDS, and most recently, the passing of Max's mother three months ago. She suffered a stroke at her job, and unfortunately, the responding medical staff could not save her. Max was devastated to learn of her passing from his sister, Sandra, when she called on the fourth Monday of May to provide the unexpected news.

Next to Brian, Betty Strong was Max's best friend. She taught him the virtues of working hard, respecting everyone he encountered, pursuing education, and loving himself and others unconditionally. Furthermore, she had treated Brian like he was her own son since the first day she met him. *In many ways*, Max thought, *she was more of a maternal figure to Brian than his own mother*.

Stretched out on his side of the bed, Max began thinking about the last time they had dinner with her. She had been invited by Brian to their apartment on the Sunday after Mother's Day to celebrate the news of Max's new position. The three of them enjoyed a soulful meal that Brian had prepared. That evening, Betty informed Max of how proud she was of everything that he had accomplished in life. For his new office, she gifted him a pair of marble bookends made up of the letters 'M' and 'B,' referencing his and Brian's initials. Reflecting on this event, Max finally felt more at ease and eventually fell asleep with Brian's pillows tucked in between his arms.

****

The desk phone rang in Max's office. "Hello," he responded.

"Hi, Mr. Webber, dean of arts and sciences," said an enthusiastic voice. "How's the new job?"

"Hey, Sandra!" Max greeted his oldest sister after recognizing the familiar voice. "Our student enrollment is up by ten percent, so the first day of the semester seems busier than usual. It does feel awkward, though, not being in the student advising department. That's a mental adjustment I'll have to make over time. I already miss my old staff, but things are decent in my new role so far. My new staff prepared a welcome breakfast in my honor this morning, but enough about me. How are you and the family?"

"We're all doing fine. Kevin was recently hired full-time at our church as the assistant pastor, so you know I can't tell him anything since he's no longer a deacon. Now Junior, on the other hand, he talks nonstop about this girl he likes. They attend the same school, but she's in a different sixth-grade class. He hasn't spoken to her yet according to him, but he watches her all the time during recess and band practice. This is his first actual crush. Kevin's supposedly working with him on his approach, but so far, Junior hasn't budged."

"Sounds like his father to me," said Max, eager to hear his sister's response.

"Oh, hush, Max. You know Kevin is a good man. How's Brian?"

"I never said he was a bad guy. He just has

roaming eyes. That's all I'm saying, Sandra. Just make sure Junior doesn't creep the girl out with all that staring!" Max teased. "Anyway," he continued, "Brian is in San Francisco for a conference on mental health and people of color. He'll be back on Friday afternoon."

"That's right," said Sandra. "I remember. He's giving a presentation, too, right?"

"You got it. He's providing a summary of his dissertation. I can't wait to hear how it goes."

"I keep telling Brian that he needs to present his research to some of our staff here at the hospital. In any event, we'd love to have you over for dinner sometime this week. I'll see if Mike and Tonya are free as well."

"Girl, *please*! I doubt they'll come, but that sounds like a plan to me. Just let me know what day and time you're thinking. I can be there any day of the week except Wednesday. That's our official convocation for new students at the college. Brian won't be able to join us until Friday when he returns."

"Remember," said Sandra. Max gave a small sigh and prepared himself to be convicted by his sister's words. She had a way, much like their mother, of piercing a person's heart when it came to serious issues. "We're still a family, Max, regardless of whatever hang-ups there might be. It'll be nice for all of us to be together for the first time since Mother's funeral. How about Saturday at 6:00 p.m.?"

"That should work for the two of us. We'll see you then." They hung up, and Max returned to his computer to read his emails. While opening a message from President Nelson, he learned that his new boss wanted to review his speech for Wednesday's convocation by 9:00 a.m. the next morning. This request was unexpected. Max leaned back in his leather swivel chair and breathed deeply. A few seconds later, he placed a reminder in his phone to complete a draft after finishing dinner with his friends tonight. He already had some idea of what he wanted to say, but he needed to structure his thoughts on paper away from the office.

He wished that he had more time to prepare the draft. Public speaking frightened Max, but backing out of this responsibility wasn't an option. It was the college's tradition during the convocation for the dean to provide the welcome, whereas the president always delivered the main address to the new student body in attendance. In response to President Nelson's email, Max promised a draft first thing in the morning.

****

As usual, Max was ahead of schedule when meeting his two friends, Salt and Pepper. This time they were having dinner at a popular restaurant known for its cheesecake in an eastern suburb of the city. Max wondered as he drove his red hybrid why he was always so early to their dates, knowing that the two of them would be running at least ten to fifteen minutes behind. Arriving ahead of schedule, however, was habitual for Max just as much as being tardy to planned social gatherings was customary for his two friends. They were a black and white lesbian couple that he and his husband had met shortly after Brian started working at Cleveland's LGBTQ Resource Center, commonly referred to as The Center. Upon connecting with Salt and Pepper during a social event for professionals at The Center, the two couples hit it off immediately. Andrea, or "Pepper," taught high school math at a Cleveland public school, and her partner, Samantha, known as "Salt," had established herself as one of the most sought-after yoga instructors in the city.

At first glance, Salt and Pepper were an odd-looking couple, but the ten years they had invested into their relationship became immediately apparent to anyone who chatted with the two of them together. Pepper, a forty-year-old African American woman with short hair, was of average height and "thick," as she often described herself. Generally, she dressed conservatively apart from those rare occasions when she hit the town, at which point she wore trendier and borderline risqué outfits. Salt, forty-two years of age and white, was three inches taller than her partner and noticeably thinner. As a redhead, Salt typically wore exercise clothing that revealed her slim body.

While he searched for a parking spot near the restaurant, Max laughed to himself as he thought about the first and only time they had gone to a straight bar in the Flats. Having decided to switch things up for the sake of spontaneity, Max danced with Pepper, while Salt and Brian, making more of a believable couple, grooved with each other. Though ordinarily outspoken, Pepper held her tongue a few times that night as heterosexual black men ogled her wife with conspicuous desire. It was Max who reminded her that they were out just having a good time, helping to soothe her simmering temper and avert any potential altercation between Pepper and Salt's admirers. During their next group outing, both couples expressed the relief they felt that evening to return home where their closeness and intimacy were protected from outside judgment or heteronormative expectations. Max remembered that Pepper was particularly adamant that they never impersonated straight couples again, as she had directly experienced how such antics could backfire.

Walking toward the restaurant from his car, Max received a phone call from Samantha. "Hi, Max. Sorry, we're running late."

"Hey, Salt," replied Max. "It's okay. What happened this time?"

Salt laughed. "Yeah, I know. Traffic is awful right now. We're only one exit away, but Andrea is over here having a fit at the cars around us. Some of the words coming out of her mouth are just unladylike."

"Yeah, that sounds like Pepper to me. You don't have any breathing exercises to calm her down?" Max chuckled to himself, hoping that Salt's wife wouldn't hear his sarcastic remark.

"That's not going to work for her, and you know it," replied Salt. Max could vaguely hear Pepper in the background complain about another driver's slow speed. He laughed to himself as he walked into the restaurant, shaking his head at Pepper's road rage tendencies.

"Well, I'll see you two once you arrive. I'm heading into the restaurant now. At least I'll get the chance to figure out what my dessert will be."

"Okay, dear," said Salt. "We'll see you shortly."

Max entered the restaurant and welcomed the cool air that greeted his body and enveloped his arms and legs with a pleasing sensation in contrast to the sweat-inducing humidity outside. He wore a button-up white short-sleeve shirt, a pair of khaki shorts, and black leather sandals he had purchased when he and Brian spent a week in Orlando for their third anniversary, revealing his pedicure from the weekend. He walked casually over to the cheesecake display counter and contemplated what he would enjoy after dinner. Max always ordered grilled porkchop with a side of asparagus at this restaurant, but he usually made a point to try a different dessert.

"Can I help you with anything, sir?" asked the handsome twenty-year-old named Jason, who stood behind the counter. Jason was an average-height guy with blond hair and friendly blue eyes. He was in the process of cleaning the back counter along the wall where carryout and online orders were held. Max briefly looked up at him and then fixed his eyes on a sweet treat near the front display. "How's the key lime cheesecake?" he asked.

"Lime doesn't appeal to me that much, sir," replied Jason. "A lot of our customers say they like it, though."

"I see," replied Max while thinking that someone needs to coach this employee on being sales-oriented. *It's not that Jason is rude or even dishonest, but his response lacked a proper sales approach*, Max reflected. Once he realized that he was not at school, he decided against making this conversation what would normally be a teachable moment. *Maybe Jason's a new employee or ready to head home after a long day. Either way, it's not that important*. "Thanks anyway, Jason. I'm sure I'll figure out something for dessert," said Max, redirecting his attention to find somewhere to sit until his friends arrived.

"Have a good evening, sir," the worker replied, turning his back to finish wiping down the countertop.

While walking over to the seating area on the opposite side of the cheesecake display and carryout checkout area, Max overheard Pepper's laughter as the front door of the restaurant opened. She was apparently snickering at how one of the drivers she had flicked off on the highway had honked his horn while she took her exit. Max knew that it was part of Pepper's nature to get people riled up.

As he approached the couple, Salt declared, "You can be quite a handful sometimes. I just hope that you didn't cause any issues back there in all that traffic by giving that fellow a stiff one."

"He's a man, Samantha. He'll be fine. Did you see that tag on the back of his truck with the guy peeing? He can't be *too* sensitive!"

"You truly need help, Andrea," Salt joked with her partner.

When they were all together, the hostess asked them if they needed a table for three and immediately directed them to a table after Max nodded in affirmation. At 6:45 p.m. the bulk of the after-work dinner crowd had already departed, leaving the better part of the dining room empty. Only a few parties remained in the dimly lit space, and they were finishing their desserts and having drinks. Walking past these stragglers and a score of empty tables, the hostess escorted the party of three to a secluded booth in the rear area, where Salt and Pepper sat across from Max, who faced the restaurant's entrance.

"How's everything going, my friend?" began Salt. "It seems like you and Brian have recently had a lot on your plate."

"We're getting through everything one step at a time," replied Max. "Brian has been such a huge support for me emotionally with my mother's passing, even in the midst of his own work at The Center and with him working on his dissertation. I have no idea where he finds the strength to do it all."

"Look who's talking!" interjected Pepper. "You'll be the president of that college soon, or at least another one if not at Greater Cleveland Community College. Besides your work, you still find the time to volunteer with youth at The Center and maintain your athletic figure."

"What I meant to convey," said Max, "is that I don't know what I'd do without Brian. This week is the first time that we've been separated since his father's health scare a couple of years ago, but I'm dealing. He won't be back from San Francisco until this Friday."

"What's he doing there?" asked Pepper. Although occasionally regarded as short-fused by strangers and even associates, she was generally warm and thoughtful, especially with her friends and relatives. Salt grabbed onto Pepper's hand at the dinner table and held it as they listened for Max's response.

"The National Coalition of LGBTQ Centers is holding its first conference on the issue of mental health in communities of color there this week. Brian was invited as the interim executive director of Cleveland's LGBTQ Resource Center. However, his current research on the coming-out process for black men and its impact on their emotional well-being provided him with a platform to hold his own workshop. After registering for the conference and learning that they were still seeking presenters, he applied and was ultimately approved."

"Sounds fascinating, but there's just one problem," said Salt, stealing the addled glances of both Max and Pepper. "No one invited *me* to talk about the positive effects that yoga and exercise can have for folks in our community. What a shame!" They all laughed. While Max personally understood the cathartic benefits of physical activity on one's mental health, he also knew that Salt was not so self-absorbed to believe that she should have received a personal invitation to San Francisco.

"Geez," said Pepper in response. "And you tell me I'm the one who needs help." Max smirked at their humor, wishing that Brian was there beside him.

A tall, skinny Latino waiter in his mid-twenties approached their table and informed them of the special that evening. "May I start you off with some beverages and appetizers this evening?" he asked. Following his friends' orders, Max requested calamari and a bottle of white wine for the table.

"I swear this place is becoming more of a modeling agency every time I come here," Max whispered after the server left.

"You're just missing Brian," Salt said. Max was quiet. *Is it that obvious that I miss Brian? I need to pull it together*, he told himself.

"So, what have you two been up to?" Max inquired.

"With the housing market being what it is, we've been thinking about purchasing a new home," Pepper responded. "Ideally, we'd like to stay on the west side if we find something suitable in our price range. For the past few weeks we've been looking at places online and then actually visiting the ones that really stick out during our free evenings. Nothing has prompted us to make an offer yet. For now, we're just getting our feet wet and seeing what's out there."

"I see," said Max. "That's exciting nonetheless – what about your current property?"

"We'd like to ideally rent it," replied Salt. "Since my work schedule is flexible during most of the year, tenants would have an easier time contacting me if an urgent issue arose. During the summers, however, Andrea would be able to take the lead on more pressing matters. This side venture would be totally new to us, but it's something that we think is feasible." Salt and Pepper looked at each other and smiled, gripping each other's hand more firmly. Max sat there and admired what they had achieved as a couple.

"Sounds like you're on the right track," Max said. "I hope everything works out for you."

At that moment, the handsome Latino waiter returned with a bottle of Riesling and placed their order of calamari at the center of the table with a stack of three ivory white dishes. He then took each of their entrée orders, moving briskly since more customers were being seated in his section. By this time, the folks who generally avoided waiting in lines were now trickling into the restaurant. Max stared at the entrance, watching carefully as these new patrons entered. He secretly wished that Brian was next to him so that they could share their thoughts about these arrivals. It was a game played between them wherein they imagined storylines about random people they saw based solely on their overall appearance and mannerisms. Purely for entertainment, this pastime drew them close to one another as a result of their shared creativity and laughter.

After a couple more drinks and their meals had been served, Max finally prepared to announce the reason behind their dinner invitation. "Okay," he said, "Brian is sorry that he couldn't be here, but he wanted me to share the news with you anyway. We haven't shared this with anyone yet," Max disclosed before taking a deep breath. Salt and Pepper gradually leaned into his presence, revealing their mutual interest in whatever news he planned to unveil.

"Well," continued Max, "Brian and I plan to adopt a child."

"Wow!" said Salt taken aback.

"Are you serious?" asked Pepper rhetorically. "That's great news! What a major step that will be for both of you and, of course, whomever you adopt."

"It's something that we've put a lot of thought into since we got married, and even more so over the past six months," said Max. "We begin the formal part of the process the week after next. But, given your busy schedules and the adoption timetable we're looking at, Brian and I wanted to make sure you were aware of what's happening."

"This is really fantastic news," said Salt. "You're going to be great dads. There's no doubt about that!"

"Thanks," said Max. "We really hope so. In addition to our excitement, there are a lot of concerns that we have as well, but those will be dealt with in due time. Of course, you two already know how difficult it is for gay and lesbian couples to raise a family in a city like Cleveland, but being two black males is going to present a different set of challenges for us. By no means are we disillusioned by that fact, but we firmly believe in our ability to provide a rich and loving environment for a child. And, oh, before you ask, we're thinking about a boy."

Salt and Pepper smiled at this update, each staying silent a little while. They didn't have any children themselves, nor – as they had freely expressed in the past – did they want any. The couple already had two beagles that they treated as their own kids, as well as seven nieces and nephews combined between the two of them. On some level, Max knew that Salt and Pepper wouldn't fully understand the challenges he and Brian faced ahead. Yet, he and Brian were certain that Salt and Pepper would be very supportive of them throughout the process based on their established friendship.

"What age?" asked Pepper with eager curiosity.

"We're interested in adopting a five- or six-year-old," Max responded. "Based on our lives at this time, it makes the most sense to adopt in that range. Having a kid in kindergarten or the first grade would be much more manageable than adopting a younger child. At the same time, we're fearful of adopting an older kid at this point because of differing values and beliefs that may already be in place when it comes to same-sex partnerships. Coming to these conclusions was a journey for us, especially knowing how many older youth, most of whom get overlooked, are in the system. We realize they need loving and committed parents, too."

"I can't even begin to imagine how strenuous that process must've been," said Salt. "However," she continued, "you and Brian have to do what is best for you and the child. I'm sure the social workers you work with will help you in determining the best fit."

"You'd be surprised how open teenagers these days are to same-sex partnerships, but I still understand your concern," said Pepper. "Just know, though, that today's youth are a generation of their own. They see, hear, say, and do everything, honey!"

"Well, getting that out sure put me in the mood for something sweet," said Max, changing the conversation to a lighter topic. "The key lime cheesecake caught my eye as I was waiting for you out by the display case. Will you two be joining me for dessert?"

"This occasion is certainly a cause for celebration, so absolutely," said Salt, turning to her partner. "What do you think, Andrea?"

"I'm in complete agreement," echoed Pepper. "We couldn't be happier for you."

At that instant Max signaled to gain their

waiter's attention as he was taking drinks to another table. He quickly came over to Max and his friends after putting the drinks down and asked if they would be having dessert. Max readily replied, "Yes, you must've read my mind, young man. I'll have a slice of your key lime cheesecake." He considered asking the waiter for his opinion of the dessert but changed his mind after recalling the unsatisfactory response he had received from Jason before being seated.

"And for you ladies?" inquired the tall waiter with a Puerto Rican accent.

"Hmm… We'll have a slice of your classic strawberry cheesecake to share," said Pepper.

"Sounds good," the waiter replied, smiling. It was clear to everyone at the table from the server's grin and slow gait on his way to place their dessert orders that he enjoyed thinking about these two women sharing their slice.

Once their last course arrived, Salt called for a toast. The three friends lifted their glasses of wine toward the center of the table. "To Max and Brian," she began, "our beloved friends, as well as their soon-to-be addition to the family – may you find completeness in your household." After expressing their 'cheers' with merriment, they speedily drank in unison.

"Thank you," said Max, preparing to bite into his cake. He could smell the subtle scent of lime as the piece on his fork drew closer to his mouth. Max found the chilled morsel pleasing to his palate, ranking it amongst his favorite cakes at this restaurant thus far. Opposite of him, Salt and Pepper casually dissected their cake with their two forks. *They look like two friends sharing dessert instead of the sensual lesbian interaction the waiter had expected,* Max thought. For a second time, he wished that his partner, Brian, was there celebrating with them.

"In light of your news, we'll take care of the bill tonight, my friend," Pepper stated.

"Thank you," said Max. "I'm just sorry that Brian wasn't here to join us."

"You know what?" Salt asked both Max and Pepper, who looked at each other in bewilderment. "There's one other thing that we're forgetting."

"What's that?" asked Pepper as Max echoed her question in his own mind.

"We must begin planning a shower! Max, please allow us to prepare this celebratory event on your and Brian's behalf."

Pepper agreed, "Oh, you're right, Samantha. We'd be honored to plan the festivities, Max. And by the time you have a child, we may be in our new house. Just think of that!"

"All right," said Max, fully convinced that accepting their offer was his only realistic choice. "I'll tell Brian when we talk tonight. He'll be equally as surprised and pleased as I am, if not more. Thank you so much, ladies."

"You better make sure he shows up to the shower, though," Salt voiced.

"Don't worry about that," Max remarked, smiling in response to her sarcasm. "You can certainly bet on it."

Pepper stopped the waiter the next time he passed their table and told him that they were ready for their check, requesting that he place their orders on the same bill. Three minutes later, he returned with the statement for Pepper, who handed him her credit card after finding no discrepancies. By this time, Max, now stuffed and pleased with his friends' reception of his announcement, looked forward to returning home to prepare for the next day.

"So, who's next on the list to find out?" Salt asked as they waited for Pepper's card to be returned.

Max gulped as he noticed that he was unprepared for this question on the table. "Brian and I," he started out slowly, "are still unsure about that right now. It will more than likely be my family since they're here in the city, but that comes with its own challenges," he stated half-heartedly. Salt and Pepper, knowing the dynamics of Max's siblings and their relationship, stayed quiet.

"We completely understand those complications," Salt eventually expressed. "I'm sure you guys will know when and with whom the time is right."

"You have a point," Max said. "Brian is a lot more level-headed than me when it comes to such decisions."

When their waiter returned, he gently placed Pepper's credit card and the receipts for her and the restaurant on the table and told everyone, "Thanks for dining with us tonight. Have a great evening. Please come back and see us soon." After Pepper signed the restaurant's copy of the receipt, the three of them stood up and made their way to the lobby area. Max hugged the two of them and promised to be in touch with them soon after Brian returned.

****

The outside view of Lake Eerie from their seventeenth-floor condo was vast. From his and Brian's bedroom, Max could see that the sun was almost no longer visible on the westward horizon. Traces of orange shades clung onto the skyline and reflected onto the massive lake's seeming stillness. While looking to the northwest from the wall-to-wall window in their room, he thought about his partner, who was in a time zone three hours behind his. *How is the first day of the conference going? How many people are in attendance? Is he prepared to deliver his topic on Thursday morning? Are any of our friends in attendance?* These questions swept through his mind as he changed into a T-shirt and a pair of shorts.

organizers of this conference were really mindful of such dynamics during their planning process. They have also started taking suggestions to increase the turnout for next year. The most impactful part of today, however, was a silent thirty-minute slide presentation of one hundred and five LGBTQ persons of all ages from around the country who lost their lives to suicide this year. Mental illness and/or trauma were underlying factors in every instance. It was an emotional presentation that hit home as to why we're here this week. They even featured our own Bianca Miles in the slide show."

Max abruptly stopped ironing his trousers and thought about Bianca. She was a popular nineteen-year-old trans woman who regularly attended The Center. Prior to taking her own life, she had been in the process of seeking regular daytime employment because she was growing tired of solely relying on weekend drag routines. Days before her suicide, Max had worked with Bianca on creating a résumé and told her to use him as a reference for her job applications. From forced sex trafficking and numerous domestic assaults by an abusive ex-boyfriend, Max reflected upon Bianca's traumatic experiences and briefly considered the magnitude of her nineteen-year-old life experiences.

"You there?" asked Brian, interrupting the dead air on the phone.

"Yeah, I'm fine," Max shared. "Hearing about Bianca just caught me off guard. She was such a nice girl who was literally fighting to turn her life around." He picked up the iron and continued with the insides of his pants. "Have you seen anyone you recognized in attendance yet?"

"The only individual that I know personally that's here is my friend, Dennis, who works with a national advocacy group in DC. You might remember him from the all-white party we attended last year. Dennis is a short, stocky white man in his early forties." Max tried, but he could not recall this person. "Aside from Dennis, I've recognized two professors from the top LGBTQ studies program in the country. Both are known for their publications on black queer identity, suicidality amongst LGBTQ youth, privilege and identity politics, and combatting nihilism through a focus on resilience."

"Sounds like a networking opportunity to me," said Max. "Any plans to meet them?"

"Oh yeah," said Brian. "There's a happy hour for presenters and volunteers on Thursday evening after workshops are over somewhere in the Castro. Hopefully, I'll have the opportunity to make their acquaintance then. How's everything back home?"

"My first day on the new job was better than I expected. The first few weeks are going to be busy with getting the foundation laid for the rest of the year, but I'm confident that everything will work out. By the way, my sister also called and invited us to dinner on Saturday evening at 6:00 after you return. She wants to have all of us over for the first time since Mother's passing."

Max finished ironing his clothing and went to hang his dress shirt and pants in his closet for the morning. From his phone that was still lying on the ironing board, he heard Brian say, "That should be fine. It should be nice to see everyone. Speaking of dinner, how did everything go with Salt and Pepper tonight?"

"Very well," Max stated, almost forgetting about their encounter this evening. "They were delighted to hear our news, babe. They even want to throw a shower for us after a match is secured. Pepper also mentioned that they're looking into the possibility of buying a new house, so the shower could even be thrown in their new place."

"A new home, huh? I'm glad for them. I knew they would be supportive of our plans," said Brian. "Sorry I wasn't there to share the news and celebrate with you all, but we'll definitely do it together next time. I promise."

"It's not a problem. We already have another opportunity this Saturday evening," said Max nervously as he thought about his sister's dinner invitation and prepared to shower before bed.

"I guess that is something to consider, but

are you sure you want all of your siblings to be there?"

After taking time to think over Brian's question, Max said, "They're all going to find out somehow, so really, it's okay with me. What I will not accept is for Mike, Tonya, or even Kevin to give one of their holier-than-thou sermons on gay couples adopting." Based on the elevated tone of his voice and the increased rapidness of his speech, Max knew that Brian was aware of his anxiety concerning the matter.

"Let's just give it some thought over the next couple of days and come to a decision together on Friday when I return," said Brian. "There's certainly no need for us to say anything definitively, one way or another, right now. We still have a few days ahead of us."

"That'll work," said Max, partially relieved to hear his husband's response. "I'm going to grab a cold shower since you're not here."

Brian laughed. "I know how you feel, baby. Get a good night's rest, and we'll talk tomorrow."

"Have a good night as well, babe."

Max hung up the phone and went into the bathroom. He needed Brian in the shower with him, but he would have to be patient. After taking a cool soak and putting on his pajamas, Max lay down on their king size bed and shut his eyes. He denied his thoughts any chance of consuming his mind tonight with worriment, knowing that the next day had plenty in store for him already.

****

Max's meeting with the department chairs lasted longer than he expected. The college was in the process of expanding its preparatory classes for students who did not have adequate test scores to begin college-level courses. More than a handful of faculty members opposed the decision to go in this direction, but it was Max's role to lead this transition, which was scheduled to start next semester after winter break. The resistance of several faculty members ultimately prolonged this morning's meeting, which was the first planning session since President Nelson announced the expansion. One of the reasons that Max was hired as the dean of arts and sciences was because of the vision he had for this initiative. Undermining statements and stalling questions from dissenters were now minor impediments through which Max was required to maneuver as the price of his promotion.

The logic behind this progressive undertaking was that President Nelson believed the college would substantially increase student enrollment as a result of making the institution more competitive with other community colleges by introducing healthcare and computer technology preparatory classes. President Nelson and Max both believed that going this route would give potential applicants a better alternative to their peer institutions and local proprietary colleges. On the other hand, the pushback from opposing faculty was that the college might be viewed as too accepting or accommodating by nearby colleges and universities, thus jeopardizing the respectable place they currently held in northeast Ohio.

It was the stance of President Nelson, though, that as a community college, they were not directly in competition with the larger four-year schools. Max and he believed their two-year institution existed to serve a specific niche, which oftentimes included being an affordable pathway to four-year programs. During Max's meeting, he provided an overview of President Nelson's objectives, introduced his own plans for bringing phase one to completion, and delegated sub-committees for the primary departments that would be initially impacted. His leadership style as a macro manager, another reason why he was hired, was straightforward.

The meeting ended at 12:20 p.m. Max was supposed to meet with Jane Budges, the assistant director of student support services, in ten minutes. Instead of walking back to his office first, he decided to go directly to the on-site cafeteria to keep from being late. Jane and Max had become close work associates since Jane started in her current role two years ago. She took the job after being an assistant principal of a public high school in Cincinnati for seven years. Unlike a lot of other staff, Max thought that Jane kept it real. Even though she was a white woman who was just slightly younger than his mother would have been, Max secretly believed that she was adopted by a black family as a child, but he knew that, historically, that was highly improbable, if not impossible. Her laidback demeanor, style of communication, and her ability to relate to most of the African American students were some of the reasons he often wondered about her upbringing. One thing, however, was clear to anyone who came across Jane in the workplace – she genuinely cared about all the students with whom she worked.

Being from a poor Appalachian community in Cincinnati, Jane could empathize with many of the situations that some of her low-income students confronted. She observed real incidents of segregation and racism in her own upbringing in Cincinnati, which never seemed acceptable or justifiable to her. Although Jane had a more profound understanding of racial and economic inequalities than most of her colleagues, Max believed she was not the type of person who accepted excuses. She encouraged and supported her students who relied on student support services and other campus resources without enabling them. Max knew that the college was fortunate to have her as an employee.

When Max arrived at the cafeteria, he found Jane already waiting to get her lunch. She was standing in the line where hot meals were prepared throughout the week. On this day fried chicken, mashed potatoes and gravy, and corn were on the menu. Max was not surprised to see his friend waiting for her southern-style lunch plate. The other options at the college's cafeteria included a salad bar and two fast-food restaurants, which were usually the most popular. A Caesar salad, yogurt, and diet soda would be Max's lunch this afternoon.

"Hi, Maxwell," Jane said as she passed by Max on her way to the check-out register.

"Hello, Jane. I'm right behind you, so just sit wherever," he said, moving briskly to grab a drink and pay for his order.

Jane found a quiet area at the east end of the cafeteria, where the majority of faculty and staff typically sat during their lunch break. Most of the students who used this section did so for studying purposes rather than eating or socializing. The spot Jane selected was ideal for them, a quasi-private table for two in a small enclave surrounded by vibrant indoor vines. Usually, she and Max would go to a restaurant in downtown Cleveland, but he decided that they should stay on campus this afternoon, considering the planning meeting.

"So, Jane, how are things so far in the semester?" asked Max.

"Student support services is honestly pretty dull. Right now, we're just focusing on hiring student tutors, advertising our services, and preparing our midterm study skills workshops. And how are things for you with the new job?"

"It's going well so far, but there are a few aspects, such as reporting directly to the president, that I'm still adjusting my mind around. As a matter of fact, I had to email him a draft of my speech for tomorrow's convocation this morning. And since today's planning meeting, I've been checking my phone to see if he's responded, and still no word yet. Considering everything, though, I look forward to getting fully immersed in the role."

"Yeah, I'm sure you'll do fine, Maxwell, unlike your predecessor, who couldn't even lead a classroom of twenty students, let alone multiple departments. It's a miracle the college was able to sustain itself for the past two years."

Max shifted uneasily in his seat and looked around to make sure that no other staff was around. While it was known to virtually all their peers that the former dean was remiss in carrying her weight during her short-lived tenure, a significant number of faculty members expected that her assistant, Amanda, would succeed her. Ultimately, President Nelson's decision to appoint Max, bypassing her and many people's expectations, resulted in a noticeable decline in the popularity of the former two.

"I hear you, Jane, but there's one thing I

definitely know, and that's this: we're beginning an exciting new chapter for the college with President Nelson's initiative," said Max. "I simply plan to focus on doing my best for the entire college under his leadership." Max picked up his soda and drank, hoping that Jane would not further belabor the subject. The two of them normally discussed college issues during their lunches when they were off-campus, but Max did not feel as though this was the time or place to have this conversation.

"Exciting is definitely the appropriate word," Jane replied fervently. "It's great to see you in this new role. You'll be the president after Mr. Nelson, you know."

"We'll see," he said before changing the subject once and for all. "Did you hear about the rain we're supposed to get this weekend? Some precipitation will be a welcome change. It's been too hot and humid these past two weeks."

"Yes, I did hear about it on the news this morning before work. I'll be in Cincinnati this weekend visiting my family, but my grass will certainly benefit from the showers. I just hope that I don't get the worst of it while I'm driving down there or on my way back."

"I totally hear you," said Max. "Be careful driving on I-71, especially if there's a downpour. I never liked driving that four-hour stretch when I worked as an admissions officer. You could always count on some sort of construction going on. It never failed." Max reflected on the countless road trips that he had made to Cincinnati, where he presented to a handful of feeder schools for the university he represented back then. He was thankful for not having to travel as much as he did at the outset of his career, especially being older and settled with Brian.

Looking at Jane as she bit into her crispy chicken leg and they talked further, he wondered about her life outside of work. To his knowledge, she had never been married and she lacked any children. Max could not recall her ever speaking about other friends outside of the community college. He initially wondered if she was lesbian, but he learned later, from conversations wherein she expressed an interest in men, that his speculation was unlikely. Truthfully, he could not see her with anyone, man or woman. Her relationships with her students were the most significant relationships that she had, as far as he knew. For an instant, Max felt sorry for Jane, but then he realized that he knew too little about her personal life to go that route. *It wouldn't be a good idea to jump to conclusions. Whatever the case, Jane never comes off as needy, overbearing, or socially inept.* He decided to disregard the subject altogether.

Max looked at his watch and thought about the response from President Nelson he awaited as they finished their meals. Although he had an afternoon meeting to attend with staff members of the health department, revising the speech, if necessary, was an action item he planned to complete by the end of the workday. Max desired to have a relaxing evening alone without having to work or allow anything else to interrupt him, apart from talking with Brian. His agenda for the evening entailed working out, taking a relaxing shower, cooking a nice meal, and watching his favorite home improvement shows. “Well, it’s time for me to get going,” Max told his colleague. “I need to see if President Nelson has responded.”

“Okay, Maxwell. I’m sure you’ll be fine. Try not to stress over it,” insisted Jane as she stood up and picked up her tray from the table.

“You’re right. Maybe I’m overreacting a little,” he said. “Besides leading the steering committee for the expansion of preparatory classes, which only started today, this will be my first deliverable. Anyway, I’m sure I’ll see you tomorrow at the convocation.”

“Absolutely, Maxwell. Enjoy the rest of your day.”

“You too, Jane.”

Max paced toward his office after their lunch ended. It was a clear, sunny day in the mid-nineties, leaving him motivated by the heat to walk faster than his normal stroll. The next appointment on his schedule was at 2:00 p.m., so he figured that, if necessary, he would have thirty to forty minutes to revise his speech. Once he arrived in his office, lightly sweating from his walk, he went immediately to his desk to check his email. Near the top of his email inbox was a reply from President Nelson. He opened the email and read:

Maxwell, this looks good. I'll see you tomorrow.

It was a familiar ending to similar stories played out in the past. Max laughed to himself as the anxiety that he had built up the day before, after reading his boss's email request, subdued. Since high school Max felt extreme pressure related to meeting deadlines and preparing for feedback from others. Most people who were not close to Max thought of him as a perfectionist. But as he matured into a young adult, he eventually sought help on his own accord and learned that he struggled with generalized anxiety disorder. While his catastrophic thinking rarely ever manifested, that hardly prevented Max from dealing with persistent worries that frequently preceded shortness of breath and sweat spells. This time, he was simply relieved to know that President Nelson found the drafted address acceptable. *I'll worry about delivering the speech tomorrow, but at least I can peacefully proceed with my plans for tonight.*

****

Driving back home from work, Max felt optimistic about his new job. Obtaining buy-in from certain faculty on the current initiative would be his greatest challenge, but Max knew that time was his strongest ally. Amongst the staff opposed to his new role, he felt certain that some of them would inevitably move beyond their present feelings and adapt to his leadership sooner or later. As for the others, performing his role well would suffice in keeping them at bay to brood in their own disappointments. In high spirits as he considered his political advantage, Max picked up the phone and called Paul, who occupied a condo a few floors above him and Brian.

Paul was a bachelor who worked out with Max off and on in their condominium's fitness facility when their schedules coincided. He practiced corporate law at a large firm in downtown Cleveland, and his evenings during the business week were usually dedicated to work. Apparently, this evening was no exception. When his voicemail picked up, Max left Paul a message informing him that he would be in the gym until 7:00. He was slightly let down that his workout buddy was unavailable, yet he was still determined to make the most of his evening.

Although he preferred lifting alone, Max enjoyed the company of his gym partner Paul as well, especially when he sought a hardcore workout. Max began working out with Paul a couple of months after he and Brian had moved into their condo. They started off spotting for one another whenever they were both at the gym while making light conversation about basketball, which eventually turned into a semi-regular routine that largely depended on both of their schedules. Practically speaking, this meant that they typically met once a week.

Max went directly to his bedroom to change into his gym clothes when he arrived home. He hoped that the fitness center would not be occupied by too many of his neighbors. Tonight, Max was in no mood for distractions or waiting to use the equipment that he would need for his upper body routine. An empty gym and his music were the only two prerequisites for the workout he had planned. When he arrived at the facility, located on the fifteenth floor, he was pleased to discover only a handful of people. Being substantially smaller than traditional gyms, a packed gym meant waiting by the most popular equipment to prevent it from being seized by someone else.

Weightlifting while listening to Chicago-style house music was one of Max's most enjoyable hobbies. To him, the act of being alone with nostalgic rhythms from his youth and the exercise equipment transcended him to an alternate universe. The demands of work, family, society, and even his relationship with Brian were suspended for the sixty to ninety minutes he typically committed to this obsession. This evening, he focused on the bench press, bicep curls, cable flyes, push-ups, chest dips, as well as tricep extensions and pushdowns. Following these exercises, he ran two miles in twenty-two minutes on a treadmill, whereafter he was drenched in sweat.

By the end of his workout, there was still no response from Paul. At 7:15 p.m., after drying himself with a towel, he entered the gym's small sauna that seated two or three people, at most, comfortably. It was there where he collected his thoughts about the convocation taking place the following night at the college's main auditorium. His mother's funeral was the last time that he had spoken in front of a large group of people, but that was in honor of his mother and directed to individuals he knew. A different set of variables were at play the next day, though. The eyes of his new boss, Mr. Nelson; the politically divided faculty; and four hundred new students would be on him for a total of five minutes. Max wiped the sweat from his forehead and chest that was beginning to develop and wished that he wouldn't swelter like that during his speech. Though public speaking was a fear of his, he knew that he would get through it and move on to other important matters.

Sitting motionless amid the high temperature that filled his surrounding enclosure, Max was confident in his ability to perform every aspect of his new job. It was his personal life, though, that would be substantially altered in the coming months based on the impending adoption process. The steps he and Brian were taking would permanently reconstruct their lives emotionally, interpersonally, financially, and – practically speaking – in every other aspect. Max looked forward to fatherhood both with excitement and a degree of fear, and he was sure that Brian felt the same way. They both wanted to start a family that extended beyond the two of them, and they were well-positioned to make that a reality. Navigating through the process would initially be challenging, but they had faith in themselves and support from their friends and a few family members.

Once Max could no longer indulge the dry heat or tolerate the dampness of his gym attire, he retreated from the sauna and wiped his face. Back in his apartment, Max immediately undressed and took a warm shower. Afterward, he made dinner and sat in front of the television to watch his favorite home improvement channel, just as he had envisioned at work that afternoon. As he reclined comfortably on the sectional, his phone rang. He expected Brian, but it turned out to be Paul returning his phone call.

"Hey, Max," said Paul. "Sorry I missed your call earlier. I'm just leaving work."

"Oh, no worries, man," replied Max. "I called to see if you wanted to work out with me this evening but it's all good. My time in the gym was well spent – got about fifteen to twenty minutes in the sauna as well."

"Nice, Max. Let's try to catch up sometime early next week. I'll be working late days until then, including this weekend."

"All right, bro. I'm gonna hold you to that. Don't work yourself to death," said Max, fully knowing that his statement wouldn't deter Paul's tenacity and ambitions of making partner at his firm. For a second, he remembered having a similar work ethic after graduating college as a single man, determined to work his way up from an admissions representative while earning his master's in higher education. Having now achieved his career goals, he knew that it was important to pay attention to his work-life balance with Brian now in the picture. There was nothing Max missed about seventy-hour workweeks between his job and school in order to get ahead.

"Well, Max, you have a good night. I need to order some takeout. Talk to you next week."

"Have a good night, Paul."

At the conclusion of their conversation, Max went back to watching the home makeover show. *Maybe it will completely come together in the end*, he thought as he lay across the leather sectional resting on his right elbow. It turned out that Max was dissatisfied with the result of the home improvements completed for a married couple in Nashville. Despite the impractical layout and bland décor of the kitchen remodel, he was impressed with the quality of the expecting white couple's three-bedroom, twenty-nine-hundred square feet home. *I wonder how long we'll be able to maintain our condo lifestyle with a child.* Urban living provided many conveniences to him and Brian as two working professionals in the first half of their thirties, but Max suspected that having a son would greatly impact their preference for downtown life in the coming months. It was, after all, a common theme that showed up time and again on many of the shows he and Brian watched on this network.

When the show ended, Max followed his normal routine to prepare for the next day. Intuitively, Brian called him shortly after he lay down in the bed.

"Hey, baby," said Brian.

"What's up, babe?" asked Max in return.

"I'm just getting in from a nearby office store to print the handouts for my presentation on Thursday. There are currently thirty people registered for my workshop, but there could be walk-ins, too. I have fifty just in case."

"Sounds good. Are you mentally ready?" inquired Max.

"Yes, now that the hand-out materials are ready to go. I plan to put my best foot forward during the presentation and hope that I'm prepared for the ensuing questions and discussion. The Q and A session is always the tricky part. Some questions can stump even the most prepared presenters."

"But, Brian, who in this country has explored the coming-out process for black gay and bisexual males like you have?" asked Max proudly.

"Not many," said Brian, sounding encouraged.

"That's right," replied Max. "You are the emerging leader on this subject. Everything will be fine."

"I wish I could hold you and kiss you right now," said Brian. "You always know what to say."

"Me too, but we only have two nights to go before you return home." Max smiled to himself as he fought to resist the erection that formed against his pajamas.

"I'm going to let you get some rest for your long day tomorrow," said Brian. "Don't stress too much, either – your speech will be over sooner than you realize."

"I won't, babe. Goodnight. I love you."

"I love you, too, Max."

Chapter 2

Droplets of cold rain pelted Max's car like liquid bullets as he waited in the passenger pick-up and drop-off area of Cleveland's airport. The day had been a miserable one due to an unrelenting storm from the southwest. Thick, grey clouds stretched as far as Max could see through his windshield, indicating no end in sight to the inclement weather conditions. While listening to his jazz playlist as he waited, Max wished that Brian would quickly arrive with his luggage in hand. Undeterred by his increasing drowsiness after waiting an hour for the delayed flight, he managed to focus on everyone who exited the automatic sliding doors of the airport.

He would recognize Brian's tall, lean build and light-skinned complexion instantly. The white framed eyeglasses that he wore, which made him look like a college professor featured on GQ, would be a dead giveaway. Max smiled to himself, thinking about how nerd-like his lover appeared in patterned dress shirts and cufflinks, bow ties of assorted colors, button-up sweaters, printed scarves, and Kangol hats. He had a look worthy of any London or New York fashion walkway, at least in his partner's eyes.

Max honked his horn when, at last, he observed Brian stepping outside into the downpour from the airport. Brian stopped and covered the brim of his black newsboy hat to block out visual distractions as he searched for Max's car amongst the line of other drivers. Max quickly escaped the protection from his car to flag down his husband, regretting that he hadn't brought an umbrella.

"Hey, baby," said Brian as he gave Max a kiss and tight embrace. Due to the intensity of the wind and the piercing rain droplets, both of their actions were quick and deliberate as they placed Brian's luggage and shoulder bag into the trunk.

"Welcome back," replied Max. "It's so great to see you. How was your flight?"

"You too," said Brian once he had taken his seat and closed the passenger door. "Let's just say that it's nice being back on the ground. You were all that I could think about during the bouts of turbulence we experienced. I have no desire to fly again anytime soon." Hurriedly, they then fastened their seatbelts, and Max pulled off into the seemingly never-ending tempest.

When Brian and Max returned to their condo, it was shortly after 9:00 p.m. Both were exhausted, wanting simply to devour the Chinese food they had picked up on their way home, shower, and get some rest. The following day would be an eventful one in their lives with household cleaning, errands, and Sandra's dinner. As they entered the front door, Brian turned on the lights and took both of their jackets to the coat closet, which was the first door on the left in the hallway that led to their bedroom. Max walked behind Brian as he shut the closet door and embraced him at the waist. Brian took Max's arms and wrapped them around his chest.

"It's good to be home," said Brian, lowering his head to kiss his lover's hand.

"You got that right," said Max. "It's nice to have you back. We have a lot coming up over the next few weeks, you know."

"Yeah, I know, but what I'm sure of is that we'll get through everything together as we've always done." As they continued standing by the closet, Brian then held onto Max's arms a little tighter and tilted his head back to gently rub his face against Max's.

"With you here in my arms, I have no doubt about that," Max whispered in Brian's ear. "Now, let's get to our Chinese food before it gets cold." He felt a sudden wave of relief knowing that Brian was home. *Indeed, everything is going to be okay*, Max told himself.

The couple fixed their plates and sat down at their dining room table. Lightning flashed periodically through the tall white blinds that covered the balcony entrance, adding occasional flickers of illumination to the open layout of their combined living and dining room area, along with the dim recessed lighting and television that had been playing since Max left for the airport.

"How did things wrap up at the

conference?" asked Max, digging his fork into the General Tso's chicken on his plate.

"It ended very nicely. This morning, before the concluding address by the executive director of the country's largest mental health advocacy group, we held a silent suicide awareness march in downtown San Francisco. There were over a thousand folks who participated in the event, most of whom were locals. Seeing hundreds of speechless marchers walking together was quite moving. The organizers really did a great job. You should come to the conference with me next year."

"I'd like that a lot," said Max.

After eating dinner, the two of them took a hot shower together and prepared for bed. Five long days had passed since they last felt each other's body temperatures in their adjustable bed. Max lay on his side facing Brian with his right hand slightly grasping the left shoulder of his partner. Brian softly caressed Max's arm that crossed his smooth caramel-toned chest. Max smiled to himself, appreciating the in-person scent of Brian that he had only managed to glean from two lifeless pillows over the past week.

The last time they had spent this much time apart occurred after Brian learned that his father had suffered a heart attack. Brian had taken time off work to be with his parents and flew to Connecticut as soon as he could. Fortunately, Harold, Brian's father, had received immediate assistance at just the right time and recovered from the incident. He had stayed a total of six nights and seven days to support his parents.

"I missed you this past week, Max," said Brian, while still gently grazing the light hairs of Max's brawny forearm.

"Well, that makes two of us," replied Max. "Just how much did you miss me?" Grinning and eager all at once, Max pressed his mocha-colored body closer to his partner. As Brian felt his lover's excitement, he began kissing Max's arm until reaching his full lips.

****

Sandra, Kevin, and Junior lived in a cul-de-sac in a burgeoning suburban community that was less than five years old. Typical of the surrounding houses, their home was a spacious two-story house with a furnished basement. Brian looked at his partner after hearing Max sigh once the car was parked in the driveway. Max sat in the driver's seat frozen, feeling the pressure of the looming dinner.

"Everything's going to be fine," said Brian. "There's no need for you to allow anyone or anything to get under your skin this evening. What more can we ask for in our lives right now?"

"Absolutely nothing, Brian," Max replied. "But I know my family, and something tells me that someone's going to try us." Max stared at the entrance to Sandra's house as he and Brian talked, admiring the pristinely manicured lawns that she and her neighbors all had. He then glanced in the direction of his sister's white front door that contained three small windows above the peephole and wondered why there was a divide in his family over his sexual orientation. *If our own mother*, Max reflected, *who raised all of us in the same household, could welcome me and Brian wholeheartedly, then why can't Mike and Tonya?* Such questions had come to him often since he and Brian began seriously dating, but deep down, he knew that there was nothing that he could do to change their hearts. "Well," said Max, "the sooner we go in, the sooner this will be over."

"Just know that if you're not ready to make the announcement, Max, we can wait for another time," said Brian.

"My problem is *not* telling them," said Max. "The issue is knowing that they'll refuse to be happy for us or for the child we'll be adding to our family."

"Unfortunately, that's nothing that you or I can change," Brian indicated with empathy. Brian placed his left hand on Max's right leg and looked him in his brown eyes. "It's going to be all right," he said. Brian took Max's right hand and kissed it. It was Brian's non-verbal way of informing Max that there was nothing to fear.

"Yeah, babe, let's go in," replied Max.

"And besides," said Brian, "after last night, you should be fine." Max was forced to grimace at

Brian's inappropriate and ill-timed wit. The two of them walked to the front door, and Max rang the doorbell. A few seconds later, Sandra opened the door to invite them inside. She was wearing an orange and yellow sundress and a pair of cherry-colored flats. Likewise, she wore a simple gold jewelry chain set on her neck, wrist, and ankle. Her hair, which she always wore natural, was combed backed and collected into a plush afro puff.

"Hey, guys," she said as Max and Brian walked into the unassuming foyer of her home. Without any delay, she greeted them both with a warm and friendly hug.

"Hello, Sandra," said Max. "Nice to finally see you again. I can't believe that the last time we saw each other was at Ma's funeral."

"That's why I recommended that we get together for dinner. We can't keep going for months at a time like this."

"You did the right thing, Sandra," said Brian. "I, for one, am looking forward to the food." They all laughed because they knew Brian's appetite was insatiable.

"It does smell good in here," agreed Max.

"Go ahead and make yourselves comfortable," Sandra insisted. "The food is all done; it's just warming on the stove now."

"Where's Kevin and Junior?" asked Max, looking around the house for signs of them.

"They're hanging out downstairs. Kevin is

watching some football game, and Junior is most likely messing around on social media. I'll tell you, they are completely different and two peas in a pod all at once." Brian and Max laughed at Sandra's unexpected remark.

"Just yesterday morning," continued Sandra, "each of them forgot something when they left home. After driving a few blocks and turning back around, Kevin came running into the house to ask me if I knew where his cell phone was. I told him I had no idea where it was, but I was able to use my phone to call his. It was still on the charger in the bedroom." Sandra paused for a moment and shook her head. "Junior, on the other hand," finishing her story, "left his eyeglasses somewhere in his bedroom. It's a good thing he realized they were missing before his bus arrived because he wouldn't have been too happy with me if I had to drive them to his school. He's essentially blind without them! After Junior left, I prayed that God would give me the strength to care for them without losing my mind."

"You've got to be kidding," said Brian, appearing astounded by her account.

"I wish," said Sandra, "but they're both forgetful. Yesterday was the first time they ever returned to the house back-to-back like that. I couldn't believe it." Sandra smiled and shook her head for a second time. The doorbell rang seconds later. "That must be Tonya and Mike," she expressed, walking toward the front door. Mike and Tonya made their way inside after being welcomed by Sandra, the eldest of the four siblings. She greeted them cheerfully with hugs, just as she had done with Brian and Max.

"How's it going, big sis?" asked Mike.

"Everything is fine," Sandra replied. "I'm excited now that everyone's here." Sandra escorted Mike and Sandra to the living area, where Max and Brian were now seated.

"It's nice for us to get together like this," echoed Tonya.

As they entered the living room area, Sandra said, "Let me go and tell Kevin and Junior to come upstairs for dinner." She quickly walked toward the kitchen, where the staircase to the basement was located.

"Hey, Mike and Tonya," said Max, hoping to start the evening off on a cordial note. "How's it going?"

"What's up, Max?" replied Mike with indifference. "I've been good. How about you?"

"Brian and I have been well," said Max. "No complaints here."

"That's good to hear," interjected Tonya. "It's nice to see you two again," she added.

"You too," said Brian, breaking his own silence amongst the awkward conditions of these three siblings being left in the same room together by Sandra. Apart from Betty Strong herself,

Sandra, at thirty-eight years of age, was the only person able to reduce the tension between her younger siblings simply with her presence. As twins and the middle children, Max believed that Mike and Tonya resented him for being the youngest and gay. He felt they only tolerated him and Brian because of their mother, who valued family more than anything. But since her passing, Max hadn't seen or spoken with them. When Sandra finally returned upstairs with Kevin and Junior behind her, everyone in the living room breathed a little easier.

"Hey, everyone," Kevin said, "it's good to see you all. I do believe that it's now time to eat."

Junior silently waved to his uncles and aunt from the left side of his father, not wanting to attract a lot of attention to himself. Max and Brian stood up from their seats and went with the rest of the crowd into the dining room area, where the table was already prepped with silverware. Just as everyone took their seats, Sandra called Junior. "Boy, come and help me with this food."

"C'mon, mom! Can't I get a break just once?" he pleaded.

"You can get a break when you start contributing to the bills around here," she replied with stern playfulness. Junior shook his head, following his mother into the kitchen to bring out dishes of baked salmon, mixed vegetables over white rice, and cornbread muffins. Being the eldest, Sandra started learning to cook at her mother's side at the age of twelve. Cooking was a skill that she easily acquired and gladly performed for her younger siblings when Betty Strong worked late nights, which became a tradition she maintained in their adulthood. Once Sandra and Junior had laid out the dinner spread and served drinks, Kevin said grace for the plentiful food on the table before them, and everyone began eating.

"Thanks for having us all over," Tonya stated. "This is really nice of you guys."

"No problem at all," said Sandra. "I know Mother would have definitely approved. Better yet, she would've been the first person here."

"You got that right," said Mike, smiling at Sandra's accurate statement.

"I'm just glad you're all here," said Kevin. "She has been talking about this dinner non-stop for the past two days. So at least I'll get some sound sleep tonight." Everyone except for Junior, who appeared aloof from the discussion, laughed at Kevin's comment.

"Well," said Sandra, "our family doesn't hold as many get-togethers as yours, Kevin. So, of course, I'm going to be excited." Kevin did not respond. Instead, he just took a bite into the baked chicken and rice collected on his fork.

"What's this I hear about you having a crush on someone at school, Junior?" asked Max, changing the subject and catching his nephew off-guard. The adult faces at the table turned toward Junior, whose own eyes widened behind his eyeglasses like he had just witnessed a tragic accident. Kevin looked at his son, beaming with pride.

"Who told you that?" Junior asked in a high-pitched voice.

"Your mom, of course," replied Max. Junior gave his mother a look of sixth-grader dissatisfaction. He had clearly been embarrassed.

"It's okay, Junior," interrupted Mike, who was visibly interested in hearing about his nephew's puppy love. "What's her name?"

After hesitating for a moment, Junior reluctantly uttered the name. "Heather."

"Heather?" asked Tonya in a startled tone. "Is Heather black or white?"

"What difference does it make, Tonya?" inquired Sandra. "Racial prejudice is not tolerated in our household."

"Who said anything about *prejudice*?" replied Tonya. "I just asked because Heather isn't a common name for black girls. That's a fact."

"She's black," interjected Junior.

"Oh, wow," said Tonya. "Well, this is a first for me. I certainly never heard of any black Heathers." Sandra rolled her eyes in silence, resolving, from Max's perspective, to leave the situation alone.

"Are you two in the same class?" asked

Max, already knowing the answer.

"No, she has a different teacher, but she's also in the sixth grade," responded Junior.

"Does she like you back?" Mike inquired.

"What little girl wouldn't like my handsome Junior?" replied Sandra, defensively. She looked at her son and smiled along with Kevin, who hadn't stopped smirking since Max broached the subject.

"I don't know," said Junior, timidly.

"We're working on that," said Kevin directly to Mike. "Trust me when I say that we'll get there in due time."

"Take your time *getting there*," interrupted Sandra, staring directly at Kevin. "I don't want Junior growing up too quickly." Max and Brian then looked at each other with mutual anticipation of this scenario playing out in their lives. Max wondered to himself how this conversation with Brian would unfold in the years to come. He knew that, like Sandra, Brian would be the more protective one between the two of them. Despite being an only child, Brian was naturally a nurturer. Brian called to check in on his parents regularly, the youth at The Center looked up to him like he was a gay superhero, and his emotional support to Max could not be contested by anyone. Max often marveled at Kevin's ability to be an anchor in the lives of so many.

"Just be yourself, Junior," said Max. "If she

likes you for who you are, then you have a keeper." Junior looked at his uncle and nodded, appearing unsure of how to respond. "You have plenty of time to understand what I mean, Junior. Don't think too hard on it." Being caught up in his uncle-role, Max looked at Brian and said, "If it's okay, Sandra, Brian and I have an announcement we'd like to share."

"Sure," said Sandra "What's the news?" she asked with curiosity. Max cleared his throat.

"Brian and I have decided to adopt a child before the end of the year," said Max. He placed his hands beneath the dinner table and began rubbing them together, feeling the light moisture of sweat form on his palms. "In fact," Max continued, "we're attending orientation for prospective foster and adoptive parents the week after next."

"That's great," said Sandra. "Are you thinking about a boy or a girl?"

"We've been thinking about a boy around five or six years of age, but in the end, we'll have to consider the best fit for us and the child," Brian answered. Max nodded his head in agreement.

"That makes sense," said Sandra. "Good for you two."

"Well, I guess if you two guys think it's a good idea, then all the best to you," said Mike. He stared at his plate as he talked, not looking at anyone at the dinner table. Max gave himself some time to think before responding to his brother's statement. Tonya, who openly loathed the fact that her baby brother was gay, remained mute as she cut into her chicken.

“Thanks, Mike,” Max stated, admitting to himself that his brother’s reaction could have taken on a more objectionable stance and tone. “We feel it’s not only the right decision for us but also for the child we’ll be adopting.”

“Tell that to God,” muttered Kevin under his breath. All eyes except Sandra’s, who was looking at her plate and shaking her head in disbelief, turned to Kevin.

“Excuse me?” said Max, raising his posture.

“You and everyone at this table heard what I said,” retorted Kevin. “My point is that nowhere in God’s word does it justify two men or two women being together. And to make matters worse, you two now want to adopt and raise a child in such a household! Frankly, I’m not comfortable with you bringing these ungodly ideas into my house and around my son. Junior, go finish your dinner in the basement.”

The eleven-year-old turned his head and looked at his mother for affirmation. Sandra reluctantly nodded to Junior in agreement, at which point, with a look of heavy disappointment, he took his dinner and made his toward the basement doorway.

“Ungodly ideas?” questioned Max after his

nephew was gone. “Brian and I are partners who have committed to one another, no different than you and my sister. And whether you like it or not, Junior is our nephew, so how dare you tell him to leave the dinner table during this conversation? There’s no need to fill that boy’s heart with hate or resentment toward his own family. There’s too much of that in our family as it is.” After hearing himself, Max secretly hoped that his last words didn’t rouse Tonya or Mike.

“Please, Max and Kevin,” Sandra interrupted. “Let’s just finish dinner and move on from this conversation.”

“Yeah, we should forget about it,” Tonya agreed, finally weighing in on the matter.

“How can I finish my dinner,” Max began as he looked across at Sandra, “after your husband sent my nephew downstairs as if Brian and I are some sort of pariahs?”

“Please, Max,” stated Sandra. “We can discuss this another time. You and Max know that Junior already looks up to you two.”

“In other words,” Max persisted, “Brian and I are supposed to *pretend* that Junior was not just sent away from the table because of our announcement?” Sandra sighed and placed her knife and fork on her plate. It was clear to everyone at the table that she was overcome by a sense of powerlessness.

“You can take it how you want to, Max,”

said Kevin. “This is my house, and that’s my son. I’ve tried to tolerate your situation, but now you two have gone too far by broadcasting this nonsense in our home.”

“Guys, can we *please* just finish dinner and talk about this later?” Sandra pleaded, in one final attempt to defuse the situation, to both Kevin and Max.

“Let’s go, Brian,” said Max, getting out of his seat at once. “So much for family,” he stated as they left the dining room and made their way to the front door.

“I knew this was going to happen,” said Max as he got into the driver’s seat from the driveway, slamming the door behind him. Brian remained silent. “The most infuriating matter was not Kevin’s religious beliefs, babe, but the fact that he asked Junior to leave the table. It’s like he was insinuating that we were untouchables or that our decision to adopt would somehow taint our own nephew. The nerve of that man!” Max shook his head continuously as he drove home in disbelief at what had just occurred. He thought about all the times that he and Brian babysat Junior, took him to amusement parks, and invited him over on weekends. Max felt that Kevin’s reaction to their news was a personal slap in the face.

“You’re right, Max. What Kevin did was completely unnecessary,” Brian conceded.

“His promotion from deacon to assistant

pastor at their church must be going to his head," replied Max. "I should have foreseen this coming, but my focus was too much on Mike and Tonya. Tonight, they were actually okay for once!"

"That's true," replied Brian. "For whatever reason, they stayed a lot more quiet than usual. I'm surprised that Sandra didn't say anything about Junior going to the basement, though."

"I'm not," said Max. "She made the choice to stand by her husband, the man of the house. And with his new position at the church, I'm afraid that things will only get worse."

"I sure hope not," Brian stated. Max knew the religious beliefs of his husband's parents were costly. Harold and Melanie hadn't attended their wedding three years ago, knew nothing of Brian's academic research or how he earned a living, and were presently clueless about the couple's adoption plans. Such was the steep price that Max and Brian, as well as many of their friends, had to pay for living their truth. When Brian came out to his fundamentalist parents, they seriously considered excommunication and disowning him altogether. Although their total abandonment was eventually ruled out, they insisted that Brian refrain from sharing any details about his private life with them or other relatives. He was also directed never to return to their place of worship unless he was willing to be delivered from his sinfulness.

"All we can do now is simply hope for the

best," said Brian. "When you're in a better place, you may want to give Sandra a call to let her know how you're feeling. I don't believe that she agreed with everything that happened today. She was initially congratulatory when you made the announcement, after all."

"I need some time to collect my thoughts before making that call," said Max. "I'm too upset to even think about what I would say to her right now. After all that we have done for Junior, that's the treatment that we're given?" he asked rhetorically. Max took a moment to pause and catch his breath. He could feel himself becoming emotional. "I was of the belief that our child would grow up alongside his or her big cousin, Junior, but now that doesn't even seem possible."

"One day at a time, Max," said Brian. "Who knows what will happen? The best we can do right now is continue loving one another, proceed with the adoption process, and hope that the two of them will come around at some point."

Brian placed his left hand on Max's right leg as they drove the rest of the way home. Max's mood began to uplift as he felt Brian's touch. Being unsure of how his relationship with Sandra would subsequently play out, Brian's hand was a reassuring reminder that he was not alone in this world. While driving home in silence, Max was certain that they were making the right decision to adopt. He resolved during the car ride that there was nothing that anyone could do or say that would convince him that their decision to raise a child was amiss.

****

A week later, Brian arrived home exhausted from The Center's routine HIV and STI testing held in collaboration with the county's health department. Saturdays were the busiest days there due to the free testing offered in addition to normal social groups and activities. Max was wrapping up his cleaning for the day when Brian walked through the door and kissed him before relaxing on their sectional.

"You look exhausted, babe," Max remarked as he retrieved a bottled water from the refrigerator for Brian.

"It was a long day as usual. Fortunately, there were no positive HIV tests today, but two people tested positive for syphilis."

"Well, at least there were no preliminary positive results for HIV," said Max, handing Brian the cold drink he had retrieved. "Y'all have certainly had your fair share of positive results during the past couple of months."

"That's true. We just hope that's not the case with syphilis over the coming weeks," replied Brian. "Sometimes, when I see the same guys frequent the clinic what seems like every two or three weeks, I cannot help but wonder if *this* is the day their test will come back positive. Many of them, especially the young ones, are constantly engaging in risky behaviors with anonymous partners that they meet online. They might have had a dozen or more partners since the last time they came in to be tested."

"The access to sex is a lot more immediate today with all the social media and hook-up apps compared to when we were younger, babe. At the same time, you must admit that we made our share of mistakes, too." Max sat next to his partner and placed Brian's ankles over his thighs in order to massage his feet, recalling the first time they had gotten tested together at the county health department when they were dating. It was a gut-wrenching experience for them both. Though Max had resolved that he would date Brian regardless of his HIV status, he wasn't completely sure what his own test would yield. They were both relieved to receive negative results, knowing that each of them had 'slipped up' before they met.

"Yes, we did," said Brian, "which means that things could have ended very differently for one or both of us." Max considered what Brian was saying and realized that he was right. He knew that as versatile men, it would have only been a matter of time before a lapse of sound judgment had caught up with either of them. As he massaged Brian's soft feet, he knew they were fortunate to have found each other and established a monogamous relationship.

"You're absolutely right," said Max.

"No," said Brian. "I'm just lucky to have you." Brian smiled and curled his toes, showing his appreciation for the generous foot treatment Max provided. "How was your day?"

"Well, Sandra called me to apologize for last night. She told me that she felt 'conflicted' being between me and Kevin but realized that things had gone too far when Junior was asked to go downstairs."

"Sounds honest of her," replied Brian. "I didn't expect that the two of you would be speaking so soon."

"Neither did I, but she called me," Max stated dismissively. "The least I could do was hear her out."

"How did you respond?" Brian asked with mild hesitation in his voice, peering into his husband's eyes.

"I mostly listened to her explain how torn she felt about the situation. She insisted, which I believe, that she was glad for us both to start our own family. On the other hand, she also sympathized with her husband in his new pastoral role at Mount Sinai Baptist Church." Max's eyes began to tear up as he recounted their discussion while he directed his foot massage to the center of Brian's feet. "She told me that while Kevin was a deacon, the two of them put up with gossip about her 'gay brother living in sin with another man.'

Until today, I had no idea that folks at their church even talked about us." Max paused briefly to catch his breath.

"As I was saying, though," Max continued, "while Sandra managed to look past those statements of people at the church who knew nothing about us, Kevin took them much more personally. As a result, his homophobia escalated to full condemnation and resentment without Sandra being able to challenge his position. After weeks of arguing, she eventually informed Kevin that for their relationship to continue, he would have to accept me as her brother and our marriage. He was entitled to his religious and moral views of homosexuality, along with the Baptist Church, but Sandra made sure he understood there would still be family gatherings, dinners, holidays and celebrations, funerals, as well as phone calls and visits…and during these times, he would have to treat us with respect."

"Now that's a bad woman for you," said Brian, who listened carefully and reached over to wipe his partner's tears. "For Sandra to make Kevin accept an ultimatum like that shows how much she cares for you and the example that your mother set for all four of you."

"Well, that was at least up until now," Max stated as he sniffed and attempted to speak without his emotions choking his vocal cords. "A lot more responsibilities and expectations have been placed on Kevin's shoulders now that he's assistant pastor, including leadership over the men's fellowship. Pastor Carter has made it quite clear that Kevin must be vigilant in upholding Biblical family values. Sandra suggested that our decision to adopt was going too far for Kevin, admitting that he feared the impact this would have on Junior, his own image in the eyes of Pastor Carter, and the rest of the church. I tried to assure Sandra that our having a child would not be very different from the way things have been now, but she insisted that Kevin didn't want to be involved in raising 'confused children' and that the backlash from the church would be unpredictable once they found out."

"Oh my," said Brian. "Well, that's certainly an earful I didn't expect. Our relationship has nothing to do with their church."

"Who are you telling?" Max asked rhetorically. "You're preaching to the choir, babe."

"Where do things stand at this point?" asked Brian.

"I'm not sure," said Max, pausing Brian's foot rub. "Sandra insisted that they need some time to discuss this as a couple. She doesn't have an issue with the adoption and being an aunt, but how things might develop with Kevin is a different story altogether. I told her to take all the time she needs, but our adoption orientation is next week."

"Wow," said Brian in disbelief. "I honestly

didn't expect them to be so bothered by our decision. We expected that Tonya and Mike would vocalize their disapproval, but Kevin clearly led the way on this issue." Max resumed tenderly massaging his partner's pedicured feet.

"Yes, he did. And now it looks as though Sandra is taking more of Kevin's side."

"That's not a fair judgment, Max. You know Sandra loves us and that she couldn't be happier for our plans. However, now she's married to an assistant pastor at a prominent Baptist Church whose senior pastor has made his opposition to our community very public. That's a difficult position for any woman in her predicament, especially when you take into consideration the privileges and hype that come along with leadership in black churches, big or small."

"I understand all of that, Brian, but she is still my sister. And any child we adopt will be her nephew or niece."

"True as that might be, baby, we cannot force their acceptance as a couple. If they have a problem with us visiting, attending our adoption shower, or whatever the case may be, that is *their* decision."

"It is, but why can't they simply accept us and our family?"

"It's Kevin's new role in the church, Pastor Carter, their denomination, my parent's denomination… In fact, it's most Christian denominations, other religions, fear. It's all those things. This isn't news to you, Max."

"I just feel like you're letting them off the hook. At this moment in time, it's not the Christian community or any other religion that's directly compromising our family or telling us we're not good enough! It's Kevin and my sister Sandra we're talking about."

"True, but Kevin's position – like those of my very own parents, please don't forget – are informed by church doctrine. And as long as he believes that heterosexuality is the only acceptable basis for a marriage, then his position will not change. Don't discount your sister, though. She provided him with an ultimatum that he accepted once, so she may have something up her sleeve this time around. But in the meantime, we have each other, and we'll have our own child soon enough."

Brian kissed Max gently on his full reddish-brown lips under his trimmed mustache after the foot massage ended. Max recalled the night that he held Brian in his arms after his parents learned that he was gay. He remembered the feelings of isolation and rejection that Brian expressed that night, which were painful emotions he had heard echoed on numerous occasions by friends and previous partners. Max then realized that the hook-up culture that seemed to thrive amongst black gay and bisexual men, which they had initially discussed, was partly established in response to their collective rejection from black churches and mainstream communities.

For the second time that afternoon, Max felt grateful to have found Brian. What they had lost in the ways of acceptance from parents, siblings, neighbors, professional colleagues, and society in general, they had compensated for through their mutual love for each other and their network of friends. Relaxed and seated by his partner on the couch, Max accepted that he needed to give Sandra and Kevin the time and space they required. He and Brian already had everything they needed, and much to prepare for in the future.

****

"We're set!" exclaimed Brian as Todd threw out his king of spades, earning the last book of the spades game that would have given Max and his husband board.

"That's what happens when you go up against Cleveland's best," Lamont chimed in, grinning as he and Todd laughed at their opponents' embarrassing loss.

"You guys aren't right," said Max as he shook his head and took the cards to shuffle in preparation for the next hand.

"There's a chance you may have a point there," responded Todd, "but we are and will always be the champions. How do you guys manage to sleep at night knowing that your house was turned upside down by me and Lamont?"

"We sleep just fine, thank you," Brian declared. "My Max lays it down where it counts."

"At least he's laying it down *somewhere*," Lamont jeered. "Because he certainly isn't putting anything down on this table!" The four of them all laughed hysterically at Lamont's crassness.

Playing spades and throwing shade went hand-in-hand whenever this coterie convened for an intimate social. These get-togethers began as a regular monthly event two years ago until competing demands in their individual lives necessitated gathering less frequently. After a decade of working as a hairdresser in various shops around the city, Lamont opened his own hair salon around that time. And Todd, who frequently travels to Michigan for work, met a guy in Detroit with whom he began to occupy most of his weekends. Instead of meeting on the first Friday of every month as was their custom, the group now planned their game nights based upon mutual availability, scheduling six to eight weeks out sometimes.

Max shuffled the cards intensely and hoped for a better hand this deal, needing desperately for his and Brian's luck to change. Brian looked at him and said, "We got this, baby. It's not over yet."

"Listen," Todd said, silencing everyone with his right index finger pointed vertically in front of his mouth. They all focused on the female jazz vocalist scatting in the background, hitting what Max considered inhuman notes with her mezzo-soprano voice. "The fat lady is singing loud and clearly. This beatin' is almost as good as her killin' this song."

"I'm not paying you or your partner any attention, Todd," Brian replied, trying not to crack a smile. "Just watch and see," he remarked while quickly putting on his game face as Max began dealing the cards.

"Keep praying, chil'," interrupted Lamont. "You and Max need all the prayers you can get in order to stop this disaster coming your way."

"All right now," said Max. "Y'all know we don't tolerate talking across the table in our house!"

"Ain't nobody talking across the board!" Lamont quickly remarked as he picked up his hand and assiduously began organizing his cards in a precise fashion.

"You're getting mighty close," said Max, picking up his own hand of thirteen cards. He wanted to, but refrained from, cringing as he painstakingly arranged the multitude of low diamonds and clubs in his hand. *You've got to be kidding me*, he thought to himself. *I can't seem to catch a break!*

"What's it looking like over there, partner?" Todd called to Lamont, initiating the bidding process.

"Five and a possible," Lamont responded immediately.

"I see. Let's go eight and wrap this game up once and for all," responded Todd.

"Fine by me, chil'," Lamont declared.

"How are you looking, Max?" asked Brian with unhidden apprehension.

"I'll be lucky if I get two," Max groaned.

"Let's go for five," Brian said, smiling, "and if we go down, we'll go down blazing."

"Ain't no *if* about it," said Lamont. "Y'all are definitely going down! Can't you smell the smoke?"

Sitting to Max's left, Todd threw out an ace of hearts and grinned like the Cheshire Cat. He and Lamont had been friends prior to meeting Brian and Max. The duo met through a mutual friend named Rochelle seven years ago during her and Todd's senior year of college. That was the year when Lamont started doing Rochelle's hair. Thanks to their respective fraternity and sorority, she and Todd were already friends. Following her third visit to the salon where Lamont worked and having acquired a newfound comfort level with her flamboyant friend, she introduced him and Todd one evening out in the Flats. The two men hit it off from the beginning, later finding their shared interest in cards at a spades tournament held by Rochelle's sorority. As much as they enjoyed spending time with them, Max and Brian always struggled when they played cards against their skilled opponents. Todd and Lamont seemed to know instinctively what each other would play. Together, they were a masterful combination and proven competitors, while Max and Brian played for pure enjoyment and the camaraderie of the game.

“Two books already in,” boasted Todd, throwing down the little joker.

“I can’t believe this!” remarked Max as he rolled his eyes in frustration.

“Ain’t this something,” said Brian. He shook his head painfully as he released his queen of spades onto the table. His only remaining possibles were the king of diamonds and ten of spades.

“It’s time you guys get with the program,” said Lamont. “That’s how we do,” he remarked and began singing along with the male R&B singer whining a song from the ’90s. Max and Brian were compelled to laugh along with Lamont’s grandstanding as Todd beamed with pride.

“So how are things going with Tim?” asked Brian.

“Decent, aside from being at a crossroads right now,” replied Todd. “It’s been a year since we’ve been dating, but for us to take things to the next level, one of us has to relocate. I think we both realize that a move is necessary for our relationship to grow, yet neither of us has mustered up the courage to address the issue.”

“I don’t know why you’re so afraid to talk

to him about this, Todd," interjected Lamont, who had already met Tim on two occasions. "You know he cares about you deeply," he added as he picked up their third book.

"Nothing about this is trivial, though," stated Todd, becoming professional in his tone and body language as if he were chairing one of his meetings at the insurance company where he worked. "There are a lot of factors we both have to consider, such as our jobs, families, friends, property, et cetera."

"True," replied Max, "but in order for you to seriously address them, don't you think that a discussion is warranted?"

"Max is right," said Brian. "You may be surprised at what you both discover by just being honest with each other." Max reached over the table and picked up their second book.

"I've never taken this step with a guy before," replied Todd.

"It's no different than the steps you would've taken with a female when you were fooling yourself during your *bi-curious* college days," Lamont added.

"I think what Lamont is attempting to express, Todd, is that love is love," declared Max impatiently. "And two people who are in a long-distance relationship eventually have to reconcile the distance between them with their future goals."

"This fool knew what I meant!" snapped

Lamont as he rolled his hazel eyes.

"Let me ask you this," said Max, trying not to entertain Lamont's tomfoolery. "Can you see yourself settling down with Tim?"

"Yes," he stated matter-of-factly. "I just don't know how that would happen," Todd replied.

"Well, there you have it," Brian said. "You already know what you desire. By communicating with him, you'll figure out the *how*, at least if he feels the same way."

"You and these *if's*, Brian!" insisted Lamont. "Ain't no *if* about it. Tim loves this man. He would get the hell out of Detroit in a hot minute if Todd called him up tonight and asked. I guarantee it."

"It's not that simple," expressed Todd.

"It may not be, but you know what you need to do," Lamont returned while slamming his big joker on the table and cementing their victory.

"I know that I could go for another drink," pleaded Todd. "In fact, I'll just pour another round for everyone in honor of our near-perfect record against you two."

"Yes, indeed," Lamont said. "I'll second that." He circled their final score of five hundred and twenty with pride and then began clearing the kitchen table to prepare for Todd's infamous blue punch.

"Well, this round can celebrate two occasions," said Brian as he stood up, shifting into a celebratory mood despite his and Max's loss.

"And what would the second occasion be?" asked Todd with interest from the kitchen island, where he poured the remaining batch of potent teal-looking liquor into four glasses.

Brian gently grabbed onto the defined shoulders of his husband, who was still sitting at the table, and looked down upon him with the same wonderment he possessed when Max proposed. "We're attending orientation for the adoption process with the county next week. After much thought and planning, we've decided that we're ready to add to our family unit."

"Oh, my God!" exclaimed Todd as he poured the last drink into the fourth glass. "That's pretty amazing, my friends. You two are going to make terrific parents and some kid quite lucky."

"Thanks," said Max. He took Brian's left hand into his own and kissed the top of it.

"I'm with Todd on this," said Lamont. "There's not a couple that I know, gay or straight, more suitable to adopt than you guys. After hearing plenty of horror stories from my clients at the hair shop about what children in the system go through, I know you guys will make a huge difference."

"Drinks are ready," interjected Todd. "Let's toast!" he suggested, prompting the other three to join him at the black granite island on which the four teal drinks stood next to what remained of a shrimp platter. Each of them picked up his glass and held it in the air. “Here’s to the joy of friendship, health, and a good ol’ fashioned spades beating,” announced Todd as he smiled with pride. “Likewise, here’s to both Brian and Max as they prepare to transition into being fathers and growing their household. May their love, peace, and joy increase a thousand-fold.”

“Well, thank you, Todd,” said Max after making his initial sip.

“Anytime,” Todd replied.

“Tell us more about the process,” Lamont requested.

“Next week,” began Max, “we’re attending an optional informational session for anyone interested in being adoptive or foster parents. In the following week, we begin mandatory three-hour classes on Tuesdays and Thursdays, which will last a total of six weeks. After completing that requirement, a social worker must conduct a couple of assessments at our home in order to ensure that we’re fit to adopt. And once those things are handled, we should begin the process of meeting potential adoptees.”

“You guys are going to have your hands full!” said Lamont.

“Yes,” said Brian, “but we’ve both made arrangements at work not to schedule anything after 4:00 p.m. on our class days so that we’re on time. The staff at The Center are also aware that they should only contact me after hours in the event of an emergency over the next two months.

"See how prepared you guys are," said Lamont. "Better you guys than me. I couldn't imagine trying to raise a child with the load of my salon, taking care of my mother, and trying to maintain somewhat of a life for myself."

"You could do it if you wanted," said Max. "I know you would make a great parent."

"Well, let me be clear as crystal, chil'. I don't want to. That's way too much responsibility. What age are you guys thinking anyway?"

"No one younger than five," said Brian. We're thinking around five or six, but who knows. Also, we think it would be more suitable for us to raise a boy than a girl. Max swears that his sisters were a lot moodier than he and his brother were."

"It's true," said Max. "Girls can be a handful."

"So can boys," added Todd. "I grew up with my two brothers and that was it – just us three boys. My dad even prayed for a girl, but it wasn't a part of the plan. Now my youngest brother is in jail for the next seven years because he thought bank robbing was a viable career option. What a knucklehead!"

"You and your middle brother still managed to come out just fine, Todd," Brian teased. "We'll cross the gender bridge in due time. Meanwhile, we're just focused on these upcoming classes and getting this place together."

“So that’s why you all have those boxes in your office?” inquired Lamont. “I was wondering what you guys were doing when I passed there on my way to the bathroom. Neither of you had discussed moving, so I didn’t think that was the case.”

“Yes, that will be the kid’s bedroom. We’re in the process of converting it and placing a few items in storage.” Todd’s cell phone rang as Max completed his statement.

“Hey, Tim,” said Todd in a deep tone that no one had heard that evening. “You’re already that close?” Todd asked before pausing. “Okay, I’ll be leaving here shortly to head to my house. Be safe,” he concluded as he hung up the call.

“Tim’s driving down?” asked Lamont with an attitude of disappointment toward his bestie.

“Yeah, he should be at my place in the next thirty to forty minutes,” responded Todd. He began to make sure he had all his belongings after rinsing out the pitcher containing his blue punch.

“You could’ve invited him over to our place,” said Brian, jumping into the mix. “Max and I deserve the opportunity to meet this mystery companion at some point.”

“Next time,” promised Todd. “He went out to dinner after work with a co-worker to celebrate her promotion, so he couldn’t make it in time.”

“I’m gonna hold you to that,” stated Brian. “Besides, if there’s any chance that he’ll be moving to Cleveland, then we need to bring him into the fold quickly." Everyone laughed. Lamont followed suit in gathering his belongings in order to ride down the elevator with Todd. Brian and Max exchanged hugs with their friends as their gathering ended for the evening. After Lamont and Todd left, the couple looked at each other in the eyes and breathed deeply. They smiled at each other, experiencing a shared feeling of gratitude for their two friends.

****

On the following Tuesday, Max and Brian sat proudly next to one another in the classroom where orientation was being held for prospective foster and adoptive parents. Michelle, their facilitator this evening, stood in front of the classroom finalizing her presentation and checking the DVD player. She was a white female with blond hair who appeared between twenty-five and thirty years old to Max. He wondered what this thin woman, who lacked a wedding ring, knew about parenting as she opened her presentation slides on the projector screen in front of the class and welcomed the last-minute stragglers looking for open seats. *Please let her have a more seasoned co-facilitator, who just so happens to be running late,* he thought to himself. *There's no way that she can possibly relate to most of us in the room.*

Max looked around the room in amazement at his and Brian's thirteen counterparts, noting the age and socioeconomic diversity of their peers. There were two African American heterosexual couples, one heterosexual and one lesbian white couple, three single black women, one single black man, and a single white woman.

"Good evening, and welcome to our county's September informational meeting. My name is Michelle, and I've been with the county as a social worker for five years. Tonight, I'll be providing you all with an in-depth overview of what it means to be a foster and/or adoptive parent, the process, as well as the requirements," the facilitator said before identifying where the bathrooms and vending machines were located. "But before we delve into our formal material, I would like to hear from everyone in the room first. So, let's start with introductions. If you wouldn't mind, please state your name and inform us *why* you're here this evening." Suddenly a number of people sat up and shifted in their seats after Michelle's request.

"Let's start with you in the back," Michelle said, looking directly at a young African American female who was seated in a corner by herself. While still suspicious of Michelle, Max appreciated her approach so far.

"Umm," began Michelle's initial target. "My name is Tracey, and I'm here today because I would like to become a foster parent. I don't have any kids of my own yet, but I know there are a lot of kids in the system that could use a positive role-model in their lives. It's about me doing my part," she finished.

"Thank you," said Michelle as she then eyed the couple sitting in front of Tracey.

"I'm David, and I'm here with my wife. We're here today because we're in the process of exploring our options due to our inability to have biological kids. As it stands, it looks like adoption is our best choice, so we're here to learn as much as we can in order to make an informed choice."

"My name is Amanda," said David's wife. "Since we're unable to have our own children, we're looking into our options internationally, through a private attorney, or through the county. It's a big decision that we don't want to take lightly. We're just trying to be as hands-on as possible."

"Thank you, Amanda, and David as well," said Michelle. Max looked around the room, and he noticed that everyone was listening intently to each speaker. He could see people beginning to empathize with Tracey, David, Amanda, and those who followed, as evidenced by head nods and compassionate glances. As the next speakers shared their names and reasons for becoming parents, Max was impressed with the various *whys* that were disclosed. One couple spoke of their desire to parent after their kids graduated high school, another wished to add to their existing family, the African American young man discussed how his foster mother impacted his own life, and the lesbian couple expressed their goal of providing a loving household to LGBTQ youth. By the time it was Brian and Max's turn to speak, several of their cohorts were crying and using the tissue boxes that had been intentionally placed on their tables by Michelle before orientation.

"My name is Brian," Max's husband began once Michelle's eyes reached him. "My partner and I have been married for three years now, and adopting a child is something we've both wanted from the beginning. There's no one with whom I'd rather share the gift of fatherhood."

"I'm Maxwell," said Max, who was the last person to give an introduction. "Being a father is something I've desired since I was a kid. More than anything, Brian and I want to provide a child with unconditional love and the foundation to know that his or her dreams are worthwhile."

"Thank you, Maxwell and Brian," Michelle said. "Throughout tonight, as you all continue down this journey, it's important that you remember why you are here. I'm here," she paused, "because twenty-two years ago, my parents gave me the opportunity that you are now considering. I was adopted at the age of six by a loving couple who wasn't rich, but they loved me just as much as their biological son." Max acknowledged to himself that he had misjudged Michelle. He gradually leaned forward in his seat, realizing that he had a lot to learn over the upcoming weeks.

"Tonight," she continued, "my goal is to help you understand the necessity of foster and adoptive parents in the eyes of the children we serve. Just as each of you has your own reasons, our children have their own stories, needs, and ambitions that are at stake."

Max and Brian looked at each other after Michelle had finished speaking. The gravity of their commitment to being fathers suddenly hit Max. Henceforth, there would be no going back or delaying this process for anything. They grabbed each other's hands as Michelle continued speaking to the group. Although their public displays of affection were generally limited for safety reasons, they felt comfortable in this space, where Michelle had already managed to foster their collective openness and empathy. Max sensed at this moment in time, holding Brian's right hand, that their unapologetic solidarity would be required as they progressed. *This is just the beginning phase.*

Chapter 3

While Brian met the delivery men downstairs to direct them to their seventeenth-floor apartment, Max stood in the empty second bedroom, admiring the newly painted sky-blue walls. He envisioned how not only this room but their entire home would be converted by early morning cartoons, homework assignments, game nights, story time, increased laughter echoing throughout every room, and other subtle changes that would reshape their urban dwelling, whether through family photos or artwork displayed on walls and their refrigerator. As he leaned thoughtfully onto the doorway of the former office, the light blue walls of the room transformed into lenses through which he saw birthday celebrations, prom night, high school graduation, college visits, a springtime wedding, and even grandchildren. Max could feel his heart racing with pride and fear in response to their future flashing before his eyes. Without warning, Brian could be heard from the hallway directing the delivery men to their condo. Max walked to the front door and opened it cautiously.

"Good timing," said Brian as he approached the apartment entrance ahead of the two delivery men carrying a kid-sized dresser.

"I and everyone else on the floor heard you giving directions," teased Max. "Come on right in, guys," he instructed the workers. "The bedroom is just this way."

"Right behind you," the short and stocky white fellow replied while backing into the doorway. "This is a nice place you two have," he added after quickly appraising their home with his light green eyes.

"Thanks," said Brian. "We've been here for close to three years now."

"You certainly made a decent investment. It seems like everyone is moving downtown these days," replied the stocky mover, still following Max's lead.

"The room is just here on your left-hand side. And if you wouldn't mind, the dresser will go along this wall," Max signaled with his two hands.

"Where would you like the other pieces?" asked the taller black worker, breaking his silence once the furnishing was placed. Max quickly responded to his question and demonstrated exactly where they had planned each item to be positioned. Following Max's instructions, Brian provided them with the key pass needed for the freight elevator and asked if they wanted anything to drink upon their return.

"Some water would be great," promptly responded the white worker.

"Yes, that would be fine," said his reserved co-worker, nodding in agreement.

With the front door closed behind the

delivery men, the couple walked into the kitchen, where Brian grabbed two bottled waters from the refrigerator. "They seem like nice guys," said Brian.

"Did you notice how quiet and nervous the black guy looked?" asked Max.

"Yeah, but maybe he's new on the job or just not used to seeing guys like us. He didn't strike me as homophobic, though."

"You're probably right, Brian. His demeanor just seemed a little odd. I think the room's going to look great once it's finished," Max stated, switching the subject.

"Me too. It's funny how small the furniture looks in the room."

"Very true. And this is going to be one spoiled kid. I never had my own room growing up until Mike moved out and I was a junior in high school. We practically shared everything in our house, from toys to Mike's outgrown and out-of-style clothes."

Brian laughed at his husband's recollection. "I hear you, sweetheart. I had my own room as the only child, but our home was modest. It wasn't much compared to this condo. To my dad's credit, he ensured that Mom and I had everything as the sole breadwinner, but we'll be able to give our kid an entirely new experience."

"Yeah, that's how I feel about what Sandra and Kevin have created for Junior. It's a blessing for parents to improve upon what they knew as children. That's progress."

"Speaking of Sandra, how is she doing?" Brian asked.

"Busy as usual with Kevin and Junior, work, and studying. She still hasn't said anything about Kevin and her making a decision related to our adoption."

"That's surprising. It's already the middle of October. She'll have to inform us of something sooner or later. Our initial assessment with the social worker is next week," Brian stated.

"You're right," said Max. "The whole thing still makes me nervous for some reason."

"You worry too much sometimes, baby," Brian expressed while gently massaging his partner's shoulder. "But regardless of their choice, we'll get through it."

Rapid knocking outside their apartment halted their conversation. Max opened the front door for the delivery men, who returned with the chest, kid's desk, and chair. Both men carefully worked their way between the living room and kitchen toward the hallway and new bedroom, placing each item as instructed.

"Thanks, guys. Here are your waters," said Brian as they approached the kitchen where he and Max stood.

"Thank you," the young black worker expressed.

"Anytime," said Brian. "Your help is much appreciated."

"Well, we only have the bed items and nightstand left," said the stocky white mover, whose commanding voice compensated for his height.

"Sounds good. You guys just take your time," said Max.

"Yes, sir," said the black guy after taking one last sip of water before their next trip downstairs, leaving his bottle of water on the kitchen island.

"You see what I mean?" asked Max after they were left alone again.

"Why don't you leave him alone?" asked Brian. "We have no idea what's going through his head. He could be dealing with some personal issues for all we know."

"I guess that's my point," said Max. "His unsure posture and soft-spoken voice remind me of so many students I've come across at work. Typically, they're not bad students; however, a lot of them tend to struggle socially or have obstacles at home that interfere with school."

"I see what you mean, but he's our mover, and both of them are doing the job we paid them to do."

"Your practicality is one of the main reasons I fell in love with you, babe, but maybe there's something we could do."

"You do realize that you could be opening up a can full of worms, snakes, and God only knows what else, but if you feel *that* strongly then just ask," insisted Brian. "You have my support."

"That's all I needed to hear. What are you smiling about?" Max asked after his husband grinned.

"You're still as thoughtful as ever after the last five years. I couldn't be any luckier, baby." Once the movers returned for their third trip, Brian opened the door for them, and they carefully entered, pulling the remaining pieces of the bedroom set on two dollies.

"This is everything that's left. We'll get the bed set up and all the trash cleared out once we're done," said the young black mover.

"Fantastic," said Max. "Just let us know if you need anything."

Brian left Max to grab two twenties out of his wallet from the bedroom. Max stood in the kitchen, pondering if he should pry into the young man's business. His mind turned toward his mother and how she questioned him and his siblings at dinner every night about their days, friends, what they had learned in school, social and political events, general likes and dislikes, and nearly everything else under the sun. Reflecting on his mother's wisdom in her Socratic questioning at dinner time led him to a plan. When Brian returned with the tip money, Max smiled at his partner as if to convey his decision.

"So, what's your grand plan?" Brian asked, taking an interest in the implied strategy.

"Just watch and learn," said Max, who took a seat on their couch and turned on the television. "I got this," he expressed.

"Well, lead the way, baby," Brian said, sitting next to his partner, who had turned on the news to pass the time.

"You gentlemen are now all set," announced the stocky young man twenty minutes later as he and his co-worker walked out of the bedroom into the hallway, pulling the empty dollies and carrying small bags of debris.

"You guys sure moved fast," said Brian, who stood up from the couch and walked to the bedroom for his final stamp of approval.

"That was certainly quicker than we expected," echoed Max. "We really appreciate your getting everything inside without damaging a single thing. Seeing the room come together reinforces how close we are to adoption."

"It's no problem. That's what we're here for," the white delivery guy replied. "Congratulations on your new addition. That must be really exciting."

"Thanks!" expressed Brian as he reentered the area after reviewing the bedroom. "We're wrapping up the required classes soon, so we haven't started meeting potential adoptees yet.

That will hopefully happen within the first couple of weeks in November. We're just getting a heads-up on the process by setting up this bedroom." Brian handed the two young men each a twenty-dollar bill for their tip.

"Appreciate it," said the quiet worker who pulled out a tablet to obtain a signature to complete their delivery. "Can one of you please sign here indicating that your furniture has been received in new condition and set up?"

"Let me take care of that," said Max, reaching for the tablet. "We never caught your names, by the way."

"I'm Darnell," he responded while accepting the device from Max. "A receipt will be sent to the email address that's on file."

"That sounds perfect, Darnell. And your name?" asked Max as he turned his eyes to Darnell's green-eyed co-worker, who stood close to the front door.

"I'm Chad," he replied with reservation.

"Can I ask you two a question before you head off?" Max inquired.

"Sure," said Chad as he cautiously approached the kitchen island where the other three were standing. "But we don't have much time before our next scheduled delivery."

"Understood," said Max. "How did you guys get involved in this line of business?"

"My Uncle John is the store owner,"

expressed Chad. "He gave me a job when I started my freshman year at the local university so that I could earn money on the weekends and during the summer."

"That's pretty cool," responded Brian. "What are you studying?"

"I'm leaning toward political science or business," Chad expressed before sighing. "My father and his brothers are all small business owners, but I've always wanted to become a criminal lawyer."

"They certainly understand the importance of having skilled lawyers," Max advanced.

"You bet they do!" exclaimed Chad. "However, they also believe the profession lacks entrepreneurial spirit and that most lawyers end up sacrificing their soul to make a living."

"I see. At least you have this upcoming year to decide on what your major will be. Have you ever considered a double major?" asked Brian.

"Yes, I have, but that would seriously kick my ass!" Chad smiled and shook his head, grinning as he appeared to visualize the demand that would place on him. "I know my limits. A double major would totally intrude upon my relationship, intramural sports, and this part-time job."

"That's understandable. It sounds like you've got a hold on things, young man," Brian responded.

"What about you?" Max asked Darnell,

who had been listening closely to the conversation with his counterpart.

"Um, I'm figuring things out myself, I guess," Darnell expressed.

"Are you in school, too?" Max inquired.

"Not right now. I graduated high school two years ago. I've been working for this furniture store for nearly a year now."

"What are *your* long-term goals?" asked Max, leaning in a little on the kitchen island.

"I don't know," replied Darnell. Max noticed the young man's left foot tapping on their hardwood floor while answering his question. "That's what I'm trying to figure out."

"A lot of folks find themselves in that position at your age, Darnell," Brian responded. "What did you dream of becoming when you were younger?"

"It's funny," said Darnell. "I always wanted to be a policeman as a kid. They were the good guys in my eyes back then. When I was eleven years old, two police officers stopped my stepdad from beating my mother outside of our apartment after his six-pack dropped from one of the grocery bags she was carrying. Beer started shooting everywhere from the busted cans." Darnell, appearing disturbed at the recollection, briefly paused his story. "My stepdad, who was nothing but a drunk, started cursing and punching my mother uncontrollably. Being only seven years old,

I was too young to do anything other than shout and beg that he stop. If the police hadn't driven by that afternoon, he would have probably killed her that day or at some point in the future."

"Wow," said Max, wanting to dive further into the conversation but realizing that their time was limited and that, perhaps, Brian was right. "It's a good thing they arrived when they did. But anyway, we certainly need more responsive and culturally aware cops today."

"You don't have to tell me," Darnell replied quickly. "I see the need in my neighborhood every day, but I'm not sure that's the job for me anymore. After constantly hearing about unjust police shootings, I guess I'm just jaded."

Chad looked at his watch and said, "I hate to be the bearer of bad news, but it's about time for us to get ready for our next job."

"Oh, no worries," said Max. "We understand. Listen, Darnell – Brian and I are here if you're ever interested in career guidance. I'm a dean at Greater Cleveland Community College, so these conversations are right up my alley. My husband directs Cleveland's LGBTQ Resource Center, and he has worked with a lot of folks your age. More than anything, we want you to feel supported if you need it." Max grabbed two business cards from his wallet, handing one each to Darnell and Chad. "Feel free to call whenever you'd like."

“I want you to know that Max really means that, Darnell,” Brian reinforced to the young man who was still reading the business card, appearing unsure of the motivation behind this gesture.

“Thanks,” said Darnell.

“You’re welcome,” replied Max, “and thank you both for the help today. You guys were great!”

“Anytime,” said Chad. “Take care.”

Max sighed as the two of them left and the door closed. “There’s definitely a lot more beneath the surface. I can see it in his eyes.”

“True,” said Brian. “He needs some direction, but he also may need a professional counselor. Don’t put more on your plate than you can chew!”

“You got a lot of nerve,” said Max. “How many calls have you taken after work from youth at The Center going through some crisis?” he asked rhetorically. “Besides, I honestly doubt that he’s going to reach out and call. He seems pretty comfortable where he’s at right now.”

“Speaking of comfort, come and check out the room with me. It looks amazing.”

Brian reached for Max’s hand, and they walked to the converted kid’s bedroom. Standing behind his partner, Brian softly dipped his chin onto Max’s right shoulder and held his arms around his muscular chest. Silence permeated their apartment as they looked onto the light blue walls and new furniture. Max, appreciating the security of Brian's embrace, sensed that their space was slowly changing into the home of their dreams.

****

Max awoke bewildered from an unsettling dream about his mother to the sound of their alarm, breathing rapidly now that he was awake. He stood up on his hands in the bed and sat motionless before kissing his lover good morning. Betty Strong's short and pudgy appearance emerged vividly in his recollection. He remembered watching her search frantically around the South Collinwood home where Max and his siblings were raised. She walked around in her favorite white suit that she only wore to church, looking for an important object. Max attempted to ask her what she sought, but after numerous failed attempts to gain her attention, it became clear to him that he was invisible and inaudible. He, therefore, could only watch in discomfort as she moved about their old home in a tizzy.

If not for her meticulous nature, she would have torn up the entire home. Betty searched everywhere methodically for what seemed like hours in kitchen cabinets, under chairs and sofa cushions, beneath beds and blankets, behind varied knick-knacks, in closets, and on top of every viewable surface until her mind and body were overcome by profound fatigue. Max's phantom body followed her closely, as he cried out

'Momma' to no avail. That was all that he could do. Exhausted, she finally took a seat in her favorite bedroom chair and slowly faded into nothingness as a thinning whisper. Max woke up startled and clueless about this dream's possible meaning. This was the first time he had dreamed of her since she died.

"Everything all right?" Brian asked in a concerned voice.

"Yeah, I'm okay. I just had a strange dream. That's all."

"About what?" Brian asked, turning toward his partner to kiss him on his forehead.

"It was my mother," expressed Max. "She was wandering throughout our entire old house looking for something as if her life depended on it. Then, after a while, she got tired and sat down. That's when she completely vanished." He looked at Brian with a puzzled expression.

"I did notice you turning over a lot more than usual. If your mom was trying to communicate a message," Brian continued, "the meaning will come in due time."

"Hopefully," said Max. "I just wish my sleep would've been better. The social worker coming later today for our first home visit will be scrutinizing everything we do and say."

"Listen, the only thing required of us is to be ourselves. Unless she's a jerk, she'll have every reason to get along with us," insisted Brian.

"You're right," Max stated, as he leaned over and softly kissed his partner on the lips. "What's not to love?"

"You got that right," Brian echoed.

Their 5:30 a.m. weekday routine proceeded normally. Brian made the bed as Max prepared a pot of coffee before hopping in the shower. Smooth jazz played softly through speakers of every room, setting the mood and rhythm of their day as they groomed and prepared their clothes. A quintessential metrosexual, Brian ironed both of their attires for the day. Style was something that he prioritized more than most did, including Max. On top of frequent shopping binges, he had regular appointments for getting his hair cut, manicures, pedicures, and manscaping. It was only thanks to the technology of calendar sharing that Max was able to keep up with Brian and his self-care schedule.

Handsome and fair-skinned, Brian learned to enhance the symmetry of his face and the natural tones of his slender body as a sophomore in college. After pledging his fraternity, several senior brothers shared their insights with him on personal upkeep, which easily rivaled the time and energy spent by the most attractive females on campus. Thus, Brian's ironing and grooming habits raised the bar for Max, who was already professional and clean-cut in his own right. Whereas Max could overlook a wrinkle or two missed in his dress shirt or dress pants, such oversights were offenses to Brian. This difference in exactness took some time for them to work through when they had first moved in together, but Max's love for Brian allowed him to relinquish this chore and embrace his partner's gift of fashion.

"Did you leave me any hot water?" asked Brian as Max entered the bedroom following his shower, still drying off his body.

"I saved you a little," Max responded, laughing. "That's the cost of being such a perfectionist," he teased, while putting on his white cotton housecoat after he had dried himself.

"Well, I'm almost finished with these clothes. I need to be quick anyway so I can check on my parents before going into the office. They didn't call at all over the weekend, so something may be up."

"That's not like your parents," said Max. "Hopefully, everything's all right. When do you plan on giving them a call?"

"Right after I shower."

"Okay, let me go ahead and get breakfast started."

Max busied himself with making scrambled eggs, sausage links, toast, and grits while Brian showered. His mind drifted toward Brian's parents, Harold and Melanie, whom he had only met once. When Brian came out to his parents four years ago, he asked Max to be present because he feared their response. Max and Brian had been together for a year at that point and had already begun discussing the possibilities of marriage. During this summer trip, Brian made reservations at his mother's favorite restaurant in downtown Hartford, where he would not only come out of the closet but also introduce his lover.

Making this romantic debut and announcing this news in a neutral space was a strategic choice. His self-conscious parents would likely refrain from making a scene by verbally rebuking Brian and boisterously calling upon God's name in front of strangers. Brian's plan mostly worked; they did neither in order to preserve their own old-fashioned dignity in the crowded restaurant. Nothing precluded them, however, from walking away from the table after Brian shared his news. As the speechless couple in their mid-fifties rose from their seats, their faces were overshadowed with shame and disgrace. Harold grabbed his wife's left hand quickly, and they departed from the restaurant without so much as a glance back.

Max recalled seeing Melanie's eyes fill with tears before their departure and thinking about Lot and his wife's exit from Sodom, but in this case neither Harold nor Melanie looked back. Despite Brian's warning, Max was unprepared for their tight-lipped reaction – almost a silent protest. All he could do was comfort Brian in the wooden booth where they sat while expressing, “I’m here for you, love. Maybe they just need time, but you have family in me now.” Max tightly held onto his partner, who cried his salty tears amid their embrace.

Harold and Melanie refused to accept any calls from their son for weeks. When they finally answered the phone after three months, Brian heard what he originally anticipated: that his ‘lifestyle was sinful and incompatible with biblical teachings.’ Furthermore, Harold expressed that they were contemplating total excommunication as their only proper recourse but struggling with the fact that he was their only child. “We need more time to pray about it,” he informed Brian. After a few months of additional silence, they finally proposed their alternative to completely shunning him from their own lives. Instead of such sweeping action, they proposed to continue their relationship on very strict terms, wanting only to communicate with him without knowing any details related to his ‘unnatural partnership’ with Max or otherwise ‘homosexual lifestyle.’ Additionally, Brian was asked to refrain from speaking with extended family or coming to service as long as he was a ‘practicing homosexual.’ This ultimatum completely incensed Brian. Initially, he planned to reject it, but Max encouraged him to reconsider.

“We only get one set of parents in this life,” Max told him. “I think you have to acknowledge that they haven't gone forth with total abandonment, and this might be their best olive branch."

Ultimately, Brian conceded to his parents' conditions. Since that trip to Hartford with Max, Brian had only returned home once to show his support after Harold's heart attack. As he wrapped up breakfast, Max silently prayed that Melanie and Harold were well. Following his prayer, he admired Brian's strength to overlook the one-sided dynamics of the relationship between him and his parents. He realized that his own life would be drastically different without Betty Strong's acceptance and support.

"Fortunately, there was enough hot water remaining," Brian joked upon entering the kitchen in his yellow and white boxer briefs.

"Told ya," said Max. "You know I wouldn't do you like that anyway. Breakfast is just about done."

"It smells good! It's too bad we don't have enough time to make any bacon of our own," stated Brian as he walked up and placed his protruding briefs on the soft cotton of Max's housecoat where his buttocks formed beneath the tie around his waist.

"You are something else," said Max as he chuckled and partially smiled in agreement at his husband's not-so-subtle suggestion. "It is too bad, but I think you calling your parents is a lot more important."

"Yeah, I know," insisted Brian. "Let me go and grab a T-shirt before we eat." Max began preparing their plates, priding himself on his sizzling brown sausages and fluffy scrambled eggs. "I threw down this morning, babe."

"You always do," replied Brian from down the hallway.

Max considered how blessed he was in life as he wrapped up his cooking over the stove. He was grateful to have Brian as a life partner. Brian was equally as caring as he was attractive, smart, ambitious, loyal, and funny. Their lives were enriched by their diverse friends who rewarded them with joy and laughter, as well as their meaningful careers, modern downtown condo, financial stability, and health. As he fixed their two plates, he smiled to himself in appreciation for their well-being.

"Everything looks great," said Brian as he returned in his crisp white T-shirt to find breakfast ready for him.

"Thanks," said Max. "Let's eat, and then you need to call your parents ASAP."

"I will," agreed Brian, sitting down to say grace and dig into their home-cooked meal.

****

Later that evening, Theresa, the social worker from children's services, sat in Max and Brian's living room to complete her assessment.

She wore a grey and white turtleneck poncho and dark denim jeans with a pair of black flats. Her thin dreadlocks were tied together with a purple ribbon, matching her violet beaded necklace and the bracelet on her right wrist. Seated adjacent to Brian and Max in a beige leather chair, she had a professional air that wasn't too formal but that also conveyed that she took her job seriously. To Max, Theresa appeared to be in her late thirties or early forties, but guessing a black women's age was a skill that still eluded him. He and Brian sat next to one another closely, with Max's left hand placed on Brian's right leg.

"Welcome to our home again," said Brian. "Can I offer you anything to drink before we get started?"

"No, thank you," replied Theresa. "I appreciate the offer, though." She grabbed two yellow folders from her rainbow-striped leather handbag that sat next to her feet and handed one to each of them. "These are for you two," she continued. "They contain information about the homestudy process, including all steps and requirements that have to be met along the way toward finalization. As your assigned homestudy assessor, I'll be working with you throughout your process. Before I dive into the initial assessment, what did you think of the pre-service training?"

"It was tremendously insightful," Brian responded. "They covered some really helpful topics, including the adoption process itself, diversity and cultural circumstances, separation dynamics, and resources available for caregivers and children. I thought it was really informative."

"Yeah, I agree," expressed Max. "We originally expected that the process might be a little boring, but we soon learned otherwise during Michelle's pre-service training. The facilitator who led our required courses, Margaret, was just as effective as Michelle. Her many years in the field allowed us to receive a more nuanced perspective of the adoption process, though. Many of our classmates echoed the same sentiment to us.

"Ultimately, it was the videos of actual foster and adoptive parents that really stood out for me. They showed us how real this process is, and to some extent, how preparation can only go so far. God knows I'll never forget the white woman who caught her black fifteen-year-old adoptee using skin bleaching products because she wanted to *be* more like her adopted family. Can you imagine?" Max asked, raising his eyebrows at the thought of having to confront his own child on such a sensitive topic.

"You're exactly right in that no amount of training or assessments can ensure that prospective parents are ever fully prepared for everything that they'll encounter, but this process does provide us with a baseline to guarantee that all potential parents receive the same information and meet the state's minimum standards," said Theresa. Max observed that she spoke in a deliberate and mindful manner while smiling at appropriate times and revealing her warm side.

"Today my goal is to begin the assessment process by learning more about you two. Following this appointment, I'll provide you with some tasks to complete before we reconvene in the future. The whole process can take up to six months, but if you guys are organized, then it has the potential to go much quicker. As your homestudy assessor, though, my focus isn't on how quickly I can get you matched. My goal is to ensure that you two are fit to take on a child and that your household will be conducive to his or her needs."

"That makes sense," said Max. "I know that I speak for the both of us in saying that we're in complete agreement."

"Great," exclaimed Theresa. "Please give me a few minutes to pull the assessment up on my laptop, and then we'll begin." Sensing his own increased breathing and the formation of sweat between his hands, Max decided to grab a bottled water as Theresa readied her laptop.

"I'm gonna grab a water, babe. Can I grab you anything?"

"Sure, I'll take one, too," said Brian.

"Are you certain we can't offer you any water, Theresa?" asked Max again, redirecting his nervous attention to the simple task at hand.

"Yes, I'm sure. I just finished my second cup of coffee for the day before getting here. Thanks again, though."

As Max walked toward the refrigerator to grab their water, he considered how nervous he was about this homestudy assessment compared to his opening speech at the convocation back in August. Somehow, speaking in front of four hundred students hadn't terrified him as much as sitting with one social worker alongside his own husband. At the refrigerator, he breathed deeply as he opened the door and told himself, *Everything is going to be okay. This is just a normal part of the process.* He took out two bottles of water and returned to sit next to Brian. By this time, Theresa's laptop was turned on and she was postured to begin her questioning and documentation.

"For starters," began Theresa, "How long have you two been married?"

"We've been married three years as of July 4th," replied Brian. He placed his arm around Max and let his hand softly land on Max's right shoulder."

"A July 4th wedding, huh?" stated Theresa. "That's a memorable date."

"Exactly. The reason for that date was the mutual fireworks that we both felt while dating," continued Brian. "It was and still is an incredible experience."

"That's so sweet," Theresa replied with

sincerity. As Max watched her closely, he observed an air of sincerity and, seeing no wedding ring, assumed that she was either a lipstick lesbian or had a close friend or family member who was gay. His breathing eased as he realized that she would more than likely be an ally in this process and not the homophobe he feared. "How did you meet?"

"We met at a brunch event during Cleveland's Black Gay Pride two years prior to our getting married. Both of us attended the event with our respective groups of friends, and it just so happened that our tables were relatively close. We couldn't keep our eyes off each other. Brian was someone that I wanted to get to know as soon as I laid my eyes upon him. His laughter was contagious. Watching him interact with his friends made me smile. There was just one problem," stated Max before pausing and looking at Brian. "He and his company wrapped up their meals as my friends and I were the middle of ours, so there was no other option for me but to act. That's when I got up from my seat and approached Brian as they were leaving their table and said, 'Excuse me, but I couldn't help but notice how handsome you are. My name is Maxwell and if you're single, I would really like to get to know you.'"

"You left out how you were sweating up a storm, baby. He always leaves that detail out," Brian said teasingly, looking at Theresa, who was smiling as she typed her notes.

"Who wouldn't be nervous approaching this fine man?" Max returned playfully, talking directly to Theresa. "Anyway," Max continued, "Brian extended his right hand and introduced himself. He asked for my cell phone and placed his number inside. I texted him later that day after getting home, and we met up for drinks at his favorite bar that same evening. We ended up talking and laughing until about midnight, despite having to work in the morning. At that time, I was the assistant director of the academic advising program at Greater Cleveland Community College, and Brian was working as a TA during the first year of his PhD program. After our first date, a good portion of our time was spent texting, talking on the phone, and seeing each other in person as often as we could. That's when those fireworks took off."

"So, then you two have known each other for five years?" asked Theresa for clarification.

"Yes, that's correct," said Max.

"Okay, so what have been some of the ups and downs you've faced together?" asked Theresa as she stopped typing and looked at them.

"Where do we even begin?" asked Brian as he considered the social worker's question. "Our first year and a half was effortless. We were head over heels for each other. Our first test didn't come until after we moved in together. We had been engaged for a few months and thought that it was best to live with each other before getting married.

During this time, we learned a lot more about each other. I had to get used to Max's preferences for tidiness and eating home-cooked meals every night. On the other hand, he didn't realize how much time I spent on my self-care and or how meticulously I followed a budget. These issues caused us to have our fair share of disagreements, but through listening and making small changes over the course of time, we both progressed.

"Several months later, we were married," Brian continued, "and that has been the ultimate milestone thus far. We got married at Cleveland's only predominantly black affirming church, New Life and Grace Fellowship. Seventy-five of our closest friends, family members, and co-workers attended the ceremony, with my parents being the only exception. I can remember standing in front of Max at the altar, dressed in our black and white tuxedos, thinking 'This is the greatest day of my life,' as the minister prepared for our vows. Looking into Max's brown eyes, nothing else seemed more important than our two-year relationship and our lives at that precise moment. Following the wedding, we had our reception at a banquet hall, where we danced like two college guys fresh out of the closet. We closed the evening by meeting up with a few friends in the Flats to watch the fireworks. It was a day I will never forget."

"That sounds really beautiful," interrupted

Theresa. “I noticed that you mentioned your parents weren’t in attendance. Any particular reason why they didn’t make it?”

“It’s not that they weren’t able,” Brian replied. “They chose not to come because of their religious beliefs.” Max gently rubbed his husband’s right leg, providing him with support.

“Oh, I see,” Theresa said. “They don’t support gay marriage?”

“Or anything else gay,” Brian insisted. “They’re strict fundamentalists.”

“Shortly after we celebrated our first year of being together,” Max jumped in, “Brian took me to meet his parents and announce our relationship, which was also his official *coming out*. Let’s just say that they didn’t take it too well. It took nearly half a year for Brian and his parents to get back on speaking terms.”

“That must have been a difficult ordeal,” said Theresa. “If it’s okay, we’ll pick back up on your parents, Brian, when we get to family history and natural supports, but this situation also represents a significant situation you two have both overcome. Are there any other similar challenges or major milestones you can think of?”

“Well, about two years into our marriage, we lost a mutual friend, Tony, to AIDS,” Brian expressed. “He was actually the person who got us involved with The Center. Before that, we mostly assumed that their programs were directed at privileged white gays and lesbians, but Tony showed us differently. Though his passing didn't come as a huge surprise because he was so outspoken about his diagnosis and distrust of healthcare professionals, it was nevertheless very abrupt and sent shockwaves throughout the local LGBTQ community. With him only being thirty-four at the time, essentially our own peer, it reminded us of just how fragile life is. I think what helped us during his loss, outside of having each other, was The Center galvanizing to honor his memory. The staff there hosted an art gallery with paintings he had donated and others that were found at his home. Additionally, one of the activity rooms was renamed in his honor."

"Is that who painted the piece behind you guys?" asked Theresa, pointing to a portrait of a black and white dove hanging on the south wall behind where Brian and Max sat, fixed squarely between the balcony glass on the right and the hallway entrance on the left-hand side.

"That's correct," said Brian. "That was one of Tony's last pieces before he died. He gave it to us for our first anniversary."

"He was very talented," said Theresa. "It seems like you've been through a lot together."

"We've had our share of difficult times, but the better part of our lives has easily overshadowed those few challenges. Brian is my best friend. We laugh with each other, support one another, and we're constantly working toward our future goals. When my mother died earlier this year, in May, I was so grateful to have Brian in my life. Second to him, she was my best friend. There's nothing that I wouldn't do for this man," expressed Max.

"I'm sorry to hear about your mom," said Theresa. "How old was she?" asked Theresa curiously, noting that Max was only thirty-four years old from the records in front of her.

"She was fifty-nine," expressed Max. "She died of a sudden stroke," he continued as he watched Theresa quickly typing her notes. A flashback to his dream this morning hit him. Once again, he visualized Betty Strong dressed in all white, desperately looking for some mysterious object. Max took a sip of water and focused on the fluids hydrating his parched throat to distract himself from the memory of his dream.

"She was young," replied Theresa. "I'm sure you miss her. It sounds like you had a close relationship."

"Yes, we did," Max reinforced. "I believe she's still looking out for us, though."

As Theresa continued with her assessment, Max and Brian took turns answering her questions. Max grew more comfortable with Theresa and the interview process, resulting in his relaxed disposition at its conclusion. He didn't expect that their 6:00 p.m. appointment would stretch for nearly two and a half hours, but the last hour was effortless. Throughout her visit, Theresa inquired specifically as to why they were interested in adoption, their families and friends, employment history and status of their finances, what type of child they were interested in, their physical and mental health, as well as their philosophy when it came to discipline. At the end of the assessment, Max sensed that Theresa was pleased with this initial phase. She concluded by reviewing a handout in their two folders that delineated the required paperwork.

"We already have some of these items for you," Brian interjected, picking up a manila folder from the center of the glass coffee table in front of them. "Here are copies of our most recent bank statements, paycheck stubs, and marriage certificate. We also have appointments scheduled with our primary care physician next week to complete our physicals. Other than that, I think we just need to have our background checks conducted."

"This is great," said Theresa. "You two are certainly on top of your business. As for the next steps on my end, I need to reach out to your given natural supports for references and schedule a return visit for the home inspection. And judging from what I see now," Theresa explained, looking around the condo, "you two will be in good shape."

"That sounds great," said Max.

"Do you have any questions for me?" she replied.

"So, after those items are taken care of, will we be ready to move forward with placement matches?"

"As long as everything returns satisfactorily, that's correct," said Theresa. "Based on all the information that's collected, I'll work behind the scenes to match you and a child. I don't foresee there being too many hurdles at this time, but the process will start once everything else is cleared. Providing me these papers is a great head start. Any other questions?"

"Do you have a business card?" inquired Max. "Just in case we need to reach out to you for other questions. And should we have our doctor send the paperwork or provide it to you when we meet for the home inspection?"

"Yes, I almost forgot. Thanks for reminding me. Here's my business card," she said as she handed it over to Max. "You can provide me with copies of the physical during the home inspection, which will likely be sometime the first week in November."

"Sounds good," said Brian. "Thanks for coming over here today. We look forward to working with you."

"The pleasure was mine," said Theresa. "I think you're going to make great dads!"

****

There were four couches in the waiting area, one lining each wall of the room. All the walls were covered with pictures of smiling families. An end table that had magazines and pamphlets about fostering and adoption sat next to each couch. Various toys were scattered about the room, likely left over from the day before, Max suspected. Sitting in this designated waiting section, Brian and Max waited anxiously for Theresa to arrive.

It had been almost an entire month since she had completed her initial home visit. During the passing weeks, Theresa had managed to complete the home inspection, wrap up their official paperwork, and obtain two possible leads. The first potential match was for a two-year-old named Demetrius. Brian and Max seriously discussed the limited information she had shared about him but ultimately decided not to proceed with a face-to-face encounter due to his age. Acutely aware of the time a toddler would require, they reminded Theresa of their preference for a school-aged child. If they were going to adopt a child that young, they believed that one of them would have to be a stay-at-home parent until he was in school. Although they had discussed such a possibility in the future, neither of them was ready to make that type of commitment.

It was during Theresa's second phone call that they had learned about Donté, a five-year-old who had recently been placed in an Akron group home following his maternal grandmother's abrupt admission into a skilled nursing facility. Max sat in the waiting room, recalling the elements of this phone call with Theresa as well as the subsequent conversation that he had had with Brian, which had led them to where they presently sat.

Donté was a biracial child who had been primarily raised by his black grandmother. Both of his parents were incarcerated shortly after he was born. The only detail regarding their imprisonment that Max and Brian knew was that neither of them would be released in the next ten years. According to Theresa, Donté's mother had no family members suitable for custody after her arrest other than her fifty-eight-year-old mother. On his father's side, none of them would consider raising a biracial child.

Without anyone readily available to care for Donté following his grandmother's turn for the worse, he was immediately taken into custody by children's services a month ago. By that time, his family dynamics were unchanged when a social worker reached out to his closest kin to discuss options, leaving these findings to ultimately cement his eligibility for adoption. Max and Brian were in complete agreement on continuing with a placement match after learning these details and privately discussing the matter.

Suddenly, the front door opened, and Theresa joined them in the waiting area, bringing in a draft of cool air with her. "Good morning, guys," she said enthusiastically to the anxious-looking pair.

"Good morning," Max and Brian replied in unison.

"How was your drive from Cleveland?" she asked.

"It was fairly straightforward – not much traffic on a Saturday morning," Brian replied. "What about yours?"

"Pretty much the same other than the cold weather," Theresa shared. "It's that time of the year when the weather, along with my dry hands, is taking a change for the worse."

"Sadly enough, it is," Max replied, thankful for her honest humor this early in the morning. "I hope we're in for a mild winter this year, but you never know here in northeast Ohio."

"It's only mid-November and we're already near freezing, so I'm not too optimistic," Theresa expressed, after rubbing a lump of scented lotion into her hands. "In any case, it's nearly 10:30, and everything should be prepared to proceed here shortly. How are you guys feeling?"

"Nervous and excited, all at the same time," answered Brian. "It seems surreal that we're even here." Max nodded his head in agreement.

"Your feelings are perfectly normal," said Theresa. "Just be yourselves and allow everything to unfold naturally. Children know when a person is being authentic. It's in their DNA. Let me go and check in with the staff here to see where we are with everything."

"This is it," Brian said as he took Max's right hand and kissed it after Theresa left.

"Absolutely," said Max. "No matter what happens, we're in this together."

Moments later Theresa returned with her counterpart from the Akron agency, who introduced herself as Laura. Easily in her mid-twenties with blond hair, Laura reminded Max of countless students, mostly eager white females, who were studying human services and planned on obtaining their BSW after receiving their associate degree and transferring to a four-year institution. She wore slim blue jeans and a red shoulderless sweater, which complemented her black two-inch heels. Her modest prettiness made her appear trustworthy to Max.

"Okay, gentlemen," Theresa said as Max and Brian stood up. "Laura is going to take us to where you will be meeting Donté. And remember," she added after holding her breath, "to just be yourselves."

Laura led the three of them out of the waiting room and down a long hallway containing six doors until they reached one labeled #3. Max inhaled deeply, being fully aware that he and Brian could potentially be making the acquaintance of their future son when she opened the door. "Here's the process," began Laura in a down-to-earth manner. "If all goes well, you two will have an hour and a half to spend with Donté. He's not in the room yet, but I'll be getting him once we're done here. Outside of my introducing you guys to him, there's no formal agenda. This time is meant to be an opportunity for the three of you to learn about each other and hopefully generate a positive rapport. The only thing that we ask is that you refrain from any touching, outside of a handshake or high-five, or discussing his family, unless he initiates a hug or brings up his grandmother. Does that make sense?"

"Yes," said Brian as he and Max nodded their heads.

"That's great to hear. This meeting is Donté's third placement match. He already has a very basic understanding of the dynamics involved, such as having to find a new home because his grandmother is ill. On the other hand, he doesn't fully comprehend the permanency of his separation from her or the adoption process. That understanding will come in time once he finds a stable home." Laura paused for a moment, giving her prospective parents time to let what she shared resonate.

"Also, Donté is a fairly shy kid. Like many of our children, he's been exposed to a lot of transitions and trauma. Neither of his previous matches resulted in a follow-up appointment.

Therefore, if he comes across as quiet or reserved, please do not take it personally. In his young mind, he's coping with his situation the best way he can. If, at any point in time, the arrangement becomes too uncomfortable for either of you, please let me or Theresa know, and we can take a break or end the session. That's the last thing that we want, but extreme situations arise once in a blue moon. She and I will be across the room monitoring the session. Any questions about anything?" asked Laura before pausing again.

"Not me," said Max. "I think you clearly laid out the process."

"I agree," Brian indicated.

At that point, Laura opened the door they had been standing in front of and encouraged them to sit down at a bright yellow table that reminded Max of elementary school. The table was surrounded by four small blue seats and covered with various coloring books as well as scattered crayons. Max and Brian giggled as they squatted in the small seats, with Max trying to recall the last time he had sat at such a small table. A bookcase filled with dozens of children's books stood on the wall to the right of where they sat. In the opposite corner, Theresa sat down in a standard-sized chair with a notepad in her hand and waited for Laura and Donté to enter. Normally talkative, she sat there quietly while Brian and Max curiously surveyed the space like they were on the planet

Mars. More pictures of radiant families and children of mixed races decorated the eggshell white walls of this room. Max silently observed to himself how he hadn't seen any LGBTQ families represented around the building. While he wasn't surprised by the absence of families like his, he found it disappointing because gay couples were legally entitled to adopt.

As he and Brian continued to examine their surroundings, Laura returned to the room holding the boy's right hand. Wearing a kid-sized blue sweater and jeans, he had dark-brown curly hair and hazel eyes. With his left hand and arm, he held a toy firetruck against his stomach, as Laura led him to the table where Max and Brian quietly sat. The boy pensively looked down at his plain white shoes and the carpeted floor until his trusted social worker spoke.

"Donté, these are the two gentlemen we've told you about," said Laura gently. "This is Mr. Brian," she indicated, pointing to him directly. "And this is his partner, Mr. Maxwell."

"Hi," said Donté softly, extending his right hand to each of them, one at a time, for a handshake.

"You can have a seat, Donté," encouraged Laura. "If you need me for anything, I'll be right over in the corner like the other times. Okay?"

Donté nodded his head in affirmation, taking a seat on the opposite side of the table from

Max and Brian. Laura walked over to the corner where Theresa was seated and positioned her legal pad to take notes just as her counterpart had done.

"How's it going, Donté?" asked Brian in a pitch much higher than his usual baritone voice.

"Okay," the boy replied, as he began rolling his red plastic truck on the yellow table.

"Do you like trucks?" asked Max.

"Yes," he replied, while making figure eights with the toy and simultaneously nodding his head.

"What's your favorite type of truck?" asked Brian.

"Ummm," said Donté, as he paused and thought about this question. "I like firetrucks," he replied with a faint smile.

"That's awesome! Those are really important vehicles," Max responded. "Do you know what they do?"

"Help people put out fires," Donté stated, looking directly up at Max and Brian for the first time before placing his focus back on the cherry red truck.

"Exactly," said Brian. "That's a really important job. Fires can do a lot of damage to people, buildings, animals, and our environment. Firefighters are brave people." Donté, still preoccupied with his toy, started making noises with his mouth to mimic a motor. It wasn't clear to Max if the distracted child was listening to them, but they continued talking.

"Do you want to be a firefighter when you grow up?" asked Max. Donté shrugged his shoulders. "That's fair," said Max. "No need to rush. You have a lot of time to figure all that out. Have you ever met a firefighter or been to a fire station?"

"No," stated Donté. He stopped moving his toy and then asked, "Do you know any firefighters?"

"Actually," said Max, "I know a couple. They attended the school where I work. They're really good people who help keep our community safe."

"Wow," said Donté. "That's cool." Max and Brian laughed at his response. "Are you a teacher?"

"No, but I work at a school for adults," said Donté. "You can think of my role sort of like a principal." Donté sat quietly, thinking about Max's answer.

"What grade are you in?" asked Brian.

"I'm in kindergarten."

"And what's your favorite thing to do in school?" Max inquired to follow up.

"I like drawing and story time," expressed Donté, who was no longer holding onto his truck. His eye contact was still minimal, though, with his eyes largely focused on the coloring books laid on the table.

"Oh, nice," said Brian. "So, that means you're an artist."

"An artist?" retorted Donté with a puzzled expression on his face.

"Yes," said Max. "An artist is someone who sings, acts, plays music, writes, or uses his or her talents in other creative ways." Donté nodded his head, smiling as he repeated the word aloud to himself.

"Can you draw us a picture?" asked Brian.

"Okay," Donté replied after initially hesitating before deciding.

He stood up from his small chair and walked toward the bookcase where there was a pile of blank paper on top, returning to his seat quickly. Taking a box of crayons, he carefully selected orange and began designing his creation. Brian and Max followed carefully with their eyes, initially not saying anything as they watched him use his right hand to draw what looked like a sun. Color by color, Donté took his time filling up the page with the image he had captured in his head. Max and Brian beamed outwardly as they leaned forward to observe Donté's illustration in the making. As he observed the five-year-old color, Max began to wonder about the boy's unremarkable heritage or how anyone could reject him because he was bi-racial.

After ten patient minutes, Donté ceased drawing with his crayons and proudly held up his finished work. Max discerned a bright sun, two people next to a house, trees, and some other obscure objects.

"What is it?" Brian inquired.

"It's my grandma and me at her house," replied the boy, pointing to the stick people. "The sun is out, and these are birds sitting on the trees near her house. And this," Donté continued pointing to a brown circular figure next to the stick people, "is Old Sebastian, Grandma's dog."

"You're a great artist!" said Max, recalling what Laura had stated about refraining from discussing his family.

"Thank you," Donté said softly, staring proudly at his completed work.

"Can we take it home with us?" asked Brian. "This will give us something to remember you by." Donté placed the picture down on the table and slid it in their direction.

"That's really nice of you," said Max. "We appreciate it." Donté nodded in their direction.

"Do you mind teaching us how to color as well as you do?" asked Brian.

"You can't color?" asked Donté, apparently shocked.

"Well, I can a little," said Brian. "But Max can really use your help." Donté laughed at Brian's joke, picking out a coloring book from the table. Max and Brian followed suit. They colored and made small talk until Laura encouraged them to wrap up. As their session concluded, Donté appeared troubled. Brian and Max handed him the images they had colored alongside him and thanked him again for the picture.

"We're going to place this somewhere special," Brian said. Donté walked from his side of the table and extended his hand to the couple, saying, "Nice to meet you, Mr. Brian and Mr. Max."

Max felt as if his throat suddenly sank next to his heart. His eyes watered, and he had to guard himself from crying.

"Hey, little man," said Max. "It was nice meeting you, too."

"Yes, it was," agreed Brian. "You be sure to listen to Ms. Laura and the staff here. Hopefully, we can see you again."

"Come on, Donté," said Laura as she extended her hand for him to grab. "It's time for lunch, and then you and I can talk about this morning afterward."

"Okay," said Donté dolefully, walking beside Laura.

As they left, Max and Brian embraced one another as tears fell down Max's face. Brian rubbed his partner's back. Max closely held onto Brian, simultaneously feeling joy, sadness, and confusion. Theresa, after completing her notes, stood up and slowly approached them.

"Nice job," she said. "This initial meeting

today went much better than I expected, and I already had high hopes. I don't think this could've gone any better." Max managed to gather himself and face Theresa while they waited for Laura to return for the debriefing.

"Wow," said Brian. "I'm nearly speechless. He seems like a great kid. It's just so unfortunate that he's going through this situation."

"Yes, it is," said Theresa. "But the turning point is when folks like you intervene in the chaos he's experiencing. That, guys, makes a world of difference."

"Okay, so where do we go from here?" asked Max.

Chapter 4

Ocean blue balloons turned gracefully on each side of the bungalow's staircase entrance, kept afloat by red strings of ribbon tied onto the top sides of the rails, reaching toward the clear late December afternoon sky. In matching grey and black peacoats, Max and Brian approached the front of Salt and Pepper's newly purchased home, admiring the outside decorations their friends had prepared, including the 'It's a Boy' banner that hung on their stained oak door. Within seconds of the doorbell ringing, Salt opened the door as the standing guests inside commenced applauding and cheering for the soon-to-be parents. Max beamed proudly as he walked beside Brian into the living area where everyone was assembled. The sight of this small crowed prompted a flashback of the electric celebration that arose outside of New Life and Grace Fellowship on his and Brian's wedding day. Instead of taking off into a waiting limousine amid raining confetti on the 4th of July, however, the two of them immersed themselves in their hosts' home that had been jazzed up with shades of blue trimmings everywhere within plain sight. A flurry of hugs and congratulations quickly followed Pepper's welcoming of their guests of honor.

"Wow, this is really awesome," said Brian as the initial celebratory activity subsided. "You guys are really too much. Thank you," he expressed, while scanning the familiar faces of those gathered.

"You're welcome," expressed Salt. "We just want you to know how happy we are for you and that you have plenty of support as this new chapter begins."

"That's right," echoed Pepper. "We couldn't be any prouder of you two in this huge step you're taking. We have your back one hundred percent. And speaking of backs, please take your coats off so I can put them away."

"Thanks, Pepper," said Max, removing his apparel as requested. "Brian and I appreciate this so much, especially since you haven't been in this house that long. It's beautiful! When can we expect a tour?" he asked Pepper while handing over their jackets.

"We promise a grand tour after the festivities, but right now it's about you," insisted Salt. "Now, let's get some drinks going before we start our first game," she suggested, moving effortlessly toward the open kitchen that was in the rear section of the first floor. Bottles of vodka, gin, whiskey, and bourbon were placed next to a bowl of spiked eggnog on a white marble countertop. Lamont and Todd, who had been acquainted with the lesbian couple at Max and Brian's wedding, quickly followed behind Salt to the staged bar. Max and Brian took their time from the tail end of the pack, holding each other's hands and admiring their friends' new home.

"May I have the honor of providing the toast?" inquired Sandra.

"Yes, of course you can!" declared Salt as she and Pepper quickly started making drinks based on everyone's preferences.

"And for our guests of honor?" asked Pepper.

"I really want to try the eggnog," said Max. "It looks delicious, and 'tis the season, after all!"

"Me too," said Brian.

"Excellent choice," said Pepper. "Salt really put her foot in that drink!"

"Yeah, I did," replied Salt. "You know if she had said that in my yoga studio, everyone would have taken her literally." Lighthearted laughs filtered throughout the group, as Max realized that the party had started early for some of them.

"Okay," announced Sandra once drinks were made to each person's satisfaction. "To Max, my dear baby brother, Brian, my lovely brother-in-law, and Donté, the newest addition to our family, may your home continue to be blessed with joy, peace, and prosperity. And may Donté magnify the love already in your home with his presence as your family grows." Shouts of 'Cheers!' immediately ensued Sandra's words.

"So, what's the first game?" asked Lamont,

already aiming for his second sip.

"Attention, folks," interjected Pepper, directing everyone into the living area. "The first game is Guess Who. Brian and Max will sit in the center of the room facing all of us," she instructed while positioning their two chairs side by side. "Each of us will take turns reading statements about likely interactions Max and Brian will have with Donté, to which they must respond by holding out a card. Their responses will indicate if each statement would best describe them individually, the other person, or both of them." Pepper then revealed six prepared cards and placed a stack of three cards on each of the two seats she staged. "For the game to work," Pepper concluded, looking at Max and Brian sternly, "you can only look at your own cards before answering."

"Got it," said Max as he and Brian sat with their respective set of laminated cards in hand. Everyone else moved the leftover surrounding foldable chairs to face the guests of honor, while Pepper handed out index cards containing the game's scenarios. "Who wants to go first?" she asked.

"I'll go," Jane Budges spoke out in her Appalachian accent, pausing to give Pepper adequate time to dish out the remaining statements. "Who will spend most of the time preparing home-cooked meals?" Jane finally asked after Pepper sat down. Max immediately raised the card that read

Me while Brian, who lagged behind, held up his card labeled *Max*. Everyone laughed at Brian's slow pace as he rolled his eyes and straightened his posture to focus before the next scenario was read. "Nice job," said Jane. "You answered the same," giving them permission to look at one another's cards.

"All right," said Todd, seated next to Jane. "This is an easy one. You guys should have this! Who will spend most of the time assisting Donté with homework?" Max and Brian each held up cards stating *Both.*

"There is a *but*, though," said Max. "Dr. Brian will be responsible for all high school science and math."

Lamont, who was now enjoying his second drink, spoke up next. "Okay, fellas. Who will go overboard with spoiling Donté?" Max raised his *Brian* card, while his husband showed *Both*. "Uh-oh!" said Lamont, as the couple looked at each other.

"Come on, Brian," said Max. "He said *overboard*. You already know that's you."

"You'll probably be just as bad," replied Brian. "I'm just going to make sure our boy is fresh every day!" Max smiled, knowing the truth of his husband's assertion. Since Theresa had shared the final details about Donté, which included his clothing sizes, Brian had already shopped for clothes and shoes on multiple occasions.

"That's exactly my point, babe."

"I think you won that one decisively, Max," insisted Lamont. Brian play-sulked at being defeated and overruled.

"Guess I'm up next," said Peter, who was Brian's friend and former supervisor. Prior to Brian becoming the interim director at The Center, Peter had directed the organization. He, in fact, had petitioned to the board of directors for Brian to follow in his leadership. After Peter's husband received a senior accountant role for a Fortune 500 company in Cincinnati, they relocated to Blue Ash last year before Brian started his dissertation. Though Peter was ten years his senior and a conservative white male, Brian appreciated their friendship and admired his networking savviness. "Who will be the primary disciplinarian?" Peter asked. Brian revealed his *Max* card, while Max also indicated himself.

"That was a tough one," said Brian. "I think Max will do most of the disciplining, but sometimes it will be both of us."

"Agreed," said Max.

"Well, you can be a handful, Max," said Peter jokingly.

"Here we go, gentlemen," said Sandra, prepared to read her statement. "Who will do most of the driving on family road trips?" Brian quickly placed out his *Me* card, as Max revealed *Brian*. "Nice job, guys," replied Sandra.

"I'm definitely the safer driver," said Brian, nudging Max in his left arm.

"You can't discipline and drive at the same time," replied Max. "Somebody has to make sure Donté is behaving himself in the back seat," prompting laughter amongst their friends. The crowd continued for several more rounds before stopping the game. After it was officially concluded, Peter proposed that Brian and Max spill the beans on the next steps in their adoption process.

"Give us the upcoming details," Peter insisted.

"So," Brian began, "our pre-placement visits with Donté are officially completed, and he has been approved to move into our home a week from Monday, two days before the new year. Once the placement is finalized, our social worker, Theresa, will complete monthly visits to monitor how things are going. Six months from Donté's move-in date, we'll then have the opportunity to petition the court to finalize the adoption and officially become his legal parents, so long as no significant issues arise."

"I see," said Peter. "I remember you telling me, Brian, about the first visit you two had, but how many pre-placement visits were there in total?"

"Since our first visit in mid-November, we've had four other weekly visits that ranged from two to four hours each," replied Max. "We could've moved forward after the third visit, but we wanted to make sure, for everyone's sake, that we weren't being too hasty."

"You two are obviously elated, as you should be," Jane Budges stated, jumping into the conversation and eager to ask her own question. "How has Donté reacted to everything? He's five years old if I remember correctly, right?"

"That's a good question, Jane," replied Max. "Yes, he's five and a really nice kid. He was extremely shy when we first met him, but he's almost a different kid now than he was then. He's a lot more talkative than he was during that encounter. It's like he has gotten used to who we are. From what I can tell – and Brian, please correct me if I am wrong – Donté knows that he will be living with us and that staying with his grandmother is no longer a possibility. He understands those basics, but the staff are now working with him to prepare for the transition."

"In fact, there's one remaining visit with him tomorrow so that we can participate in that process," said Brian. "We're going to show him pictures of the condo and ask him about things that he would like in his space to make him feel more comfortable when he eventually moves in with us. To some extent, the meetings have been the easy part. They're essentially supervised get-to-know-you sessions. However, Max and I feel that once

Donté is separated from the staff and his peers that he's been with the past few months, it will be much more challenging for him."

"Knowing how well Max works with our students at the college," Jane expressed, "I'm sure you guys will help him adjust to his new home in no time."

"How did you decide on Donté?" asked Todd, whom they hadn't seen since their last social.

"It was a mutual decision for the two of us," said Max, turning to briefly face his lover. "He melted both of our hearts during our initial meeting. We asked if he would give us a drawing he made of his grandmother, her dog, house, and himself. To our surprise, he offered the drawing to us. His eyes lit up when we told him that we would be sure to put the picture in a special place. Our subsequent meetings only confirmed what we initially felt. Also, I think that Donté has a very natural connection to Brian. It's obvious to anyone looking at their interactions. During our last visit, he immediately ran to Brian and offered to share popcorn that he brought from his snack time. It was a really sweet moment."

"Before Donté," Brian added, "Theresa also gave us a lead on a two-year-old named Demetrius. We never moved forward with him, though, because of his age. Raising a two-year-old at this point in our lives would have required too much of a drastic change for us both."

"Don't underestimate a five-year-old," said Sandra. "Junior is eleven, and you two know that he's been a handful his entire life," filling the room with responsive chuckles.

"So true," interjected Peter. "We have a nine-year-old of our own, and you would think that she's already fifteen." Max thought about Tiffany after Peter spoke and conceded that he had a point. Tiffany, who was born to a surrogate mother to whom Peter and his partner Dave paid a handsome sum of money, was a no-nonsense girl. *Her confidence level was certainly through the roof*, Max thought as he remembered the first time Brian and he made her acquaintance. She was only six at the time but spoke with the confidence and had the vocabulary of someone twice her age. That was the byproduct of an elite education and the surroundings of their Pepper Pike community. "But to the point I believe you were making, Brian," Peter continued, "raising an infant or toddler is typically a lot more demanding than a school-aged child who is substantially more autonomous."

"But if I heard you correctly," Lamont expressed, "it sounded like you were open to the idea of a baby or toddler later on."

"Yes, we have discussed the idea of having more than one child," said Max. "But currently, our focus is on Donté, Brian completing his dissertation, and my new job. That's more than enough for us right now."

"Y'all ain't fooling nobody," Lamont quipped. "We'll be having another adoption shower in a year or two."

Following this impromptu discussion, Salt introduced the group to a second game that required physical movement. This game lasted nearly thirty minutes before they transitioned to the catered meal, which consisted of a spread of chicken wings, a Caesar salad, baked macaroni and cheese, and a blue velvet cake with cream cheese frosting. Max studied his friends and sister as they chatted with each other around the dining room table. He appreciated Salt and Pepper for this thoughtful shower. Even though Tonya, Mike, and Kevin hadn't shown up, he prided himself on focusing on the guests who were present. *Donté will be blessed*, he thought, *to have these adults in his life as uncles, aunts, and simply wise guides who will nurture his growth and education.* As Max sat at the dinner table eating his cake next to Brian, Salt and Pepper brought everyone's gifts into the living room for the final phase of the party.

Max's cell phone suddenly rang. "Hello," he answered, wondering who would be calling during this inopportune time.

"Hello, Mr. Webber," replied a distressed male voice.

"Yes, that's me. How can I help you?"

"It's Darnell," the male voice indicated. "I assisted with your furniture delivery a couple of months ago. You gave me and Chad your business card."

"Oh, yes," said Max, remembering this young man and nodding his head at Brian. "We're in the middle of our adoption shower right now. Do you think I can call you back later?"

"Oh, my bad," said Darnell. "I'm sorry for bothering you. I got fired from my job yesterday and thought you would be a good person to talk to. But yeah, you can call me back whenever you're free."

"I'm sorry to hear that," said Max. "If you're free in the morning, I can call you then. Should I call this number?"

"Yes, you can reach me at this same number, and tomorrow morning is fine."

"Absolutely," said Max. "Talk to you then."

"Goodbye, sir."

"That was Darnell, the furniture delivery guy," Max discretely shared with Brian after the call ended. "He said he got fired from his job and wanted to talk to me, but we can talk about that tonight at home." Although he was eager to open the gifts Salt and Pepper were arranging, Max's thoughts momentarily drifted to Darnell and how he could've been fired. Max had sensed that Darnell was an overall nice guy who got the job done. *Other than being quiet, Darnell's interaction with me and Brian was positive. He and his co-worker seemed to get along, too. But their trip to our home,* Max admitted to himself, *was only one of many deliveries throughout the week. I can't imagine why he would've been fired, but I'll find out tomorrow. In the meantime, I need to focus on enjoying this party,* Max reminded himself.

"It's gift time!" shouted Pepper from the living room. Brian, Max, and their guests all at once transitioned from the dining room back into the living area, where a square table covered in a baby blue tablecloth was adorned with multicolored wrapped boxes and gift bags of various sizes. With Christmas being less than a week away, Max already felt as though being with his friends and family to celebrate the addition to their family was the best present he could receive. Sitting side by side, he and Brian carefully unwrapped the packages that sat at the table in front of them. In doing so, they unveiled an assortment of winter clothes for Donté that included beanies, mittens, sweaters, and pajamas; a sky-blue blanket knitted by Salt; a battery-powered race car set; a kid's tablet; a medley of children's books inside a cherry red bookbag; matching 'world's best dad' T-shirts; and a handcrafted scrapbook inscribed with *Our Family* in calligraphy on the cover.

"You guys are truly amazing," said Brian. "Thank you for these wonderful gifts," he indicated to their friends, who were all beaming with pride. Max, who shared his partner's gratitude, kissed Brian on the lips and felt as though they were reliving their marriage ceremony and reception all over again.

****

As the 8:30 a.m. alarm rang the next morning, Brian woke up refreshed, finding himself tucked in his partner's arm. Max followed suit after feeling Brian reach over him to quell the annoying clock. Feeling well-rested, Max kissed his lover gently on the lips. The two then arose from bed to begin their normal weekend routine, which was similar to their weekday routine except that Brian rarely ironed due to their casual dress and they listened to their favorite news podcast instead of jazz. Their transition meeting in Akron with Laura and Donté was at 11:00 a.m., leaving them with plenty of time to prepare and eat breakfast before their drive.

"What a great shower yesterday," Max mentioned while hopping into the passenger seat of Brian's car. "Salt and Pepper did a really nice job of pulling that off."

"So true," Brian replied. "We owe them a really nice thank you card," he continued. The habit of writing thank you cards was an artform that Brian had picked up from Peter when he directed The Center. As executive director, he personally wrote thank you cards to their board members on a yearly basis, as well as to every potential donor he met with, all major contributors to the annual fundraiser, and each of their volunteers throughout the year. Under Peter's mentorship as program director, Brian observed how well-received these cards were and adopted this practice into his personal and professional life. "It's a good thing, too," Brian continued, "that we wrapped up so early. That gathering could've easily gone on forever."

"You're no spring chicken anymore," Max joked with Brian, who was thirty-one years of age. "But you raised a good point. It was nice to have enough time to come home to put away Donté's gifts and rest up for our meeting today. I got the feeling that Salt, Pepper, and Lamont started the party a little early."

"I think you're right. Besides, you already know that Lamont could outdrink all the queens in Atlanta and New York City combined!" said Brian. "You have to love that man."

"After Donté gets settled in, we need to have another spades night," Max suggested.

"That sounds good to me. Donté will have to be adjusted, though. We don't want him being overwhelmed by too much at once."

"Speaking of Donté, do you have the pictures we took of the apartment for him?"

"Yes, they're here in the console," Brian replied. "Hopefully, they help out with giving him an idea of what to expect."

"I think they will," said Max, removing the images Brian had taken with this phone." We can even place them in the scrapbook Lamont gave us."

"That's a great idea, baby. Donté will definitely appreciate having them when he's older."

As Brian drove toward the freeway, Max remembered the unexpected call from the previous day. "I need to call Darnell back," said Max, reaching for his cell phone.

"Oh, yeah," said Brian. "I hope he's doing okay."

"We'll see shortly," Max replied. "He sounded bothered yesterday." Max reviewed his call log and found Darnell's number, listening closely as the phone rang after he dialed.

"Hi," replied Max once the call was answered. "Is this Darnell?"

"Yes, Mr. Webber. That's me. Thanks for calling me back."

"No problem, Darnell. So, what's going on?" Max heard him relinquish a heavy sigh over the phone. *Something serious must be up. Maybe Brian was right about not getting in over my head*, he thought before the young man began telling his story. "Do you mind if I place you on speakerphone so Brian can hear? We're driving to Akron right now."

"I guess I don't mind," said Darnell,

pausing briefly. "This past Monday at work, I was delivering a new mattress and box spring set to this older white lady. I was working with this guy named Kenny, another white guy who's in his early thirties. He and I never talked to each other much on delivery trips like me and Chad, but we never had any beef with each other, either. Anyways," Darnell continued before stopping to catch his breath, "Kenny drove the truck to this assignment. After he parked in front of the lady's house, I got out and began walking to the front door. That's when I heard her scream out from the back yard, 'This way, boy! Come around the back.' For a second I thought that my heart froze. I was stunned and didn't know if I should turn back to the truck or follow the directions of this old woman. But something told me to stay cool and go around to the back.

"So, when I got to the backyard, she stood in the rear doorway, holding her screen door wide open and dressed in this dingy, green nightgown. 'My front door don't work, boy!' she said for the second time. 'You got to use this back door,' she demanded. That's when I calmly told her, 'I'm sorry, miss, but my name is Darnell, and I'm not a boy.' She stood there quietly with an offended expression on her face as if *I cursed her out*. Eventually, though, she said, 'Listen, boy, I don't care what your name is. I paid for my mattress and box spring to be delivered and that's what you're here to do. So, if you don't bring my stuff in here ASAP, I'll call the furniture store and inform them that you're intentionally holding my items up.'"

"Wow," said Max as he listened intently and looked over at Brian, who was shaking his head in disbelief while he drove toward I-77. "What happened next?"

"I told her, 'Let me go so I can get my co-worker, ma'am.' By this time, I was wondering what was holding Kenny up, anyway. I walked back to the truck as quickly as I could and explained what had taken place. All he said to me was 'Let's just get moving. This trip should be finished in no time.' A part of me was pissed that he had nothing to say about her calling me 'boy,' but I thought that maybe he had a point about us simply finishing this delivery. Depending on how much she had in her house and where the bedroom was located, it could've easily been a ten-minute trip. 'All right,' I said, and then we pulled the box spring from the back of the truck.

"As we entered the backyard and approached the rear entrance to the house, she said, 'Hi, honey' to my co-worker Kenny. 'You must've talked some sense into that damn boy! You give *these people* a job, and they're too lazy to do it. It's a total shame,' she told him. Furious, I dropped my end of the box spring on the ground and walked back to the truck without saying a word.

"Kenny hollered at me to come back and

finish the job, but I was too angry. From the truck parked in front I eventually heard her on the phone complaining about me to someone at the store. After a couple of minutes, Kenny walked over and handed me the company cell phone. The owner, John, was on the other end. He said that he understood that I dropped the lady's box spring in her backyard and that I refused to complete her delivery. I told him that was true while reinforcing that it was only because she had called me 'boy' four times and implied that black people were lazy. John said that he was sorry for her words, but that I had a job to do and he expected me to complete the order if I wanted to stay employed. That's when I told him that he would have to fire me because I wasn't delivering anything to someone who was so disrespectful. I handed Kenny the phone afterward and began walking to the nearest bus stop, while he and the old woman waited on someone to replace me."

"Geeze," said Max in response to Darnell's story. "That's complete nonsense. It's not like you insulted her or anything. All you did was inform her of your name so that she could refer to you appropriately. You would really think that we would be beyond these insidious color games in this country by now, but it's the entitlement of people like this woman that lets us know the roots of racism are fresh as ever. How have you been holding up since then?"

"It's been tough," said Darnell. "I was getting pretty close to moving into my own place, but now I need to find another job or at least make other moves. Fortunately, my mom was understanding, but we still have bills to pay."

"At least you have a mother in your corner and the wisdom to realize that continuing on with your life versus holding onto the anger is in your best interest. So, how can I help?" Max asked, sensing that there was a more practical reason behind Darnell's call.

"I was hoping that maybe we could sit down in the future and discuss the possibility of my being a firefighter. I don't think law enforcement or going back to school is what's best for me right now. You may not understand, Mr. Webber, but I need to follow my gut."

"Meeting up would be fine with me, Darnell. And I respect you for following your intuition. All I ask is that you are completely honest with me. If you hold back anything that might be helpful for me to know, it not only makes me potentially look bad, but it also hurts you and my capacity to trust you. Does that make sense?"

"Yes, sir," Darnell answered.

"Okay," Max continued, "Why don't I call you this week so that we can set up a time to talk in person?"

"You got a deal, sir. I look forward to hearing from you. This really means a lot."

"You got it," returned Max. "And don't beat yourself up over this situation. Sometimes, there are tough sacrifices that come with upholding your dignity. I believe that this is an opportunity for you to mature and land something even better. Keep your head up, young man."

"Will do, sir," Darnell replied with a smile on his face that both Max and Brian heard over the phone.

"Can you believe that?" Max asked Brian after the call ended.

"Unfortunately, it's hard not to believe him. These types of instances are becoming too commonplace nowadays. We hear about these unbelievable situations nearly every other day on the news. I've got to give Darnell credit, though, for maintaining his cool. He could've lost his temper, but he walked away and caught a bus," laughed Brian.

"You got that right. Neither the old lady nor his co-worker could have been too happy after he left with the box spring on the ground," Max said as he imagined the awkward scenario of Kenny and the customer waiting for help, more than likely baffled by Darnell's actions.

It was 10:45 a.m. when Brian and Max arrived at their destination. Laura greeted both of them in her usual friendly voice and gracious smile shortly after they seated themselves in the waiting room. She briefed them on the expectation for that morning's transition meeting, which would only be an hour. The goal, she relayed, would be to provide Donté with concrete information about his new home without overwhelming him too much. She also asked if they had reviewed the file about Donté that she had delivered to Theresa. It contained official information shared with adoptive parents after a match was secured, providing a more thorough picture of Donté's background, unlike the cursory details Theresa had initially shared. Brian confirmed that they had already reviewed it twice as a couple. As Laura informed them about the resources that were available if significant issues developed related to Donté's propensity for nightmares or social shyness, a young black woman walked into the room with the boy closely by her side. Seeing both Brian and Max, he smiled and ran to them for quick hugs. Laura then led them to the familiar doorway used during their previous visits.

On this occasion, Laura escorted them to door #4, the inside of which was significantly smaller and more mundane than the others they had used. It contained a round table in the center with four chairs and a small bookcase filled primarily with picture books. There were no hanging portraits of diverse families or toys of any kind. Once they were all seated, Laura led the discussion by reminding Donté that "Mr. Maxwell and Mr. Brian" were looking forward to adopting him, which meant that he would be "leaving the group home soon to live with this new family." Donté sat quietly in between Laura and Brian, trying his best to listen to Laura as he painted pretend circles with his right index finger on the manila table. "Do you remember all of us discussing the possibility of you going to live with these gentlemen?" asked Laura.

"Yes," said Donté, bobbing his head in a spirited manner to display his sense of humor.

"Good," said Laura. "Today we just want to talk about the move so that you feel more comfortable. They plan on taking you to your new home in eight days, which is a little more than a week from today." Donté nodded his head in agreement to what Laura was saying without speaking this time. "Is it okay if they share some information with you about your new home?"

"Yes," Donté replied, leaning forward toward the table. He appeared curious to learn about this new residence Laura spoke of as Brian pulled out the envelope of pictures. With Max's assistance, he laid out eighteen photos on the table for Donté to see in plain sight. The photos showcased every room in their home, views of downtown Cleveland and Lake Erie, their thirty-story condo building, and two cars. Laura sat back and watched as Donté crossed his arms on the table and protruded his head over the pictures, carefully listening to Brian and Max describe each image. Unlike their previous encounters, Laura refrained from taking notes during this transition meeting.

"I get to have my own room?" ask Donté eagerly. Max and Brian were aware that he hadn't had a room of his own since leaving his grandmother's.

"Absolutely," responded Max. "You will have your very own room that you can decorate however you want."

Donté initially beamed as he considered this possibility, but then his facial expression expressed concern. "What about my friends?" asked Donté. "Will any of them be moving in, too?"

"Unfortunately, they won't," replied Brian. "We're starting off with one kid as new parents right now, and that's you. Hopefully," Brian continued, taking his time to explain such circumstances to a five-year-old child, "your friends will move into a home of their own soon like you. But you will make new friends at your new school and maybe in our condo building." This realization obviously made Donté sad. He withdrew from looking at the pictures and pouted as his eyes stared down at the floor in front of him.

Suddenly, Max had an idea. "Do you remember the picture that you drew us the first time we met?" asked Max. Donté nodded his head slowly, not up to the task of talking. "You can ask your friends here to draw something like you did for us. And after you move in, you can hang their pictures anywhere inside your new room," Max suggested.

"It's not the same," said Donté.

"You're right, Donté," said Max, humbled and heartbroken by his insight and honesty. "It's not the same as having your friends by your side as they are now, but having something of theirs, like a picture, is a way to hold onto them. You don't have to if you don't want, though. The picture that you gave us is something that we held onto to help us remember you and the family we want to have. It's already hanging in your room above your bed." Donté listened to Max's words without responding this time.

"Hey, Donté," said Laura, intervening for the first time during any of their sessions. "Leaving friends or family is really, really tough. The good news is that you have one week left to enjoy them as much as you can. It may not feel like it, but your moving into a stable home is a wonderful opportunity. Like they said, you will make friends at your new school, in your neighborhood, and through your new family. Do you think you can trust me on this?"

"I don't know," said Donté hesitantly.

"I'm not saying that it's going to be easy," Laura conceded, "but being with two caring parents like these gentlemen until you are all grown up means a whole lot." Max wondered to himself how much of what they were saying was actually getting through to Donté. He tried to imagine how difficult this situation must be for him.

"Is there anything that you would like to have in your room or bring with you that would make you feel better?" asked Max.

Donté sat in his seat, deeply contemplating the question posed to him. "A puppy," Donté expressed, shyly.

Being as obsessed with cleanliness and orderliness as he was, Max smiled at himself and understood the *be careful what you ask for* look Brian conveyed after the boy answered.

"A puppy?" Max slowly repeated as Donté nodded in affirmation.

"Well, I guess that settles it," said Brian. "But it won't be right away. We'll move forward with that after you're settled in. How does that sound?"

"Okay," said the hopeful-looking boy, seemingly pleased with this agreement.

****

"Wake up, Donté," said Max, gently tapping his knee. Donté had fallen asleep during the forty-five-minute drive to Cleveland from Akron eight days later. "We're home," Max said with a smile on his face as Donté stretched his arms and yawned, curiously looking out the windows to observe his surroundings. Donté appeared to have a confused expression, not fully understanding how the enclosed concrete structure filled with vehicles was home.

"This is the parking lot," Max explained to the five-year-old. "Everyone who lives in the condominium parks their cars here, but we stay up on the seventeenth floor." The tired boy looked at Max and Brian without speaking. Max realized that Donté was likely experiencing a sense of uncertainty. "Everything's going to be okay, Donté. We're going to get all your items from the trunk and then head upstairs after Brian parks. Hold onto your truck," encouraged Max as he picked it up off the floor beneath Donté. Quickly taking the toy from Max, the child turned his attention to one of the remaining connections that linked him to his grandmother as well as the group home. He held it close against his chest.

Recognizing Donté's protective posture, Max reassured him, "It's okay, Donté. We know your truck means a lot to you. You'll be able to store it safely in your room once we make it to the apartment." After Brian found a parking spot, Max encouraged Donté to release his safety belt. Brian, who sat directly in front of the boy in the car, assisted him with getting out of the vehicle. Max took it upon himself to carry Donté's remaining possessions, consisting of one large duffle bag and a small backpack.

This is it, Max thought to himself in partial disbelief as they walked toward the elevator. *Everything that Brian and I have planned for is unfolding right in front of us. It's almost too good to be true.* He sensed that his and Brian's life had now catapulted into new territory that he couldn't quite fathom. Keenly observing the cold and damp parking lot, it was evident that Donté was now fully alert as his eyes darted to the four elevator doors in front of them, the numerous cars neatly aligned in countless rows, as well as the partial view of the falling snow outside.

"All right, Donté, here we go," Brian announced as the second elevator buzzed upon its arrival. Its doors opened clumsily. "It's okay, that's normal," Brian insisted, extending his hand for him to grab. Accepting the gesture, he carefully followed Brian into the elevator, with Max in the rear.

"This is our floor here, number seventeen," Max said pointing toward the button. "Would you like to push it?" he inquired. Donté raised his free arm and pointed his index finger out toward the clear button with black numbers, tapping it and withdrawing his hand quickly. When the elevator floor suddenly jolted beneath them, Donté stood closer to Brian for security. Max watched him as the elevator ascended and gave him a high-five for taking the initiative to hit the button. Donté smiled at his accomplishment and the recognition being provided.

"Is this it?" Donté asked as the doors jerked themselves open.

"You got it," said Brian. "Just right this way," he finished. The two of them now followed Max to their front door.

Three big red balloons were fixated above the peephole, just above a sign that said 'Welcome Home, Donté' in royal blue lettering. Max read the words aloud to the boy, who responded with his second smile since his nap.

With his two hands full, Max stepped aside for Brian to open the door leading into the living room and open kitchen. Donté's eyes expanded while he examined the household from left to right after taking his first step into the apartment. Brian, still holding Donté's left hand, began introducing him to the front side of the condo as they walked toward Donté's room.

"And *this* is your room," said Brian after taking the first right in the hallway. "It's just like the picture we showed you."

Donté's eyes grew even larger this time upon seeing the furnished room decorated with his name on the main wall facing the doorway, unopened toys and books, as well as a closet full of clothes. "This is really my room?" he asked.

"All yours," said Max. "What do you think?" he asked, wanting to make sure they laid a foundation for him to become comfortable expressing his own ideas.

"I like it!" he returned, reaching out to give them each a hug. At that instant, Max felt confirmation for his and Brian's decision to adopt. It was a deep knowing that informed him that he and his husband were exactly where they needed to be. Max kissed Brian on the lips as the palpable stirring in his soul lingered a while longer, only to be caught off guard by Donté's unexpected reaction.

"Ewwww," replied Donté. "You kissed him," the boy expressed in such a way that left Max unable to determine whether his quick remark was a question or observation.

"Yes, that's what married couples do," said Brian. "But why don't we show you the rest of the house before we unpack your stuff and get you officially settled in?" he continued, decidedly changing the subject of their perceived intolerable behavior to something less awkward.

"Okay," said Donté.

"Across the hall here is going to be your bathroom," said Max.

"I get my own bathroom, too?" he inquired with astonishment.

"Yes," replied Max. "It will be all yours most of the time. But when we have guests over, like your Aunt Sandra or your cousin Junior, both of whom you'll meet soon, they'll also use this bathroom."

"All right, on to our room," said Brian to Donté, who was now walking independently. "This is our bedroom. We have a really nice view of Lake

Erie and some of the city from here," he said, walking along the wall that consisted mostly of a custom-built window. Brian picked Donté up and placed him on his shoulders to provide an unobstructed view of the outside.

"Wow," said Donté, fascinated at the enormous body of water before his eyes.

"All of the water you see is called Lake Erie. It runs along the north part of our state, Ohio. Most lakes are not this big, so we're fortunate to have this nice view. These tall buildings you see," Brian continued as he pointed, "make up downtown Cleveland, the city where you now live. Downtown is full of restaurants, museums, a few parks, and other attractions we'll take you to." Donté sat tall on Brian's square shoulders, placing his two hands at the top of his bearer's heads and taking in the view of the unfamiliar landscape.

"This is our bathroom here," said Max, leading his family in that direction.

"You have two sinks?" Donté inquired after noting the double vanities.

"Exactly," said Max, who was starting to become impressed with their son's attentiveness. "Brian's sink is this one on the left, and this one is mine."

"Why don't you guys have a bathtub?" asked Donté.

"That's because we both prefer taking showers instead of baths," Max responded, totally not expecting that question, while at the same time understanding the logic behind it.

"Well, I have a question for you," said Brian.

"What?" inquired Donté.

"If you have to go to *any* bathroom but the door is closed, what do you do first?"

"Knock?" Donté answered.

"Great job," said Brian as he reached up to give him a high-five, with Max following suit.

"That's correct," said Max. "When it's just the three of us at home, your bathroom will always be empty. But just knock any other time."

"Okie-dokie," responded Donté, causing both Brian and Max to laugh – they had never heard him use that phrase.

"Where did you get that expression?" asked Brian curiously.

"My grandmother said it when she was happy."

"I see," said Brian. "Well, I think that's great," said Brian as they all walked back to Donté's room to start unpacking his belongings.

Back in Donté's bedroom, they showed him where everything was placed before unpacking, including the picture he had drawn for them. Donté quickly discovered his kid's tablet, collection of various trucks, assorted picture and coloring books, a mini-basketball hoop behind the bedroom door, and a trove of clothes and shoes stored in the closet and dresser. While unpacking, the couple gave Donté the opportunity to place his toys according to his preference. Unsurprisingly, he placed his favorite firetruck on the center of his nightstand, giving it the distinguished honor in the room. As for Donté's packed clothes, Max sorted through them as Brian and his little helper determined the best places between the closet and the spaces left in the junior dresser. Max carefully observed them in action, acutely realizing that he would have to significantly relinquish his nitpicking tendencies and accept Donté's naive understanding of order. It dawned on him that nurturing Donté's creativity and individuality was far superior to a few books or clothes being awry.

When Donté was sufficiently acclimated with the space of his new home and his belongings were organized, Max fixed ham and cheese sandwiches for everyone. During lunch, the couple noticed that Donté appeared sleepy despite his short nap on their trip home. Seated sluggishly in his chair after consuming most of his food, he rocked his head back and forth to fight off his unconcealable fatigue.

"Okay, kiddo. It's officially your nap time," Brian stated in a matter-of-fact tone that sounded natural to Max's ears. Brian stood up and positioned Donté in a pretend flying position, mimicking a plane's take off as the boy spread his arms in flight toward his new bedroom. Max was proud to see Brian handle their new role in such an effortless capacity. For the boy's descension, Brian pulled off a forward flip, causing Donté to land on his feet on his bed. Exhausted and overwhelmed with his new surroundings, Donté flopped down onto the bed. Max reached into the closet for a knitted blanket made by Salt – just one of the shower gifts from her and Pepper – and covered Donté up to his shoulders.

"It looks like you need some rest," Max expressed. "Go ahead and take a nap. You've had a full day so far. We'll be right outside if you need anything."

"Welcome home, Donté" said Brian.

"Door open or closed?" asked Max as they left the room.

"Open," Donté replied quietly before closing his eyes.

"We're parents, baby," Brian said softly as they entered the living room area. "This is unbelievable."

"I look forward to the journey ahead us," said Max. "You're such a natural. I couldn't ask for anything more in life."

"Neither could I, baby."

At their kitchen island, the two of them sat down to discuss the two weeks ahead. Since they were both off work, this time would be used to enroll Donté in kindergarten, schedule his initial pediatric appointment, make introductions with family and friends, complete the first post-placement visit with Theresa, have family pictures taken, and take care of various other tasks.

Sandra was scheduled to stop by in two days after picking up Junior from school, but Max wasn't sure if Kevin would be joining them. Brian, who still hadn't communicated anything to his parents about the adoption, discussed broaching the conversation with them soon. Based on his parents' reaction to Brian coming out, Max fully understood his reluctance to share their news. Though not his doing, Max regretted the fact that Brian didn't have any relatives with whom he could share this part of his life. His fraternity line brothers all lived in different cities. Peter and their mutual friends were the closest thing Brian had to a family, except for Max and now Donté.

"I fully support you either way," said Max. "If you want to call them, I'll be right here with you."

"Let me think about it," said Brian. "At least Sandra and Junior will be visiting this week. After what happened the last time we were at their house, I still don't know how she managed to have Kevin change his mind about being involved in our lives. She really is incredible."

"Me neither, but she gets her determination from our mother," Max replied, thinking about Betty Strong's ability to stay laser-focused on her priorities after his father admitted to having another family. Despite the pain she endured from being left with four children, he witnessed his mother achieve the near-impossible task of completing her bachelor's degree and working full-time without ever going on public assistance.

"You all do," said Brian. "That even goes for Mike and Tonya, too. They're like my parents, though – sometimes too caught up in religion to consider real human needs and circumstances."

"Speaking of those two, Sandra told them when she and Junior would be stopping over to meet Donté, but I don't expect them or Kevin to come with her. That's not a bad thing, now that I think about it, though. Theresa doesn't need to see any negativity during her home visit. It will give her an opportunity to see Donté interact with Sandra and Junior. That should be plenty."

"You've got a point there," replied Brian. "Can you remind me of when you're meeting up with Darnell?"

"Next Thursday at 10:00 a.m. We're meeting at the coffee shop on campus. We shouldn't take more than an hour."

"Okay, if you want, I can bring Donté by after he's out of school so that he can see where you work and meet some of your staff."

"That's a great idea," said Max. "I'll email my assistant to let her know that we'll be stopping by. She'll be excited. Do you want to stop by The Center afterward?"

"Sure, I think Donté will enjoy that a lot," said Brian as he updated his phone calendar with their discussed plans.

As he and Brian talked at the kitchen island, seated on two red stools updating their schedules, Max slowly sensed a maturity that he had never experienced. Though he had worked with more high school and college students than he could count, led an entire department, and was now directing the entire arts and sciences division of the college, he had never assumed responsibility for another person in the way that Donté required. That made him nervous, but he also realized that he wasn't in this situation alone. On their couch together, he felt like more of an adult than ever before as they planned out their next two weeks. *In the big picture, this is the easy part*, Max considered.

"Life's gonna be even more consumed when we return to work, but it's nice to have these two weeks as a transition period," Max stated. After completing his sentence, a frightening scream emanated from Donté's room. The two of them hurried there to determine what was happening. Upon entering, Donté's screeching suddenly stopped, but he sat up looking around in a terrified manner, sweating and sobbing silently as his chest heaved forcibly with every breath.

"What's the matter?" asked Max, fully certain that he was experiencing the sort of nightmare that he and Brian had read about in the boy's official paperwork. He and Brian seated themselves on each side of him. "Did you have a bad dream?" Max asked with concern. Unresponsive, Donté sat frozen and continued crying.

"You're okay now. We're right here," said Brian, rubbing Donté's back.

"Everything's going to be fine," Max stated, echoing Brian's tone and feel-good sentiments. "Let me grab you something to drink," he said, hoping that a cup of warm milk would have a calming effect on Donté, who still appeared to be in a state of shock.

In the kitchen Max was on autopilot as he prepared his mother's remedy. Betty Strong swore by its soothing abilities, although his father dismissed her concoction of milk, cinnamon, vanilla, and spoonful of sugar as a hoax. Without fail, "Just deal with it," was always his solution for insomnia or any type of ailment that didn't require immediate medical attention. Max had consequently promised himself that when he had children of his own that he would never dismiss their feelings so coldly.

Though he never knew definitively one way or the other if his mother's warm milk worked, he vividly recalled her being with him on a sleepless night before a middle school city-wide spelling bee. After making her homemade cure-all, just the way that he preferred, Betty Strong sat next to him in bed and told him stories of how she and her brother taught their mother to read when they were in high school. She expressed how proud she was of Max for being in the spelling bee that evening. Although he didn't fall asleep until after midnight, he still placed second in the spelling bee and, more importantly, was left with a memory of his mother at his side that he never forgot. As he completed the finishing touches of the milk, he missed her presence.

Max found Donté resting his head on Brian's shoulder and breathing at a normal pace when he returned. He slowly offered the cup of milk to Donté, who accepted it. "This should help," said Max. "It's my mother's secret recipe," he teased.

"Where's she?" asked Donté.

"She's in Heaven," said Max, realizing that he should now expect the unexpected with their inquisitive kid.

"With God?"

"Absolutely," replied Brian. "She was a really good person."

"Are your parents in Heaven too?"

"No, they live on the east coast in Hartford, Connecticut," Brian replied.

"They must be nice people, too."

"They raised me to be a good person," said Brian. "But speaking of good people, your grandmother must be pretty amazing herself."

"I miss Granny," Donté stated, carefully sipping Max's borrowed remedy. He smiled for the first time since waking from the terrifying dream.

"I'm sure you do," said Max. "That's perfectly normal. And even though she's sick, I'm sure she misses and still loves you."

"What did your granny do when you had nightmares?" asked Brian with curiosity.

"She would sing to me and let me pet Old Sebastian. Are we still going to get a puppy?" Donté inquired, referring to their promise from the transition meeting.

"Yes," said Brian. "Right now, our first priority is getting you settled here, but we'll choose a puppy together soon."

"I can't wait," exclaimed Donté.

"Now that you're up," said Max. "We have a surprise for you. Would you rather go to the aquarium or the zoo to see the holiday lights?"

"Let's go to the aquarium," Donté said without hesitation. "I want to see a shark."

"Good choice," said Brian. "There are plenty of them there. And compared to the zoo, we'll be inside and won't have to worry about the snow that's starting to pick up."

As the family prepared to leave, Max thought about Donté's nightmare. *Reading something on paper isn't quite the same as confronting the real deal. This incident will have to be shared with Theresa later in the week.* Moreover, he hoped that another bad dream would not present itself before then. By the same token, he felt they had responded to Donté's first sleep disturbance satisfactorily. Until now, it wasn't clear to Max that such events could occur during a nap. That meant, Max realized, this information would have to be shared with the new school and anyone who babysat in his and Brian's absence. In the meantime, Max hoped that the frequency of these terrors would be rare and committed himself to learning about the most appropriate responsive techniques for Donté, not being sure if he and Brian had simply lucked out with this afternoon's outcome.

****

Sandra and Junior arrived just after 5:30 p.m. without any sign of Kevin senior. Max, who was in the middle of preparing snacks for their guests this evening, promptly answered the door. His face lit up after seeing his sister and nephew for this introductory gathering. Still dressed in her maroon scrubs from the hospital where she worked, Sandra hugged Max tightly and kissed him on the right cheek. Junior patiently waited for his turn as his mother and uncle exchanged a prolonged hug, gently waving back and forth as people often do at funerals or other somber occasions. But this was no sad occasion. Sandra embraced her baby brother in celebration and thanksgiving that he and Brian had achieved their goal.

"It's so great to see you, little bro," Sandra said. "Where's Brian and Donté?" she asked while looking around the kitchen and living room.

"Brian is helping Donté get dressed for this evening. He's been in his pajamas all day. Come and give your uncle a hug," Max told Junior, who also appeared curious to meet his first cousin. "You just keep getting taller every time I see you." Junior grinned and slowly pushed his glasses back toward his eyes.

"Hey, babe," Max called out, "Is Donté almost ready? Sandra and Junior are out here."

"Here we come," Brian answered. Within seconds, he walked out of the room, holding Donté by the hand. The boy was now dressed in jeans, a miniature blue sweater vest over a red long-sleeve shirt, and a pair of brown boots.

"Aww," said Sandra, as the two approached where she, Max, and Junior stood between the kitchen and living room. "Look at all that curly hair. You're adorable!" she told Donté. Obviously embarrassed by her comment, Donté looked down at his feet and remained quiet.

"This is your Aunt Sandra and your cousin Junior," Brian indicated to the bashful kid.

"Can Aunt Sandra have a hug?" she asked as she bent down and opened her arms. Donté, after looking at Brian and Max for approval, acquiesced to her request with reticence. "And this is your big cousin, Kevin Junior," she informed Donté as she released him from her squeeze.

"Hi, Donté," said Junior, who appeared relieved to meet a family member relatively close to him in age. Junior gave him a hug as well, prompting Donté to grin, although he remained silent.

"Your outfit is really nice," said Sandra.

"Thank you," Donté replied modestly.

"Where's your room?" Junior inquired, deciding to take the opportunity to abandon the adults. Donté turned his torso slightly to the left and pointed toward the room.

"Do you have any games or toys?" asked Junior. Donté nodded his head in affirmation, seemingly pleased that Junior was interested in playing. "Cool, let's go and check them out. I also have games on my phone if we get bored." Donté ran toward his room, with Junior walking swiftly behind.

"Slow down, guys. No need to rush," warned Max, who was surprised to see Donté run. He and Brian had witnessed Donté take off at the aquarium while watching stingrays swim, but there had been other kids running around wildly. Remarkably, that had been the first time that he and Brian witnessed Donté having the opportunity to play freely without the parameters of social service workers. This time, it pleased Max to witness his and Junior's youthful engagement, notwithstanding his quick safety caution to them.

"Junior has been talking about meeting Donté all week long," said Sandra after the kids vanished from their sight. "I know he really wants a brother or sister, so hopefully meeting Donté will help with his patience."

"Is that something you and Kevin are working on?" asked Brian while offering to take her coat.

"We want to have at least one more after I finish school, which will be in just a few more months," she said.

"That's not too far at all," replied Brian. "You'll be changing diapers and working in a promoted role in no time."

"Amen to that," Sandra said. "It could be a lot worse."

Max, who had returned to the kitchen counter, where he was preparing snacks for the evening, offered Sandra a glass of wine. While accepting the drink, Sandra informed them that Kevin was unable to make it tonight because of a church board meeting. Unconvinced that he would've come otherwise, Max chose to hold his tongue. Instead, he focused on updating her on their first week with Donté, including their trip to the aquarium, enrolling him in kindergarten, his probing personality, and his scheduled pediatric visit the next week with Dr. Jones, whom she had originally recommended. Sandra listened carefully as Max and Brian provided their updates with enthusiasm. In the background, they could hear Junior teaching Donté how to improve his basketball shots.

"Let me go and check on these boys," said Sandra, as their commotion increased.

"Good idea," said Max. "I'm glad that Donté feels so comfortable with Junior. He hasn't played with anyone like this since leaving the group home."

"Well, you can adopt Junior too," joked Sandra before walking toward Donté's bedroom as Brian and Max chuckled behind her.

The condo's doorbell rang as she left, and the couple immediately knew it was Theresa. Brian buzzed her into the first-floor lobby while Max checked on the children with Sandra. They had stopped shooting basketball hoops, and Junior was now showing Donté how to play a video game on his new tablet. Relieved that they were interacting with less fracas, she and Max returned to the kitchen with Brian. Sandra, who appeared from Max's perspective to be beside herself with this brief respite from work and her own household, poured herself a second glass of wine. Max sensed his sister's feeling of liberty as she sat down at the island stool, already giddy from her first glass.

"Girl, you need to come over more," Max said to her. "You know that you're always welcome."

"I would if I could, Max, but you know how life gets."

"All the more reason to ensure you take some time for your own self-care, if you ask me," Max rebutted, knowing that his loving advice was unsolicited.

Theresa's rapid knocking interrupted the conversation. Brian opened the door for their expected visitor, welcoming her into their home as usual. Since their initial homestudy assessment, Theresa had grown fond of Max and Brian, having shared a handful of personal details about her own life. She had informed them that she was a divorced mother of two and had adopted her youngest child one year prior to officially separating from her husband. After seeing so many children in need, she explained feeling obligated to do her own part. Unfortunately, her husband was not supportive after the adoption was finalized. He decided to end their marriage, putting her through a rigorous custody battle over their ten-year-old biological daughter. Ultimately, Theresa indicated that he was awarded guardianship during summers and was required to pay child support for the adopted child, who was only four years old. Max and Brian admired Theresa for her commitment to her two children on top of the fact that she had found a high-powered lawyer who she was now dating.

"Good evening, gentlemen," she expressed

in her usual down-to-earth fashion. "How's everything?"

"Great," Max indicated. "Allow me to formally introduce you to my sister, Sandra."

"Hi," said Theresa. "It's nice to meet you in person. I remember us talking when you provided a reference for them during the initial home visit phase."

"Yes," said Sandra, who had left her glass of merlot on the table and joined them near the entrance. "Max and Brian have spoken very highly of you. They credit you for placing Donté into their lives."

"I wish I could take the credit," said Theresa, "but the spark they had with Donté is something that can't be manufactured. The three of them deserve the credit. Speaking of Donté, how's he doing?" she asked after looking around for him from their location.

"He's doing well," said Brian, leading everyone toward the child's bedroom. "Right now, he's playing with Sandra's son in his room. It appears that they're really hitting it off as cousins."

"I'm glad to hear that," said Theresa, who was eager to see Donté in his new environment.

Once they had approached Donté's bedroom, Brian reminded the boy that Ms. Theresa was visiting to check in on him and their household. Donté waved and appeared to recognize the social worker but made it clear to everyone from his body language and engagement with Junior that his focus was on learning the video game at hand. Savvy and observant, however, Theresa observed that Donté appeared well-adjusted and that his room exceeded all the state's required standards. After asking him a few questions that he answered satisfactorily, albeit while mostly distracted with his new tablet, Theresa informed Brian and Max that she only needed to follow up with the two of them to discuss the past week in more detail. Leaving the two cousins to resume their gaming, the adults went into the kitchen and surrounded the granite-topped island that contained assorted cheese and crackers next to the half-empty bottle of merlot.

With her yellow legal notepad in hand, Theresa documented the new parents' responses to her questions on how they were all adjusting to Donté's transition, the fact that he would be starting at his new school, and his upcoming pediatrician's appointment. Theresa's only expressed concern was the recurrence of Donté's nightmares, as he had had three since his move-in date. She encouraged them to continue implementing a bedtime routine and supporting him as soon as possible after he woke up, informing them that developing a new norm would likely result in decreasing terrors, as his experience at the group home had shown. Additionally, Theresa instructed them to inform Dr. Jones so that she could decide on a proper course of action based on Donté's history and her medical recommendation, which could possibly lead to a psychiatric referral.

Although Theresa explained that most adoptees struggle to adjust to their new homes, whether through oppositional behavior, anxiety, bedwetting or depression, Max still worried that this issue might hinder or delay their formal adoption six months later. Since he and Brian were finally experiencing fatherhood, he couldn't imagine the devastation that would be caused by the anticipated formality being thwarted. Sitting beside his husband and sister at their kitchen island, Max internally battled the anxiety he felt as the worst-case scenarios played out in his mind.

Chapter 5

Brian fumbled with his cell phone, turning it to-and-fro as he second-guessed his resolve to update his parents about their adoption process as Max sat closely beside him at the kitchen island. It was the Monday after Theresa's home visit and Donté's introduction to his Aunt Sandra and cousin Junior. The only time Max recalled seeing such angst in his partner was during their mutual trip to Connecticut, where he had paced nervously around their hotel room on the afternoon before coming out to his parents. Observing Brian in this state was near déjà vu for Max, who was now rubbing his partner's back for comfort. After a couple of deep breaths, Brian finally composed himself and looked up his dad's number. He placed the call on speakerphone and inhaled deeply once the phone starting ringing.

"Hello, Brian," Harold answered.

"Hey, Dad," Brian responded. "How's it going?"

"We're just fine, son. Your mother is over here clipping coupons as usual, while I'm watching the sports network. What about you?" he asked concerned. "We usually catch up near the end of the week, and it's only Monday. Is everything okay?"

"There's something important that I have to share," stated Brian slowly as Max rested his hand upon Brian's right shoulder.

"You ain't sick, are you?" asked Harold.

"No, Pa, Max and I are both in good health."

"Okay, so what's going on with *you,* son?"

"I wanted you and Mom to know that we're adopting a kid. He's a five-year-old boy named Donté. He moved in with us last week, and we hope to finalize the adoption process in about six months from now." Brian paused to catch his breath and give his father space to respond.

"Dear God!" Harold said in almost a whisper, as if the wind had been knocked out of him. After taking a moment to formulate his response, he proceeded to ask, "Why, Brian? Isn't your relationship enough?"

"For the same reason that you and Mom decided to have me, Dad. Max and I love each other. Like you, we also want to build a family of our own and leave something in the world that will extend well beyond ourselves."

"Don't compare your homosexual relationship with me and your mother, boy," Harold said sharply. "A male and female complement one another for reproduction. Two males or two females, for that matter, are nowhere near the same. It's only out of God's gift of free will that you can live this lifestyle, but now you're bringing someone else into the picture to grow up thinking that's okay."

"I knew you would be opposed to our decision, but, as my parents, I figured that you and Mom should know since he's essentially your grandchild," Brian said firmly. Max looked at his husband in admiration, overcome with pride that he remained focused on the purpose of the phone call versus being distracted by his father's theological perspective.

"Geez, boy," his father said with contempt. "You need to talk to your mother. I just can't seem to talk any sense into you." Brian and Max could hear Harold mumbling in the background as they waited for Melanie to pick up the phone. Max, still holding onto his husband's shoulder, was surprised that they hadn't hung up the phone as he expected. *Maybe having the conversation over the phone made it more palatable for them rather than having to face their son again in person,* he wondered.

"Brian?" Melanie asked after taking the phone from Harold. "What's this about you two adopting a child?"

"Yes, Mom," Brian stated calmly. "We're in the middle of the adoption process right now. His name is Donté, and he moved in with us last week. If all goes well, the adoption will be finalized at the start of this summer."

"That ain't right, Brian. That just ain't right," Melanie repeated. "You two just can't live your lives together without getting anyone else involved, especially a child?"

"Thanks to the passing of marriage equality, Max and I are entitled to this basic right as much as any heterosexual couple, Mom. And besides, Donté is a great kid who really needs a loving and stable home. We can provide that for him, and I think that it would be great if he knew you as his grandparents. He was being raised by his maternal grandmother before she was suddenly admitted to a nursing home, so now he's part of our family." Max's lower jaw briefly dropped as Brian fluently recounted their son's history, momentarily rendering her silent.

"Listen, Brian, your father and I have always dreamed that you would settle down with a godly woman and have children *the right way*, but you chose this homosexual lifestyle instead. What you are telling us now, however, is well beyond the scope of God's will. We've already continued to accept you as our son instead of excommunicating you against our better judgment, but this is something entirely new. We just can't condone it."

"I understand, Mom, but Max and I aren't asking for your stamp of approval. The decision has already been made. Donté's now part of our home. More than anything, I just wanted you both to know that you were grandparents, even if it didn't come about in the manner you had dreamed. And if you two decide to come around, then you have a beautiful grandson who would desperately appreciate getting to know you. Goodbye, Mom. I love you."

"Bye," Melanie said in a startled tone.

"I'm so proud of you, babe," said Max after the call ended. He embraced Brian with a tight hug, feeling as though his husband had triumphed this time by stating his case so maturely. Neither of them had expected his parents to accept their news with open arms, but Max was grateful they had heard their son out.

It's a good thing, he also thought, *that Donté isn't home*. Prior to Brian calling his parents this morning, the couple had dropped their son off at Mrs. Simmons' Elementary School of Excellence, where Donté was eager to meet his classmates and start making new friends on his first day. *How ironic it is that Donté, a five-year-old, could be so open to meeting new parents and friends while adults like Melanie and Harold were so hostile to accepting him as their grandchild. Even if their rejection of Donté was precipitated upon their opposition to Brian's sexuality, what has Donté done to them? The truth is that he hasn't done anything.*

"That went better than I anticipated," said Brian. "Now we'll just see if they'll ever talk to me again. You already know that it took months for us to get back on speaking terms after I came out."

"Well, at the very least, you were given the opportunity to share what was in your heart," Max replied, still holding onto Brian.

"After having Sandra and Junior over and addressing Donté's questions about my parents last week, I really tried to entertain the possibility, however remote, of them being involved grandparents. Is that too much to ask?" Brian asked in a dispirited tone.

"Not at all, babe," Max stated, as he rubbed Brian's back in solidarity. "But for them and folks like Kevin, it's a complicated matter. You've told me the very same thing yourself. Today you gave them the opportunity to ask themselves what sort of grandparents they'll choose to become. Now all we can do is give them time to answer that question."

"You have a point, Max. Now, what are your thoughts on this puppy we promised Donté?" Brian grinned, wiping away his tears after he and Max released each other.

****

On the following day, a line of people snaked around the cozy café located in the Center for Student Life. Max stood in the middle of the queue, periodically looking back for Darnell to arrive so he could order for the two of them without the young man having to linger behind the growing line of customers.

As he waited, Max reflected on the shocking details that had led to Darnell's termination. If he had been placed in that situation, Max wasn't sure how he would have reacted. The instances of racism he had encountered within his own work environment were disguised with more sophisticated expressions such as “inexperienced,” “different,” “my *African American* colleague,” and others that wantonly referenced his otherness. None of his counterparts, he believed, would ever call him – a former department head and now dean of arts and sciences – *a boy* without incurring formal reproof.

Darnell entered the café just before Max made it to the counter to place his order. “Hi, Mr. Webber,” he said as he approached the front of the line.

“Hey, Darnell, you arrived just in time. What can I get you?”

“I’ll just have a coffee… Black, please,” Darnell requested while looking at the abundance of options on the large chalkboard on the wall behind the cashier.

“All right. Why don’t you grab us a couple of seats, and I’ll meet you at the table shortly?” Max suggested, sensing that some of the people behind them were displeased with his guest skipping ahead.

“Yes, sir,” Darnell said, quickly making his way to the last available table in the confined joint. The young man sat down patiently and began looking out the window at the students walking casually by with a perceptible sense of importance inside the energetic Center for Student Life.

"Thanks again for taking the time to meet with me, Mr. Webber. I really appreciate it," Darnell expressed when Max approached the table with their orders.

"It's no problem," Max replied. "I was surprised that you actually called. How've you been since the job incident?"

"Life is getting more and more stressful at home. My mother's been putting a lot of pressure on me to find a job this past week. I've applied to a couple of places so far, but to be honest, I've really been looking forward to this meeting today. You and your husband seem like guys who have it together. I figured that talking with someone of your stature could help. A part of me is still upset with how the store owner and my co-worker responded to what took place. It's like," Darnell hesitated before speaking, "neither of them cared to see my side of the story. Everything that happened that day keeps replaying in my mind like a merry-go-round. And now my mother is getting frustrated with the fact that I play video games to distract myself. It's not like I'm selling or doing drugs, or anything like that. She even said it was a waste of time coming here to talk with you.

"I honestly want to work, Mr. Webber, but I don't want just any job. If I had my choice, I'd like to become a firefighter. Now that's a respectable job. I've told my mother, but she doesn't seem to be taking me seriously. She's too concerned with me finding something right away so I can help her with the bills. I feel trapped right now," Darnell expressed, sounding exasperated.

Max was caught off guard and humbled by Darnell's willingness to share, which stood in stark contrast to his reserved nature when he and Chad had delivered Donté's furniture. After closely listening to the young man lament his perceived misfortunes, it became clear to Max that Darnell lacked a plan to regain momentum in his life. *It's almost like*, Max reflected, *he's become paralyzed from the whole situation.*

"I hear everything you're saying, Darnell," Max communicated. "You're obviously dealing with the pain of being placed in that unfortunate predicament by your employer and your mother's complaints about you not working. There's a lot on your plate right now. On the other hand, you have this goal of becoming a firefighter that will likely not be an overnight process. Do you know the steps required to become one?"

"Umm," said Darnell, surprised by this question. "All I know is that there's a written and physical test required."

"Yes," said Max. "Those are two of the components required. If you are seriously interested in becoming a firefighter, go to the city's website and research the process. That's an absolute must, Darnell. If you had to take either of those exams today, how prepared would you be?"

"Good question, sir," said Darnell as he considered Mr. Webber's inquiry. "To be honest, I wouldn't feel all that prepared for either one, especially the written examination."

"Keep up that honesty, Darnell. Remember what I told you: I can't be of any help to you if you're not honest during this process. So, definitely keep that up. Here's what I propose," said Max as he corrected his posture and leaned in toward Darnell. "After you're able to clearly inform me of those steps and write a five-hundred-word essay on what becoming a firefighter will mean for your life, I'll connect you with a tutor here at the community college who can help with the exam preparation, as well as a firefighter to inform you about the volunteer program. In terms of the physical exam, you may want to get a gym membership or at least start exercising at home."

"That would be great, Mr. Webber," said Darnell excitedly.

"Any legal trouble that might be a barrier?"

"No, sir. My record is clean."

"That's good. In that case, I'm happy to do this, Darnell, but believe me when I say that the bulk of the responsibility will be yours. The people that I introduce you to will only be able to do so much. In terms of studying, working out, and learning as much as you can about the job before completing the city's application process, and everything thereafter, the onus will be on you."

"I understand," said Darnell, "and I promise not to let you down, sir."

"It looks as if we have a deal, then, but this isn't about you letting me down. This game plan is about your life. I do have one other question, Darnell. I know you mentioned feeling like your mother is getting on your back for not working right now. I do believe, though, that she may be coming out of a place of legitimate concern as your mother. If, as you've indicated, you were going to be in a position of moving into your own apartment soon, that would've been a significant step toward your independence. From her perspective, seeing you hanging out at home and playing video games all day isn't the same. She knows you're capable of more, trust me. Having said that, what's your game plan for working toward your own place again?"

"I wish my mother could explain things like that instead of snapping at me all the time," Darnell insisted. "As for your point, though, I'll have to keep looking for a new job."

"Awesome. There's no need to rush your main goal right now. Part of your research needs to include when examinations will be offered by the city. In the meantime, if you work with a tutor, get yourself in physical shape, learn as much as you possibly can by volunteering, and receive a solid recommendation from a new employer, I believe you really have a shot at making this happen."

"Thank you so much, Mr. Webber. This

means more than you realize," expressed Darnell.

"You're welcome, Darnell. I look forward to hearing back from you about the requirements and reading your essay."

The two of them departed after shaking hands. Max hoped that his potential mentee would follow through on the action items they discussed, yet he realized the need to accept Darnell's responsibility in the matter. He could neither force the young man to research the employment process for firemen on the city's website nor extract a five-hundred-word vision statement from him. *If, and when, Darnell does respond*, he thought, *is totally outside the parameters of my control.*

As Max pondered the young man's predicament, his thoughts transitioned to parenting Donté. These recent conversations with Darnell had enhanced his motivation and commitment to providing the most secure foundation for the boy. Knowing the challenges that Donté had already endured – from losing his biological parents and maternal grandmother to being rejected from paternal family members and dealing with night terrors – Max pledged to create a stable foundation for their son's healthy development and long-term success.

Jane Budges of student support services walked up to Max while he was adding reminders in his phone to reach out to potential tutors for Darnell as well as one of his former students who now worked as a firefighter. Because Jane was wearing a heavy black coat with a matching cloche that concealed her brunette head, Max almost did not recognize his friend. Though pleased to see her, he hoped that no other staff would stop by his table, as he was technically on two weeks with pay. Before Max could motion his invitation, Jane promptly sat in the seat that had been vacated by Darnell.

"Well, what do we have here, Maxwell?" she asked in a surprised tone. "Aren't you on vacation?"

"Hey, Jane," Max replied. "Yes, I just had a quick meeting with a young man in need of a little guidance right now."

"Oh, I see. Is he a student?" she asked curiously.

"Not at this time. He's someone that Brian and I met a little while ago. It's a long story. How are things here?" asked Max, seeking to change the subject.

"Now that the second semester is here, we've kicked into high gear since these new preparatory classes are in place and student enrollment is up, yet again."

"Your boss, Dr. Whitmore, seemed to have everything under control before I left," Max said.

"He thinks he does," said Jane, "but it's the student advisors who are concerned. Their caseloads have increased by twenty percent, and they're required to provide two additional informational sessions in their respective concentrations without any raises."

"I totally hear you," said Max. "The college has already committed to hiring additional staff during the summer if phase one succeeds this semester. Your department, as you and Dr. Whitmore already know, is one of our top priorities. You've seen the planning documents."

"Yes, I have, but managing six advisors who already feel overworked places my ears directly to the ground. All of my staff support the college's expansion in theory, but from their perspective, they don't want to be set up for failure."

"Dr. Whitmore and I have looked at the analytics of your advisors a few times, and I can promise you that what we're asking for this semester is doable, Jane. You know that I wouldn't mislead you. If you'd like, I can set up a meeting for all three of us to review these initial weeks and discuss the concerns of your advisors. How does that sound?"

"That's fine, Max. I'd appreciate that. And you already know that none of this is personal. We all know that this expansion is part of the legacy that President Nelson wants to leave before passing the baton to you. How are you and Brian adjusting to being parents?"

"It's been an adventure," said Max. "Donté

is really latching onto us, which we didn't expect to happen so soon. Yesterday was his first day of school," Max said proudly as he showed her a photo of Donté and Brian on his cell phone. "And Brian has been amazing. It's like he's been a father all his life."

"He's absolutely adorable," Jane responded, looking at the picture of Max's family in front of the private academy. "It's nice that he's adjusting so well. Any major plans as a family before you return to work next week?"

"Actually, he and Brian are stopping by later this afternoon after Donté gets out of school so that I can introduce him to my staff, and then we're headed to The Center so Brian can do the same. Tomorrow we plan on surprising Donté after school by going to a rescue shelter to look for a puppy. His grandmother had a dog named Old Sebastian. He's going to be thrilled when he gets to the shelter," said Max, imagining Donté's reaction.

"I'm happy for you and Brian, Maxwell," she said. "You've always been a joy to be around, but now there's this new vitality in your spirit that's even more endearing, my friend."

"Thank you, Jane. That's good to hear," said Max. "It's about time for me to head out. I have a slew of errands to run before meeting them back here this afternoon. But, as usual, it's a pleasure to see you. I'll shoot my assistant an email later today to schedule that meeting after I return to the office."

"Okay, Maxwell. I'm glad we had this brief encounter. Enjoy the rest of your time off."

"Will do," said Max as he buttoned his smoky grey peacoat and prepared to enter the blistering January temperature that awaited him outside of the Center for Student Life.

****

At 2:45 p.m. the next day, when the school bell rang at Ms. Simmons' Elementary School of Excellence, Max and Brian picked up Donté at the designated location of the cafeteria for kindergartners. Donté, already snug in his bright red coat, mittens, and knitted beanie, ran toward his parents for afternoon hugs. It was clear to Max that their son, at least for now, was oblivious to the grimaces of his peers and others throughout the cafeteria, including staff, as he cheerfully embraced his two dads. Being only one of three black children in his kindergarten class out of twenty-one students, Max wasn't sure whether their onlookers were confounded by the fact that they were an African American family or that two men, as opposed to a heterosexual couple, were picking Donté up.

Feeling relatively sure that their puzzled stares would persist if they were either a gay white couple or a heterosexual black couple, Max was already learning on Donté's fourth day of school to dismiss the stupefied stares of their son's largely homogenous cohorts. *Their eyeballing,* he reasoned, *is probably rooted in the fact that we're a black gay couple.* Until the reality of racism and homophobia inevitably revealed their ugly heads to Donté's developing cognizance, Brian and Max had decided not to speak on such issues.

"How was your day?" Brian asked Donté as they walked toward the cafeteria exit.

"It was great, Dad. I made two new friends, Eric and Sarah," the boy declared proudly. "Eric shared some of his cookies with me during lunch."

"Oh, really? That was nice of him," Max indicated. "Did you share anything with Eric in return?"

"Yes, Papa. I gave him and Sarah a piece of my rice krispie treat."

"That's your favorite snack," said Brian in a surprised voice. "You must really like them to share that."

"They were really nice to me," said Donté. "I can't wait until school tomorrow."

"Great to hear, son," said Max. "It looks like you're having a really good day. We have a surprise for you."

"What is it, Papa?" Donté pleaded with excitement as they entered the busy parking lot.

"You're going to find out soon," Max shared as he smiled, holding the kid's hand for safety in this busy section of the urban academy.

"Is it inside the car?" Donté inquired of his imminent fortune.

"We can't tell you anything else," said Brian. "You'll just have to wait and see for yourself. Think of it as an exercise in patience."

"C'mon, Dad!" Donté insisted, trying a different tactic by pulling on Brian's arm with his free hand to garner his dad's favor.

"I told you we can't provide any more details," said Brian. "You'll find out soon."

Donté dropped his dad's arm in disappointment and turned to Max for one final attempt. "Papa?" he gently asked. "Can you please tell me?"

"That's not going to work, either," Max said. "You heard your dad."

"Okay," Donté muttered, resigning himself to his fathers' united front.

By the time they approached Brian's car, Donté's curiosity exceeded his initial response. Once seated, he searched diligently in the back of the car and peeped his head in the front for any visible signs of a surprise. Max smiled to himself as Donté squirmed around the back seat looking for clues. On the drive to Cleveland's Animal Rescue Shelter, Max attempted to distract Donté by asking about what he learned in school and his new friends, but Donté's laconic responses conveyed his intolerance of irrelevant small talk. Brian, who had been quietly observing their interaction as he drove, proposed a game of twenty questions to give Donté an opportunity to guess at the mystery. Fortunately, his idea kept the boy engaged until they arrived in the parking lot of the rescue shelter, outside of which a mural of dogs and cats was painted on the front wall.

"We're getting a puppy!" Donté shouted with confidence this time, preparing to take off his seatbelt as Brian parked the vehicle in the nearly vacant lot.

"That's right, but keep your seatbelt on until the car's parked," said Max, turning around to face their son. "A dog, as you already know from Old Sebastian, is a lot of responsibility. Brian and I are going to be counting on you to help with taking care of him. Are you up for the task?"

"Yes, Papa," Donté stated sincerely.

"I think you will do a fine job of looking after a puppy," said Brian. "That's why we're here right now." Donté beamed with pride at his two dads after he had unbuckled himself, ready for Brian to unlock his door.

Inside the spacious facility, they slowly walked around the canine section, looking at diverse breeds assembled behind rows of metal enclosures. A cacophony of squeals and rowdy barks reverberated around them, seemingly to catch their attention and that of a few other strollers looking to adopt a pet of their own.

Within five minutes of their arrival, the

sound of soft yelping caught Donté's attention. It was a young Jack Russell Terrier who sprinted back and forth in the front part of a cage shared with two fully-grown and disinterested basset hounds. He was all white apart from two golden-brown spots that covered his eyes and ears, leaving the remaining part of his face to resemble an hourglass. After spotting the puppy dart tirelessly in his confined parameters, Donté walked directly to the cage. The youthful terrier ceased its playfulness upon Donté's approach and genuine display of curiosity.

"I like him," said Donté with assurance.

"I think you mean *her*," corrected Brian. "But by the looks of her wiggling tail, she really likes you too."

"She does look like a great choice," said Max. "Let me go and find someone to let them know that we've made our decision," said Max before walking away. Soon enough, Max returned with a female staff member whose name tag read 'Assistant Manager: Elaine.' She smiled widely as she walked up to the cage where Brian was standing and Donté was squatting in front of his new playmate.

"What a delightful choice," said Elaine. "She belongs to a litter that was recently brought to us from a family who couldn't afford to care for them all. The last of her four siblings was adopted yesterday. Puppies, as you might imagine, tend to go very quickly."

"Does she have a name?" Donté wondered aloud.

"Not currently. We typically like to leave naming to families unless we know for certain what a pet's name is when they arrive. So, that will be your decision as a family," Elaine indicated.

"Let's call her Pickles," exclaimed Donté, who was visibly delighted with the idea of naming their new puppy. Elaine and his parents burst into laughter at the unconventional suggestion.

"Pickles?" asked Brian, wanting to make sure that he heard his son correctly.

"Yeah, Dad," the boy replied.

"Where on earth did you come up with that name, Donté?" Brian asked, still smirking at the idea.

"Everyone loves pickles!" Donté said in a silly voice. Max, who wasn't fully convinced of the factuality behind Donté's assertion, could not think of anyone who hated pickles. *In any case*, he thought, *the Jack Russell Terrier is undeniably lovable.*

"The name does have a peculiar ring to it, *Pickles*," said Max, repeating the name for his own confirmation.

"Well, Pickles it is," agreed Brian. Donté seemed pleased to watch his fathers settle on the chosen name. Upon the family's approval, Elaine opened the cage and picked up Pickles, placing her carefully in Donté's arms, where he cradled her like a baby. Pickles greeted her new friend with tiny slurps on his chin.

Elaine, who looked as if she had had a long day, then led them to an area lined with shopping carts, where Brian and Max could buy their new pet's essentials. An outspoken dog owner herself, Elaine recommended the brands and products that she deemed superior in quality. When their shopping cart was full of everything that Pickles would require and more, she led them near the entrance, where they completed the official paperwork and received Pickles's shot history. Max, who felt a sigh of relief after swiping his credit card, was proud of his family's second addition. He felt a sense of completion and satisfaction at seeing Donté's zeal as he walked Pickles out of the building with her new hot pink leash.

By the time the family made it home, it was after 5:00 p.m. While Brian and Max carried Pickles's supplies, Donté continued leading her by the leash from the condo's parking lot into their apartment, where she was released to explore the unfamiliar environment. Determined to ensure that their son quickly assumed responsibility for their new puppy, Max requested Donté's assistance with organizing the newly purchased pet items. He carefully followed the instructions without any gripe, while Max closely monitored Donté's progress as he prepared dinner and Brian laid out Donté's school clothes for the next day. Meanwhile, Pickles conveyed her allegiance to the family by staying in Donté's shadow wherever he traveled.

After her walk that evening, beginning what Max knew would be a long and tedious process of house training, the couple encouraged Donté to commence his bedtime routine. This developing ritual currently consisted of him using the bathroom, brushing his teeth, changing into pajamas, saying a bedtime prayer, and choosing a book to read with at least one of them. With the arrival of his new pal, Donté stalled this evening by making every excuse he could concerning Pickles. Brian and Max redirected him back to his bedtime program several times, letting him know that there was nothing left she required at this point, until he finally acquiesced.

Once Donté had finally settled into bed, Max started reading this evening's storybook. The boy dozed off at the half-way point. All the excitement of making two new friends at school and choosing Pickles, Max figured, had finally caught up to him. To Max's amazement, Pickles swiftly jumped onto the mattress after he kissed Donté on the forehead and walked off. As he left the door ajar, he hoped that her presence would help deter or at least mitigate their son's reoccurring nightmares.

****

On the last Friday of January, nearly a full month after Donté's official move-in date, Brian and Max hosted their friends for cards night. Max and Lamont played against Todd and his boyfriend, Tim, who joined this tradition for the first time. Brian was officially on daddy duty and watched the spades match close by from one of the kitchen stools. Tim's presence made it much easier for Brian to respond, if necessary, to Donté, who was sleeping soundly in bed, and double as bartender. Max, now teamed up with his normal nemesis, closely focused his attention on the game at hand, given Lamont's advanced skill level.

"That's really some kid you guys have," said Todd. "I'm seriously proud of you. However, I hope that he doesn't learn spades from this one," he said, cutting Max's king of clubs with a three of spades. Lamont simply shook his head in dismay.

"Thank you," replied Max to his friend's initial words about their son. "He's definitely a special kid. We couldn't be any luckier, but there's no need to show off in front of your boyfriend," Max stated, refocusing on their game. "We're still far ahead."

"I got my baby's back," said Tim. "Maybe the little guy shouldn't learn from you. Do you play better than he does?" he asked, turning toward Brian. "If so, you should let Max assume daddy duty while you take over his hand."

"We're actually about the same," said Brian to his own husband's defense.

"You *can't* be serious," replied Tim, obviously taken aback.

"Yes, chil'. Unfortunately, he is," said Lamont, who was far less talkative this evening compared to their normal social gatherings.

"Hey," said Max. "You're supposed to be on my side." Todd and Tim laughed at the in-feuding they had inspired.

"If the shoe fits," Lamont said. "Anyway, Donté now has Uncle Lamont to teach him how to play and take care of wanna-be players like you," he said while fiercely eyeing their two opponents.

"Just as long as he isn't learning from these guys," Tim expressed. Max, who was still determining his opinion of Todd's boyfriend, had to stop himself from taking too much offense. Tim, it seemed to Max, was not one to hold anything back. *It's just a spades game*, he reminded himself. Max quickly looked at Brian to communicate his irritation with their visitor as Lamont earned the book on the table.

"How about focusing on you and Todd's need to catch up?" announced Lamont, picking up the hand he just won. "Uncle Lamont is here to the rescue!" Todd and his partner were briefly silenced.

"Is everyone good on drinks?" asked Brian, taking this quiet interval to make himself helpful.

"If so, I'm going to check on Donté."

"You know I never turn down a long island, honey," said Lamont.

"I'll take one, too," said Max.

"All of them drinks are the reason you're going to lose," said Todd. "Drink up," he jested. Tim and Brian laughed at Todd's wisecrack.

"Y'all ain't seen nothing yet," Lamont said emphatically, slapping down a queen of spades to snag yet another book. Brian returned from the kitchen with the two requested drinks before going to Donté's room.

"So, a little birdie told Brian and me that you might be moving, Todd," said Max, who had been waiting to see if his Michigan-bound friend would address the elephant in the room.

"Well, we planned to make the announcement to you and Brian tonight, but it looks like *someone* beat us to the punch," Todd replied, rolling his eyes at his best friend, Lamont.

"Huh?" asked Brian after making a quick check on Donté, "What's this about an announcement?"

"Last week, my job officially approved my transfer request to Detroit so that I can relocate to live with Tim. My position there, which is basically the same as our local office, starts in three weeks from this upcoming Monday. I'll be moving into Tim's place and renting out my house here, at least for the first year."

"That's huge," said Brian. "It's great to see you guys taking this next step. I'm sure you must've weighed your options seriously."

"No kidding," said Max. "I just wish we had the opportunity to meet you sooner," he communicated to his and Brian's new guest.

"Same here," Tim indicated. "My schedule has been hectic, but Todd's regular visits to Michigan made it a lot easier for us to stay in contact throughout this time. Believe me, though, with his family and you guys being here, we certainly won't be strangers. And as I mentioned earlier, a true spades champ needs to teach your son how the game is played." This was the first time that Max smiled at one of Tim's remarks. *All right*, he thought, *maybe this guy is okay after all*.

"So how are your preparations coming along?" asked Brian.

"I start packing this weekend, actually. Lamont's coming over tomorrow to assist me and Tim. I would've asked you, but you two obviously have your hands full now with Donté and Pickles. Man, it feels like we just attended your wedding yesterday. Now here you are living the American dream."

"If we'd known earlier," Brian responded, "one of us could've definitely made plans to join you guys. Just let us know if you want help next weekend. Between the two of us, we'll figure something out. And from the looks of it," he added, "you and Tim are on your way there."

"I think we have the packing covered, but I could definitely use one of you guys when I move in three weeks. The more manpower, the better."

"You didn't hire movers?" asked Max with a stunned look on his face. "You make way too much money, and all of us are getting too old to be carrying furniture," Max joked, looking around the table at everyone.

"Tim and I have a future to think of, so I'm saving everywhere I can. And besides, as much as you work out, Max, you got a lot of nerve talking about 'getting old.'"

Before Max could respond to Todd and pick up his newly dealt hand, Donté screamed from his bedroom. Max and Brian immediately looked at each other and hastened toward the bedroom after excusing themselves from the kitchen table. Their three friends sat frozen in their seats while the couple attended to their son. In his room, Donté lay in bed crying and holding Pickles tightly. He looked frightened as his fathers approached, staying mute as they began comforting him with their gentle words and hugs. Feeling sorry for Pickles, who was obviously alarmed from Donté's screaming, Max slowly loosened her from the restrictive grasp around her small body and placed her at the bed's foot end.

"You're okay," said Brian in a soothing voice. "You are one brave kiddo," he said. "Papa and I are right here with you."

"You sure are. We love you so much," said Max as he took a tissue from the nearby bed stand and began drying Donté's face. "Would you like me to make grandma's special recipe?" he asked, referring to the homemade remedy he had acquired from Betty Strong that Donté now thoroughly enjoyed. His son, starting to gain control of his breathing, slowly nodded his head in agreement. Max returned to the kitchen area, where their friends appeared concerned.

"Is everything okay?" asked Lamont while Max began to warm a cup of milk.

"Yes, he's all right. He had a nightmare, which he has from time to time. There's no way of predicting them, though. In all honesty, that's the primary reason why Brian and I aren't playing together."

"I'm sorry to hear that," said Todd. "Is there anything that we can do?"

"No, thanks, Todd," Max said. "Brian is taking care of him now, and I'm making a cup of my mom's famous warm milk. We're slowly getting the hang of responding to his needs during these situations."

"Your mother made that, too?" Tim inquired. "Anytime my siblings and I had a headache or had trouble sleeping, our mother would make us cups of warm milk with cinnamon and vanilla. I loved that stuff."

"You're the only other person I've met who knows about this remedy!" declared Max. "Brian thought that I was nuts when I offered him a cup after we first moved in with one another. He had this awful migraine that came from nowhere. He tried it and told me that it tasted strange, saying that he 'couldn't get mentally beyond the idea of drinking anything but cold milk.' See, that's what you have to look forward to, Tim, when Todd moves in." Max gently added each ingredient into the cup and stirred, as Lamont and Todd watched with intrigue.

"It doesn't look *that* bad," Todd expressed while Max returned to Donté's room, where Pickles was now doing most of the comforting. In fact, Brian had moved down the bed and placed the puppy back in her original position, while ensuring that the boy's grip wasn't as restrictive this time. He and Donté were both playing with her as she soaked up all the attention she could. Donté slowly sipped from his cup after Max offered it to him.

"Thanks, Papa," he stated softly.

"You're welcome, son," Max said. "Are you feeling better?" Donté nodded and grinned as Pickles poked at the cup with her paws. Max knew that he couldn't have received a better answer.

"It's okay if you go back with the guys, baby. Everything, I believe, is going to be fine. I'll stay here until he goes back to sleep." Respecting his husband's decision, Max kissed Donté on the forehead and wished him goodnight. Upon seeing Todd and Tim, as he reentered the kitchen area, he felt glad for his friends and their decision to live with each other. It had been clear to Max the entire evening, from how they played cards with each other and communicated, that they were in love. He hoped for their future engagement, but in the meantime concerned himself with guaranteeing that he and Lamont would walk away with bragging rights this evening.

****

On the following afternoon, Max traveled to meet Darnell at a soulful café in East Cleveland. Mourning his loss of sleep from the previous night, just one of the many adjustments that he and Brian were making since Donté's arrival, Max drove carefully down Euclid Avenue until he arrived at Superior Avenue, where he turned left. He recalled holding Sandra's hand and catching the school bus at E. 125th in this resilient community that his family had called home before his mother was able to purchase a house in South Collinwood. Betty Strong took a great deal of pride in becoming a homeowner in their predominantly working-class neighborhood, albeit a modest upgrade from East Cleveland. The biggest upside of their relocation, for Max, was the significant decrease in the drug transactions and gunshots that they had regularly witnessed in their former community. Contemplating the challenges that plagued so many residents in this area, he was pleased that Darnell had followed up with him earlier in the week and requested that they meet.

Over the phone on the previous Tuesday evening, he had accurately walked Max through the steps of becoming a firefighter from the initial application through the apprentice program after becoming a cadet. The essay required of him, according to the young man, was three pages hand-written, which Max encouraged him to type before they met. The energy in Darnell's voice, Max recalled, had differed vastly from their last in-person meeting. He sounded confident and hopeful this time around. Max looked forward to seeing him and reading his essay. Max noticed as he searched for a parking spot that the café was full, catching him by surprise, as it was late on a Saturday afternoon. Once parked, he quickly texted Brian to let him know that he had arrived despite the slushy road conditions and then proceeded to trudge through the sloppy snow toward the warm and inviting community enclave.

Inside, Max was overwhelmed by the smell of baking brownies and a lively crowd of people – standing and seated – making it difficult for him to locate Darnell. Eventually, he spotted the young man waving his hand in the back of the café behind several rows of packed tables. Considering all the clamor, Max was relieved that his mentee had arrived in time to claim seats. The busy café showed no sign of letting up anytime soon. He signaled to Darnell that he would be over shortly after buying a coffee, fighting the temptation to purchase one of the café's redolent brownies.

A friendly light-skinned woman with shoulder-length dreadlocks took his order and quickly poured him a cup of house coffee, informing him that he was in for a treat this evening. The café was hosting the first round of a statewide spoken word contest that was starting in two hours at 6:00 p.m. Disappointed, Max confessed that he was meeting someone and had to be home by 5:30 to make dinner. The thoughtful barista handed him a flyer with upcoming spoken word and open mic events for him to take. Despite the growing audience and loud talking around him, Max felt at home as he fought his way toward the rear of the café.

"Hi, Darnell," Max began. "It's good to see you again."

"Hello, Mr. Webber," Darnell responded before sipping his own apple cider. "You made it just in time. This place is getting packed."

"It definitely is," Max agreed. "The barista informed me that they're having some type of poetry slam contest later. And, by the way, you can call me Max from now on, Darnell. I appreciate the respect, but there's no need to be so formal."

"Okay, Max. I can respect that," said Darnell, nodding his head in agreement. "The spoken word slam is a yearly event that takes place at this venue on the first Saturday of February. The first round is always here in Cleveland before it moves to Columbus and Cincinnati over the next couple of weeks."

"Oh, wow, I had no idea," said Max. "It's been a long time since I've heard spoken word," he continued, trying unsuccessfully to recall the last event he attended.

"My best friend Mike is a poet, so that's why I chose this spot when you mentioned Saturday afternoon. This is his first year participating at this level. There's no way I would ever miss his event. He's crazy talented, but he has some serious competition."

"That's awesome," Max responded. "I promise not to keep you too long. You probably have other friends joining you later, so let's get to it. How've things been for you?"

"Let me start off by saying how much I appreciate our last meeting. It really helped me focus my attention on what I want in life. You really have no idea how much it meant to have someone like you hear me out. I'm so used to my mother always telling me what to do. I know she means well, but it's like my opinion hardly ever counts for much around her, even when it's about my own life." Darnell shook his head while Max sat listening quietly.

"The day after we met up, I made a trip to

the library and researched the process of becoming a firefighter until it was completely memorized. I also started applying for jobs to earn some money like we discussed. Luckily, the manager of a nearby bakery was willing to give me a chance. This past Monday was my first day on the job. So far, I've been learning to bake all kinds of items I never imagined as well as how to operate a cash register.

"I have to admit that I didn't start writing the essay until last week. I just assumed that it was something that I could rush through. And, truthfully, I thought that it was something that you really didn't care about. Instead of writing, I stuck with the job applications and played video games until I asked myself *why* I was procrastinating on something that seemed so trivial. On top of that, I also knew that you wouldn't meet with me again if the essay wasn't complete. I was torn, but then it hit me. No one ever seriously asked me what I wanted out of life. Aside from knowing that being a firefighter was a respectable career, I was lost. It took me three days to write this essay," he stated, holding up the typed document.

"What I can now say is that writing these five hundred words gave me the opportunity to articulate what type of man I plan to be, and the title of firefighter is only one component. Other than being a respected professional, I want a family and to set a positive example for my children. I want to be the type of dad I never had in my life growing up, someone that will make my mother proud."

As Darnell finished explaining his arduous self-reflection process, he handed over his typed two-page document to Max, who started reading it without delay. Darnell sat nervously as his personal statement was read, looking periodically toward the front entrance to see if his friend had arrived. Virtually every seat in the café was occupied at that point.

"So, what do you think?" asked Darnell after his essay was read.

"You hit the bull's eye," Max replied earnestly. "I see everything you listed as being possible, but that doesn't mean that achieving those things will be easy or quick. Now it's time for my part of our deal," he said before pausing. "It's clear that a tutor will be helpful for the written exam, so let's start there. I'll put you in touch with Emily next week. She's one of our adjunct professors and really knows how these city exams are put together. I think she'll be quite helpful. You two will have to arrange when and how often you meet based upon your schedules. Once she provides confirmation of your progress, I'll put you in touch with Reggie. He's one of our graduates who can school you on the position and the city's volunteer program."

"That sounds great, Mr. Webber," said Darnell. "No, excuse me," he corrected himself, "I meant Max."

At that moment, Max's phone started ringing. "Hello?" he answered, curious who was calling from an undisclosed number.

"Is this Maxwell Webber, husband of Brian Webber?" a monotone voice asked.

"Yes, it is. Is everything okay?" Max asked apprehensively, feeling that something was off.

"I'm afraid that your husband Brian has been physically assaulted and has sustained serious injuries this afternoon. He's being treated here at the main campus of Cleveland University Hospital. We have Donté here with us as well. He's physically okay, but he's in a state of shock, to be honest."

"Oh, my God!" Max nearly shouted from his seat as tears filled his eyes. "What happened? Can I please talk to Brian or Donté?"

"Right now, Mr. Webber, the best thing you can do is get here as soon as possible. Brian is currently unconscious in our ICU. He's in room 314. I can assure you that Donté is in good hands with one of our nurses."

"I'm on my way now," said Max, nervously hanging up the phone with trembling hands.

"What's wrong?" asked Darnell with a worried expression on his face.

"It's my husband, Brian," said Max, who was already standing and putting on his coat. "He's apparently been assaulted. I need to hurry to the hospital. I apologize, but we'll have to continue this conversation later."

"I'm sorry to hear that, Max. I totally understand, and my prayers are with you."

Max walked forcefully through the horde of people gathered in the café, indiscriminately pushing his way through the strangers around him. His face winced and tears flowed down his cheeks as he resisted the full onset of a panic attack. *Unconscious? This can't be happening*, he told himself. *Why Brian and Donté? They, of all people, don't deserve this. Who would attack Brian? He's never harmed a soul. And poor Donté... I hope he's all right. This is the last thing he needs with everything he's been through. I should've been with them instead of being here!*

Oblivious to the bitter coldness inflicted on Cleveland this afternoon, he walked with an unshakable determination to his car. Nothing mattered to him at this moment except for Brian and Donté. He prayed fervently to God for their health, especially for his unconscious husband. Hurrying to his car, it seemed to him a cosmic and tragic irony that the very world they just started building was on the verge of collapsing. He pleaded with God to spare Brian's life while opening his car door and getting inside, wishing all of this was a bad dream.

Chapter 6

Max had loathed hospitals since he was eight years old and had broken his ankle on the playground. He and a group of friends were playing dodgeball during recess when his right foot twisted while trying to pivot after a ball was launched in his direction, incurring the double agony of embarrassment and a grotesque ankle injury. Everything proceeding his fracture, from the loud and traumatizing ambulance trip to his panic-inducing surgery procedure, had terrified him. He pleaded uselessly with Betty Strong during his hospitalization to take him home to their cozy two-story house, where life was familiar and less eventful.

Due to his own hatred of hospitals, a part of Max was grateful that his mother did not have to endure any trauma at a medical facility after the stroke she suffered at work. Although he recognized such thoughts were selfish, he justified this line of thinking based upon the distress of patients and their loved ones who waited in emergency rooms or ICUs, hoping and praying for a positive outcome, often to no avail. At the same time, Max desperately missed his mother and wondered if she still might be alive had the first responders intervened sooner.

Now Max sat beside the hospital bed where Brian lay unconscious with bruises covering his face and arms, nasty remnants from the attack this afternoon. "Babe, I desperately need you to get through this and come back to Donté and me," Max expressed to his unconscious husband. "We both need you, Brian. Every day I look forward to kissing you in the morning and knowing that you'll be next to me when it's time for bed. I love how you light up a room with your sense of humor, connect with everyone you meet so authentically, maintain your coolness and patience in rocky times, inspire the youth at The Center, and still manage to make me feel like I'm the only man in the world. And now that Donté is in our lives, you've been showing me how great of a dad you are. It's way too early for you to let go. I won't ever give up on you, so don't give up on us – *please Brian*," Max implored, holding his husband's limp hands.

As Max finished his words, the minute and hour hands of the black and white clock in the sterile hospital room inched steadily toward twelve, which would signal midnight and the longest seven hours of his life. Still holding Brian's hands, Max looked over at Donté sleeping soundly on the small couch next to the bathroom. He was grateful that their son hadn't been physically harmed during the attack that occurred as they were walking Pickles, who had been taken to a local animal shelter. Unable to fall asleep beside his comatose husband, Max recalled the events leading up to his present state of insomnia.

Detective Roberts, the first person to greet Max once he reached the ICU just after 5:30 p.m., confirmed that Brian's assault had occurred several blocks away from their condo in a small park near the theatre district. Donté and a second witness who arrived at the scene after hearing the boy's scream both described three male suspects, all wearing black ski masks. The detective informed Max that their investigation would include looking at cameras in the vicinity of the incident to obtain a lead on the culprits. He encouraged Max or someone from the hospital to call him once Brian, hopefully, regained consciousness so that he could be interviewed. Brian, he surmised, would likely be able to provide the most detailed account and information about the attackers, given Donté's age and the fact that they fled immediately after the second person arrived on the scene.

What stood out more than anything for Max was Detective Roberts's warning that Brian's situation could have been deadly. He stated that based on the injuries and dozens of attacks he had personally responded to over the course of his seventeen-year tenure, the combination of Donté's screams and the arrival of the second witness likely saved Brian's life. Stunned at hearing what could have been a fatal outcome, Max sat down next to Brian's bed, placed his face in his hands, and wept as he felt the full impact of this revelation. Before leaving, Detective Roberts also told him that since the incident appeared to fit the pattern of a hate crime, the FBI would likely take over the investigation at some point. For the time being, however, his department was taking the lead while working in partnership with them.

It was not until after Max initially saw Brian and met with Detective Roberts that Donté was eventually brought into the room. While he desperately struggled to hold onto any semblance of sanity himself, Max couldn't imagine what Donté's state of mind must have been after witnessing the assault and seeing his dad lay unconscious on a hospital bed. Max had therefore resolved that he would *stay strong* by supporting Donté. Practically speaking, that initially meant hugging him, holding his hand, and verbally reassuring him that neither he nor Brian had done anything to deserve what happened in an effort to mitigate the boy's state of shock, and most importantly, reinforcing that he was now safe.

According to his son, the attackers repeatedly screamed the words 'fag' and 'homo' as they collectively struck Brian with their fists and feet. Listening to his son, Max remembered the unwelcoming stares at Donté's school, as well as the video clip of the black teenage adoptee caught using bleaching cream. *Theresa was right. No amount of preparation could've ever fully prepared us.* He never imagined that he would have to explain such homophobic terms to Donté at his current age, especially without Brian at his side. Rather than go into depth, though, he informed their child, "They were mean terms used to make us gay and lesbian people feel bad about ourselves." While Max observed that his son understood the hurtful intent behind the words, his puzzled and melancholy demeanor conveyed confusion as to *why* someone would attack his dad, who was nothing but kind and loving to him and everyone Donté saw him encounter.

Fortunately, Max wasn't left by himself to support Donté during the initial hours of his arrival at the ICU. Nurses and patient assistants cared for the boy by bringing him snacks and coloring books, turning the television to cartoon stations, talking to him about baseball and firetrucks, as well as answering a barrage of questions pertaining to the medical equipment and interventions being used on his father. It was during these short intervals when Donté was distracted that Max methodically began making telephone calls to inform their friends and family of Brian's predicament. Sandra, Salt and Pepper, Todd, Lamont, and Peter, who lived outside of Cincinnati, all confirmed that they would be on their way. By 8:00 p.m., Max had managed to make the bulk of these calls except for the one to Brian's parents, Harold and Melanie.

Max had never spoken to them directly since his initial greeting at the restaurant in downtown Hartford. They had made it clear to their son that they wanted no involvement in a gay relationship, including any communication with Max. Now following Brian's most recent discussion with them about the adoption, their rejection also seemed to include Donté. Sandra, the first to arrive at the hospital, encouraged Max to call Brian's parents after they hugged and briefly chatted. "As his parents, they deserve to know," Sandra expressed, agreeing to look after Donté while he made the call. Knowing that his sister was right, he left Brian's room and wandered the ICU's chilly halls until he found a suitable place to make the call.

"Hello," Harold answered the phone.

"Hi, Mr. Webber," said Max slowly. "This is your son's husband, Max. Please do not hang up. I'm afraid that I have some bad news about Brian," Max expressed before pausing.

"What's the matter?" Harold inquired.

"This afternoon Brian was attacked by three men while he and our son were walking our puppy not too far from where we live. He has sustained four broken ribs, a broken clavicle, bruises all over his body, and trauma to his head. He's currently in a coma here at the hospital, and the doctors aren't sure if he'll regain consciousness." Harold gave a deep sigh over the phone. From the ensuing silence, Max wasn't sure if he was crying or just needed time to find his words.

"Did they catch the attackers?"

"No, they haven't caught them yet. The detective on the case informed me that he and the FBI would be investigating cameras near the park where the assault occurred. There are only two known witnesses right now, one of which is our son, Donté. The second person is a woman who heard Donté's screams during the attack and warned the attackers that she was calling the police, causing them to run. The detective said that Brian would've likely been killed on the scene if she hadn't arrived. Based on the reports from her and Donté, they believe the assault may have been because of Brian's sexuality. If that's true, it would legally be a hate crime."

"Oh, my Lord," Harold expressed. "When did all of this take place?"

"I got called this afternoon just before 5:00, so it probably happened sometime around 4:00. The video surveillance will hopefully help them determine the exact time."

"It's this type of stuff that Melanie and I were afraid of," Harold replied in a heavy voice that was infused, Max sensed, with a familiar hybrid of subtle judgment and fear.

"I'm sorry?" asked Max, who was in no mood to tolerate disrespect toward his husband.

"What I meant to say is that he wouldn't be in this situation if he was living according to God's word."

"Mr. Webber," said Max, reminding himself to stay calm. "Brian and I both understand your position on homosexuality, but with all due respect, I don't think this is the time to talk about your son's sexual orientation or the Bible. What I do know is that Brian's now fighting for his life in a hospital bed, where he's been unconscious for the past three hours. And to top it all off, we don't know if he'll even come back," Max paused to catch his breath. "This may be a hate crime, Mr. Webber, but this type of random attack could happen to anyone, gay or straight, at any given time."

"My wife, Melanie, should be home soon from choir rehearsal. I'll let her know what's going on when she returns. Believe me when I say that we'll put Brian in our prayers so that God can handle everything. Can we reach you at this number if we need to?"

"Yes," said Max, who struggled to keep himself from expressing his true feelings to Harold. "If anything changes with Brian's condition, I'll be sure to let you know immediately. And, oh, I almost forgot…he's at the main campus of Cleveland University Hospital in room 314 of the ICU."

"Thank you for the call and everything you've shared, Max," Harold expressed. Surprised that the fifty-seven-year-old man said his name,

Max felt a sense of helplessness with everything taking place. Not only was his lover and best friend's life in suspension, but Brian's father had seemingly responded with more indifference than grief or anger. With Donté now in his life, he couldn't fathom having such a nonchalant attitude as a father. After a few deep breaths, Max stood up from the freestanding bench he had located in the ICU and walked back to Brian's room, struggling to hold in his tears. When he returned, Sandra informed him that Lamont and Salt and Pepper were seated in the waiting room. Meanwhile, Donté was seated on her lap, fighting to stay awake as he watched a cartoon playing on the television. Looking at his son, Max realized that resenting Harold's response wouldn't do him or Brian any good. The people who truly counted were already rallying in support.

Outside in the waiting lobby, the three newcomers greeted Max with extended arms and shared tears. Max informed them that Brian's condition hadn't changed since he had initially called them and shared all the details that he had received from Detective Roberts earlier. Lamont, usually the life of the party, abdicated his outspokenness in favor of a comforter role to Max and their female friends. He stood quietly between Max and Pepper, rubbing their backs gently as Max explained that the attack was being considered a hate crime in consideration of the known facts.

Max's friends listened and latched onto every syllable that he communicated, signaling an unspoken yet palpable devastation in each of them for Brian and their own susceptibility to such hostility. After relaying everything he knew, Max informed them that only two people were allowed in Brian's room at a time. Once Sandra and Donté joined them in the hallway, Salt and Pepper were the first pair to visit Brian. Max and the others welcomed Todd and Tim upon their arrival, inspiring a second wave of hugs, tears, and more updates.

****

Shortly after 7:00 the next morning, Max and Donté were awakened by Dr. Wu, who was completing his morning rounds. Despite his short and skinny appearance, Dr. Wu exhibited a confident, direct, and amiable personality. He informed Max that Brian's vitals were stabilizing, but they were still concerned about the head trauma and would thus continue monitoring him closely throughout the day. As for the coma, Brian's status remained uncertain. Observing that Max and Donté had slept in the hospital room overnight, the doctor encouraged Max to ensure that he and their child took some time for self-care. Max laughed to himself as he thought about the doctor's statement, knowing that Brian would normally be instructing him along those same lines. Given the current state of affairs, Max partially resented such a notion. He felt compelled to be there every minute with his husband, although he also recognized Donté's own needs. But deep down inside, he knew that Dr. Wu's suggestion was wise. He and Donté would eventually have to tend to their own needs. Before leaving, Dr. Wu informed him that a nurse would check on Brian hourly and that another attending doctor would stop by in the afternoon.

"Is Dad going to wake up today, Papa?" Donté asked after Dr. Wu's departure.

"I don't know, son, but I sure hope so. His body needs a lot of rest right now," Max replied. "The best we can do is stay by his side and show him our love, pray for his recovery, and make sure we take care of ourselves because that's what he would want."

"Can I say a prayer to God, Papa?" asked Donté.

"Of course, you can," said Max, surprised, taking his son and sitting him on Brian's bed. "Give me one of your hands and place your other hand on Dad's," Max instructed. Together they bowed their heads.

"Dear God, please bless Daddy and allow him to wake up. We miss him and need him a whole lot. Thank you. Amen."

"Amen," echoed Max. "That was beautiful, Donté. I believe that God and your dad heard that prayer."

"Are you going to pray, too?"

"I think your prayer was perfect, son. You said exactly what was needed. As for today, I just want you to know that we likely have another long day ahead of us. Later this morning we'll go home so that we can freshen up and change our clothes. We can make sure we also bring some of your toys here. How does that sound?"

"What about Pickles?" Donté inquired. "Can we get her also?"

"Right now, she's in a safe place. Since we're spending so much time at the hospital, I think it's best that we let her stay where she is. However, we can stop by the shelter to see her for a little while on our way home."

"Okay," said Donté. "I can't wait to see Pickles," he said, smiling.

"I bet she misses you, too," said Max.

After Max informed Donté of their plans for later, he took his son to the bathroom to wash their faces and brush their teeth with items that had been thoughtfully left by a third shift nurse. Max was impressed at how far along Donté had come with these activities during the past month. He scrubbed his round face and brushed his miniature teeth confidently compared to the initial hesitation he had exhibited after moving in. These developments, Max noted, were only two areas of growth he and Brian had begun witnessing. Donté now conveyed a genuine interest in reading, expanded his vocabulary daily, and grew more comfortable with individuals he regularly encountered. Max imagined the confidence that Donté would possess a year from now when he was six and preparing for the second grade. He desperately hoped that Brian would be there with him, watching the milestones and achievements that awaited him next year and beyond.

"All done, Papa!" Donté insisted, showing off his white teeth.

"Okay, son," remarked Max. "Now, let's head to the cafeteria to quickly eat breakfast so that we can spend a little more time with your dad before heading home."

"I'm not hungry, Papa" Donté insisted.

"Me neither, Donté," Max acknowledged, "but it's really important that we put something in our stomachs. You had an eventful day yesterday, and there's a lot in store for us today. So, I need you to try and eat, if only a little, son." To Max's surprise, Donté conceded instead of frowning in disapproval. As they left Brian's room, it was clear to Max that his son was getting used to his lecturing. Right now, Donté's tell-tell signs of frustration were pouting and sighing, but Max expected that in the coming years, Donté would start vocalizing his annoyance. Moping or not, however, Max was grateful to have his son as they proceeded to the cafeteria with Donté seated on his shoulders. As he walked and the boy played on his bald head like a drum, Max sensed, for the first time since he received the call the day before about Brian, a calming peace.

In the cafeteria, Donté managed to eat a couple of bacon strips, a few apple slices, and one pancake that Max had cut up for him. Considering his son's initial comment that he wasn't hungry, Max decided that Donté's effort was better than nothing. While eating his own omelet and a bowl of oatmeal, his mind drifted toward Brian's parents and the conversation he had had with Harold the day before. He wondered if they would make the trip to Cleveland or, at the very least, call to check in on their son's condition. Sitting next to Donté, Max struggled to imagine how they could cut their son out of their lives for any reason.

Even though they managed to ultimately continue communication with Brian after he came out, their overall relationship, Max believed, was unbalanced. Harold and Melanie disclosed nearly every facet of their lives and marriage, while Brian was relegated to sharing mere generalities of his existence. *Here in the middle of a full-blown family crisis, it's up to me to serve as the intermediary between Brian and his parents*. A better recipe for resentment couldn't exist for Max. Until Brian's condition changed, however, he figured that there was nothing else that could be done. He had told Harold everything he knew. *Whether they come to visit or call is their choice*, he thought as he watched Donté blow translucent bubbles in his glass of milk. Max felt that he was exactly where he needed to be.

After returning to the ICU, they found Peter in the waiting area chatting with two strangers. He had a cup of coffee in his right hand as he sat with his legs crossed on a bench across from an older heterosexual white couple. Peter, a socialite wherever he went, introduced the pair to Max and Donté. Their names were Susan and Bartholomew. Max judged that they were in their mid-sixties based on their grey hair, eyeglasses, and outdated midwestern dress. According to Bartholomew, they were waiting to see their grandson, who had been in a car accident three days earlier. He had left a bar in downtown Cleveland before falling asleep at the wheel while driving northeast on I-90.

The hapless young man, Dustin, broke his left leg from the impact and sustained bruises on his face. Bartholomew explained how 'lucky' Dustin was to end up with only a broken leg and minimal scratches considering his irresponsible choice of driving under the influence. He relayed how they were a praying family and how they considered Dustin's accident a wake-up call for him. Max listened carefully to the older man as he held Donté's hand and watched Susan nod her head to nearly every other word her husband uttered.

It was clear to Max that Peter hadn't been there too long before Bartholomew asked him who he was visiting. Upon hearing this older white man ask that question, Max stopped himself from cringing in the face and committed to a few heavy breaths. Peter directly answered his question by stating that he was visiting his friend and former co-worker Brian, who was also Max's husband. He told these new acquaintances that Brian had been attacked the night before in downtown Cleveland and that he was currently unconscious. When he finished speaking, a noticeable silence overcame the table where they were all seated.

"Susan and I believe," Bartholomew said, breaking the awkward ice, "that all of us are God's children. Can we pray for your husband, young man?" he asked Max.

"Why, yes, you certainly can," said Max in disbelief at the outcome, acknowledging to himself that he had unfairly judged the older gentleman. "That's very thoughtful of you."

"In that case," said Bartholomew looking at his wife, "do you mind leading us in prayer for this family?" Susan, an ordinary appearing woman, transformed into a charismatic preacher when she started praying. It turns out that she was a pastor of a non-denominational church. Donté thanked the woman for her prayer and asked if they could visit her church sometime, to which she graciously obliged. She handed Max her business card and said that she looked forward to meeting Brian once he was better. That placed the largest grin on Donté's face that Max had seen since they had adopted Pickles. Max assured his son that they would visit her church at some point, before thanking the couple for their kindness and telling them goodbye.

The receptionist sitting outside permitted Peter to go back with Max and Donté since it was just the three of them. Brian remained in the same position that Max had found him in this morning. His face was tilted to the left toward his shoulder, while his left palm faced upwards toward the ceiling. His right arm, protected by a sling, lay on his stomach underneath the blanket covering his body. Slightly bent over his old coworker, Peter began talking as he took Brian's left hand in both of his.

"Hey, Brian," he said. "I believe you can hear me. You're going to get through this, buddy. Whoever did this may have hurt you physically, but they certainly didn't kill your spirit. You have far too much to live for, and we all need you, especially Max and Donté.

"Don't even get me started on The Center," he continued, slightly laughing. "We both know that place would be in big trouble without you. Your leadership was desperately needed after I left. Now you've managed to not just keep the ship afloat, but you're steering it into uncharted territory with mental health programming, trans advocacy, and employment readiness programs. Your staff and community members really need you, Brian.

Take all the time you need as you rest your mind, body, and spirit, but just don't quit on us. There's no shortage of work for you, my friend."

Tears ran down Peter's cheeks. "Any update from the police?" he asked Max, who was seated on the small couch beside Donté.

"No, the detective just told me to contact him once Brian regains consciousness," Max replied.

"If that isn't lazy policing then I don't know what is!" Peter expressed in disbelief. "In an active investigation where the victim is lying in the hospital unconscious – they should be reaching out to *you* and giving a heads-up on where they are." Max listened carefully to Peter, who had had more than his fair share of encounters with police officers, being The Center's previous executive director. In his role, he often advocated on behalf of assault victims whenever homophobia was the clear motive, helped to identify a handful of trans women who were murdered during his seven-year tenure, and worked with the police to help with missing person reports. Max was certain that Peter wasn't just saying this to feign empathy.

"Do you mind if I go to the police department to inquire about the status of their investigation?" Peter asked.

"That's fine with me," said Max. "But you know me, Peter. The one thing I don't want is for our family business to garner too much attention.

So far, Brian's situation has only been disclosed on a need-to-know basis, although I'm sure the word will spread tomorrow after The Center opens."

"I totally respect where you're coming from, Max. My goal in talking to the police is simply to assess where they're at with the case. That will let us know if we need to set a fire under them – which is likely the case if this so-called detective told you to contact him."

"All right, Peter," Max said, seriously. "If you respect me, then you will keep your conversation just between you and the police. It would be nice to know if they were able to find any helpful video footage around the park. Those criminals need to be behind bars before they attack someone else."

"I'm with you there," said Peter. "That's exactly why we need to proactively stay on top of whoever is working this case."

"You know what?" said Max. "I blame myself for not being there with Brian and Donté that evening. If I had been there, maybe those crooks would've thought differently about attacking two grown men."

"The truth of the matter, Max, is that you have no idea what would've happened if you were there. What if that would've led to both of you laying here in the ICU? Beating yourself up for not being there is absolutely the last thing you need to do. You and I both know that Brian wouldn't dare hold any of this against you, so neither should you."

Max sighed as he listened to Peter, reluctantly agreeing. He considered various scenarios that could've played out at the park if he had been with Brian and Donté, realizing that there would inevitably have been factors outside of his control in any situation. With his son at his side, he rubbed Donté's head and considered how thankful he was for the boy's safety. Peter looked at Max and smiled, nodding his head at the two of them.

"There's your blessing in disguise," said Peter. "Just keep holding out for Brian. I have a strong feeling he's going to pull through."

At that moment, a nurse came into the room and informed Max that two additional visitors had arrived in the waiting area. Wondering who else would come so early, Max left Donté with Peter and went to see who was waiting outside. He secretly hoped that it was Brian's parents but also recognized the improbability of such optimism. *The two of them showing up would be a miracle*, he thought.

As he walked through the doors that opened into the waiting area lobby, he saw Salt and Pepper holding hands, looking outside from one of the room's large windows onto the medical campus below. They stood there in silence as Max approached them. It was evident to him that they were fearful for Brian.

"Hi, ladies," he said as he reached out to give them hugs.

"Good morning, Max," Salt said as she embraced him.

"Hey, my brotha. How are you holding up?" Pepper asked during their protracted hug.

"It's been a long night," said Max. "But we're keeping our faith that Brian's going to pull through. The doctor informed us earlier that his vitals had stabilized. While he's unconscious, the best they can do is monitor him every hour."

Tears started flowing down both of their faces as Max's words of incertitude sank in. Max knew, from the ten years this couple had been together, that they understood his suffering. In unison, the three of them stood in a circle and held each other for support. Memories of their recent adoption shower, their wedding, birthday parties, fundraisers for The Center, and other occasions – each of which Salt and Pepper had been involved in – raced through Max's mind.

"If there's anything that we can do for you and Donté, please let us know. We're here for you," shared Pepper.

"You got that right," said Salt. "Let us know if you need anything."

"I really appreciate that," said Max, recalling his plans for this morning. "Actually, if you wouldn't mind staying with Brian for a few hours while I take Donté home to freshen up, that would mean a lot. I think it would do us some good, especially Donté, to have a couple hours away from this hospital. Sandra and Junior should be here by 11:00."

"You got it," Pepper replied. "We can certainly stay here until they arrive. I think you're making a good decision by giving yourselves a little space."

"Honestly, I wouldn't know what I'd do without friends like you and Peter. He's also here watching Donté in Brian's room right now, but he plans on stopping by the downtown police station later this morning to get an update on the case."

"Good for him," said Salt. "That should help move things along with all of his connections in the department. But, in the meantime, Andrea and I are happy to stay with Brian until your sister arrives."

****

Max was overwhelmed with a mixture of emotions once he and Donté walked inside their lifeless apartment. He felt as though an internal part of himself was missing without Brian there. Despite this emptiness, he had promised himself on their way home that he wouldn't give Donté any reason to detect his emotional fragility. Their son's stability was paramount, and that required Max to manage his feelings and not allow them to erupt at any given time. Nearly everything throughout the apartment reminded him of Brian and their five-year history with each other, making this trip home for Max nearly just as overwhelming as being at the ICU. For Donté, on the other hand, he expected that walking into their home would provide a constant and familiarity that the boy desperately needed. This suspicion was confirmed after Donté immediately proceeded toward his room and retrieved the firetruck off the nightstand. Max sat next to him and watched as Donté rolled the toy around on his comforter, seemingly deep in thought.

"Are you doing all right, son?" Max asked. Donté nodded his head without looking up. After a few seconds, he placed Donté on his lap and said, "Hey, buddy, it's okay if you're not feeling too well right now. It's normal to feel sad when someone you love is in the hospital and they're not doing too well. What I want you to know, son, is that we're going to get through this time together. I promise you. And if you need to talk or cry, I'm here for you. Just remember that your dad is a trooper. And if I know anything about Brian, he's fighting for you and me even though we can't see it."

"When Daddy gets better, will he have to go away like Granny?" Donté asked. Suddenly the reason why he seized the red truck became apparent to Max.

"When your dad gets better," Max said, "He may have to stay in the hospital for a little while, but eventually he'll return home to be with us. Fortunately, he wasn't hurt too bad physically. His injuries will all heal in due time. Are you scared that he could go away like your grandma?"

"Yes," replied Donté, nodding his head once again. This time he looked up at Max and placed his head on his father's left shoulder.

"Your grandmother and dad are dealing with different health conditions, Donté. In your grandmother's case, a disease called Alzheimer's made it really difficult for her to take care of you because she was losing her memory and the ability to take care of herself. Your dad, though, will still be able to take care of you. He just may need a little help from us before he's fully recovered." Donté remained silent and continued resting on Max's shoulder.

"I can't wait until he gets home," Donté said quietly.

"That makes two of us, son. Let's get you washed up and changed, though, so we can stop by and see Pickles before heading back to the hospital." Donté raised his head after hearing their puppy's name and found the motivation to heed Max's words.

After Max had bathed Donté and aided him in putting on a clean set of clothes, he turned on Donté's favorite cartoon in the living room for him to watch. Mindful of his own need to freshen up, he decided to take a hot shower for himself.

Standing in his and Brian's roomy double shower, Max permitted himself to finally give in to the pain and agony he had been staving off since he was first called by the hospital. His tears streamed down his face as he squelched his moans, not wanting to alarm Donté in the living room. Exhausted from the ceaseless travail of worry in his mind, he leaned against the metal bar on the sliding door, grasping it tightly, and cried until he was overcome with numbness. As the heated shower water drizzled upon his bare body, the knowledge that his and Brian's shared life now hung by a thread tormented him.

Within twenty minutes, Max had managed to shower and change into a fresh set of clothes that made him feel slightly more prepared to deal with the day ahead of them. Somehow, the act of self-cleansing and putting on new attire restored a hopeful outlook in his mind. He found Donté smiling and staring at the television screen when he walked into the living room. *At least*, Max thought, *Donté is also experiencing a slight reprieve from the chaos in our lives*. Max smiled and prayed that Donté's return to school the next day would offer him another healthy outlet. While Max had already determined that he would not return to work until he knew Brian's condition was improving, he planned to ensure that Donté maintained some normality.

"It's about time for us to get ready to see

Pickles," Max stated, interrupting Donté's cartoon. "Are there any toys you want to bring back to the hospital? We'll stop somewhere for lunch afterward." Donté slowly looked around their apartment. Finally, he grinned and ran into his room only to return with the blue and white blanket that laid at the tail end of his twin bed.

"She liked to sleep on this," Donté said.

"That's nice of you," Max said, taken aback by his thoughtful gesture. "I'm sure this will comfort her until she's able to come back home."

"Yeah, I know she misses us," Donté replied. "Hold on before we go," he insisted, running once again away from Max, who held out his small red coat. "I forgot something," he called out from his room.

"Hurry up, kiddo," Max replied, thinking about how Brian used that term more frequently. Donté walked out of the room proudly holding his red truck.

"You're giving that to Pickles, too?" Max asked, confused.

"No," insisted Donté. "This is for Dad. I want him to have it. Can we put it by his bed?"

"Yes, of course you can. That's really sweet of you, son," said Max, who was now starting to help Donté with his coat. "Your dad is going to be touched by this gift."

"I hope so," said Donté.

"Trust me when I tell you that he will," said

Max, zipping up Donté's coat. Max was blown away by the boy's thoughtfulness. He couldn't imagine Theresa finding a more suitable kid. The connection that Donté and Brian had established reinforced this reality for Max, whose hypervigilance for the boy's safety and protection had been augmented to a new level. As far as he was concerned, he never wanted to see their son in this predicament again.

On their way to the animal shelter, Donté chatted nonstop out of his excitement to see Pickles. Donté questioned if other dogs or people were being mean toward Pickles and if she was being walked, eating doggy snacks, sleeping on a comfortable bed, or making puppy friends. Max responded to these concerns with as much agility as he could while simply saying, "I don't know, but we'll soon find out" on those matters about which he was completely clueless. Enjoying the opportunity to play detective, Donté didn't mind his Papa's uncertainty. He instead focused on the fact that his inquiries would soon be revealed at the facility where he could see with his own two eyes.

When they reached the animal shelter, Max found himself gravely disappointed with the place. His displeasure evidently rubbed off on Donté, who asked, "Are we in the right place?" after seeing the crumbling bricked building once Max parked. It was a small, modest one-story building situated just east of downtown with a large, concrete yard full of discarded animal cages and old car tires. Inside the brick building was a tiny office area in the front and a black door to the right of the entrance that led to rows upon rows of cages. Dogs were on the left side of the room, and cats were on the right. Every animal had its own cage with small bowls for water and food. There were no signs of toys, treats, beds, or anything that would've made the room less monotonous and more comfortable for the deprived animals. One of two workers in the shelter walked Max and Donté to Pickles's cage. She immediately started barking and wagging her tail once they approached her cage.

"Can we hold her?" asked Donté. The young man who worked there nodded his head in affirmation at Max before opening the cage.

"Just let me know when you're ready to leave," he said before walking off to return to the lobby area. Max assumed that he went there to chat with his female co-worker stationed at the front desk. He grieved the fact that Pickles and the other animals had to live in these bland conditions. Feeling sorry for Pickles's current situation, Max, alongside his son, began rubbing all over her short-haired coat. He and Donté stood next to her cage and played with her for thirty minutes before leaving. As they wrapped up, Donté ran to inform the laggard employee that they were ready to depart. Max realized that he hadn't thought about the hospital once while they were there. Pickles's charm had allowed him and Donté to briefly relieve their minds of Brian's dire situation. While Max appreciated the reunion with their puppy, he also was determined to find her an alternative boarding option.

****

When Max and Donté returned to the hospital shortly after noon, they found Sandra and Junior sitting in the waiting area of the ICU. Sandra, whose hair was braided and tied behind her back, greeted her brother and nephew with warm hugs while Junior watched. When it was his turn, Max squeezed his nephew and lifted him up. Junior smiled and laughed at this unexpected action and began squirming, as if to signal that he was too old for these types of hugs. In any event, Junior returned the favor to Donté who was ecstatic to see his big cousin after their initial encounter two weeks ago. Unlike Junior, Donté didn't mind the attention of being elevated in the air. After their exchanges, Sandra informed Max that Lamont, Todd, and Tim had arrived nearly thirty minutes earlier and were in Brian's room.

"Have you seen Peter?" Max asked.

"No, I haven't. Was he supposed to be here already?"

"He was here earlier this morning with me and Donté. He asked me if it was okay for him to stop by the downtown police station to get an update," Max informed his sister.

"What did you say?" Sandra inquired.

"I told him that was fine as long as he didn't make that much noise about what was going on. The last thing we need is the media getting involved."

"Do you trust him?"

"Brian does," said Max. "He's never let Brian down, so I guess that counts for something."

"I see your point, Max. Honestly, that's how I feel about some of Kevin's friends and even Pastor Carter's influence on him. I couldn't see myself being friends with many of them if it wasn't for our marriage, but I have to respect their relationship with my husband."

"Exactly," said Max. "Speaking of your husband, is he coming by later?"

"Don't count on it," Sandra said. "It was nearly a battle getting Junior to come with me until he remembered having to attend a senior team meeting after this morning's service." Max watched Donté and Junior play a game of checkers in a corner designated for children where there were board games and coloring supplies. He hoped that the bond their children were forming wouldn't be upended by Kevin's bigotry.

"Well, Donté and I appreciate your being here," said Max. "I pray that Brian recovers from this coma soon. I need him so much, Sandra." She placed her hand on Max's back and began making small gentle circles with her right hand to encourage him.

"You guys are going to get through this ordeal for the better," she said. "Just take Donté, for instance. This entire situation must be really difficult for him, but he's learning that he can depend on you and that you're in his corner, no matter how hard life becomes." Max considered the wisdom of his sister's words as he listened. "Despite Kevin's quirkiness at times, he was there for me in ways that I never anticipated after Mom died. That drew me closer to him."

Max could relate to what she was saying. Brian had been there for him during that time as well. While Sandra's words resonated with him, he hadn't considered how Donté might internalize their relationship. After all, it had only been one day. Still, in Max's mind, twenty-four hours was far too long to be solo parenting. He wondered, to his mother's credit, how she was able to raise four children on her own after her husband's betrayal.

"I guess you're right," said Max. "That's a perspective that I hadn't considered. What Mother achieved in raising all of us is nothing short of a miracle, Sandra."

"I think about her every day," she replied. "If Kevin and I ever have a daughter, we're naming her Betty."

"Now that would be special, sis. Honoring someone through a namesake is one of the greatest ways to pay homage." After Max spoke those words, his phone started ringing.

"Hello," Max answered, seeing that the caller was Darnell.

"Oh, my God, Max," the young man's voice said. "I'm so sorry to hear about your husband's attack near the theatre district yesterday afternoon. It's like there's no such thing as a safe place anymore. Anyway, I hope they find the three guys who attacked him. How are you and your son?"

"What do you mean?" said Max, confused about how the young man was able to reference such specific details.

"That was your husband who was attacked last night, wasn't it? Brian Webber? Now I see exactly why you had to leave the café so soon. The 12:00 news just aired his story. Some white guy talked to a reporter about what happened to Brian. He made it sound like the police were dragging their feet with the investigation, although he mentioned the FBI was somehow involved, too. He said he was a close friend to you and Brian."

"Are you serious?" asked Max, fully aware that Darnell had no other way of knowing these particulars and to whom he was referring. At that moment, Max's phone received another incoming call. It was Jane Budges from the college. Max let the phone go to voicemail, expecting that she was calling for the same reason. In the meantime, his heart rate started to increase, but he decided to ascertain as much information from Darnell as he could.

"Yes, sir. There's no way that I'd ever make this up."

"I believe you," said Max. "Was the guy's name Peter, by any chance?"

"Yup," said Darnell excitedly. "That's him. He was a tall, balding guy with a beer belly. He also wore an expensive-looking leather coat."

"That's the guy," said Max, laughing at Darnell's highlighted details. "What all did he say?" Max asked, wanting to arm himself with the full report before ending their conversation and calling Peter.

"Well, he basically said that Brian was attacked yesterday by three men while he and your son Donté were walking your dog in a park by the theatre district. He stated that it seemed like it was a hate crime because the attackers made homophobic statements. He called out the police for taking their time because they hadn't obtained any video footage from the area. He also questioned whether or not they'd work this slowly if the victim was white." Darnell paused to breathe as Max listened carefully. "Oh, the last thing he mentioned is that there would be a vigil at the gay center tonight in Brian's honor."

"I can't believe this," Max stated, realizing that he didn't mean for Darnell to hear his words.

Sandra, who was still sitting next to him, looked at him with concern.

"You didn't know?" asked Darnell.

"I had no intention for this to be on the news," said Max plainly. "But listen, Darnell, I need to go so that I can handle this situation. Your call is really appreciated."

"Anytime, Max. I'm babysitting my sister's kids right now, but maybe I can stop by the hospital later this afternoon to visit. It's the least that I can do, given everything you've done for me."

"All right," said Max. "Just stop by room 314 in the ICU."

"See you later, sir."

When Max hung up the phone, he took a deep breath and shook his head in disbelief. *Being in this situation is exactly what I was trying to avoid*, he thought. *How could Peter be so dismissive of my one and only request?* Max quickly brought Sandra up to speed on Peter's betrayal and the budding public relations crisis. With Brian being the interim director of The Center, Max knew that this story would now garner the attention of Cleveland, if not also Columbus and Cincinnati.

As Max shared his thoughts on responding to the situation at hand to Sandra, a barrage of beeps and rings from incoming text messages and calls stormed his phone until he turned off the volume. After glancing at Junior and Donté, who were still playing checkers, he was grateful for Sandra's company. The stress of Brian being in the hospital was already more than what Max wanted to accept, but now he would have to deal with everyone else outside of their small circle of family and friends. Max could feel his anxiety increase as he considered how this new element would deepen the entanglement he already faced.

Just as Max was preparing to call Peter to reprehend him for going to the media, a familiar lady pulling a small suitcase walked into the room. It was Brian's mother, Melanie. She wore a long, brown wool coat with a white church-lady hat that had a single flower in the front. Max couldn't believe his eyes. He elbowed Sandra lightly before getting up and whispered, "That's Brian's mother. I can't believe she came." When Max stood up, she looked in his direction, and it was evident that she remembered him from their single encounter in Connecticut four years ago. *I guess a mother never forgets the first man her son introduces as his boyfriend*, Max thought. Poised and conveying a restrained sense of dread, she walked slowly in his direction.

"Hello, Mrs. Webber," Max said cautiously, being unsure how she would respond. "Thank you so much for coming," he stated, before reaching out to hug her. Initially hesitant, she finally let go of her dark grey carry-on luggage and placed her two arms on his back, as Max squeezed her affectionately.

After observing his papa's unexpected interaction with this unfamiliar woman in her fifties who was now crying on his shoulder, Donté left the board game and cautiously approached them with Junior at his side. As she and her son-in-law hugged, Melanie released a painful wail as her knees slightly bent with Max catching her before she fell to the ground. It was a familiar bodily reaction Max had seen in his youth at church when women, and sometimes men, were overcome by the Holy Ghost. *Being in Cleveland, Ohio, in the arms of her son's male lover, at a hospital where Brian was lying unconscious, must have broken something in her*, Max reasoned. He rocked her slowly side-to-side in their steadfast embrace before introducing her to his son.

"Donté, this is your Grandma Melanie. "She's your dad's mother." Donté's entire face lit up with a smile after hearing this news. Instantly, he reached out his short arms toward Melanie for an embrace of his own.

"Hi, Grandma!" Donté nearly shouted. "I've been waiting to meet you."

"It's a pleasure to meet you, Donté," she replied, reaching down to him in return, as tears flowed down her sand-toned cheeks.

Chapter 7

Max was relieved once the mass of people who had flocked to the ICU after seeing the midday news began dissipating. Most of them were going to the vigil that Peter had managed to organize on such short notice. The gathering was due to start at 6:30 p.m. outside of The Center, where Peter was still active as a board member despite no longer being the executive director. As the thoughtful crowd of people who showed up to express their concern started leaving, Max looked forward to spending time with Melanie. Until now, she had primarily looked after Donté and her unconscious son in Brian's room, away from the busy waiting area, after Sandra and Junior left earlier that afternoon.

To maintain some degree of crowd control, Max took it upon himself to provide a sense of comfort and medical updates to everyone who had heard about Brian either on the news or through social media. There were far too many people for Max or anyone else to escort back and forth to Brian's room, especially since the two-person maximum remained intact. For their part, Lamont, Todd, and Tim assisted with comforting and updating the sympathetic visitors for as long as they could. Given Todd's approaching move next Saturday, though, they left at 4:00 p.m. to do some more packing. Todd promised that he would return on Friday to say goodbye before finally hauling his belongings to Detroit the following morning.

After shaking hands with and expressing his thanks to Darnell, the last of the worried bunch, Max sighed and allowed his shoulders to ease into a relaxed position. He was pleased that the young man had kept his promise and stopped by the hospital. With everyone now gone, Max figured an intimate evening with immediate family would be an ideal transition before going home. Inside Brian's room, Donté sat comfortably on Melanie's lap with his head laid on her chest while she told him stories about Brian as a kid.

Max watched and listened as Donté relaxed on his grandmother, seeming to picture her description of Brian's youthful defiance. She shared how Brian, when he was twelve years old, had taken advantage of having his tonsils removed by refusing to eat anything at the hospital but ice cream. He ate scores of the chocolate-flavored frozen treat for two entire days. Melanie emphasized, however, that she and Harold only agreed to Brian's diet at the hospital. When he returned home, there was no more ice cream, only chicken noodle soup, mashed potatoes, and creamy corn. After Brian's throat had healed, she said that he refused to eat anything soft or soggy for an entire week because it reminded him of being in the hospital. Ice cream was his one exception to this rule, but Harold required that he eat all his food.

Therefore, in order to resume eating his favorite dessert, Brian finally acquiesced after realizing that his father was not giving in to his stubbornness. It was clear to Max, from watching Melanie's personality come to life, that Donté enjoyed hearing her stories.

"Are all those people gone?" Melanie asked as she wrapped up.

"Yes, ma'am. I didn't think they were ever going to leave," Max indicated.

"Thank God! That goes for you and me both." Max laughed at Melanie's sense of humor.

"It just so happens that most of them are headed to a vigil being held for Brian by one of his good friends named Peter. It's starting in about thirty minutes. If it wasn't for the vigil, I think most of them would still be here."

"I honestly had no idea that there would be such a turnout. But, if I may be honest, it's nice seeing all those folks show their support. In moments like this, it's good to know love isn't hard to find."

"You may not be aware of this, Mrs. Webber, but your son has inspired a lot of people from all walks of life from his PhD program to The Center where he works. If Peter hadn't taken the story to a news outlet, the word of his being in the hospital would've begun spreading tomorrow when he failed to show up for work."

"So, what *exactly* does he do for a living?"

Melanie inquired. "The only thing that my husband and I know is that he's working on completing his PhD in sociology and that he directs some agency."

"Currently, he's the interim executive director at Cleveland's LGBTQ Resource Center, where he's responsible for managing an entire staff of people who put together vital programs for our community. After Brian's friend Peter stepped down last year, Brian was asked to direct the agency until they found a suitable replacement. He's been doing such a good job, though, that the board of directors hasn't really prioritized finding anyone else. I believe that they're going to officially offer him the position after he earns his doctoral degree."

"I see," said Melanie. "And when you say LGBTQ…" Melanie started before Max completed her sentence by saying what each letter of the acronym meant. Max carefully observed Melanie attempting to make sense of Brian's life, which has largely been shaped and defined by his own sexual identity. While she reflected on these details that she was learning for the first time, Donté fell asleep on her chest. Max knew that Brian's contribution to the LGBTQ community was inversely correlated to the acceptance he felt from his parents. At this moment, he could tell that Melanie was just starting to see the picture for herself as she stared at Brian helplessly from her seat.

"May I ask what sort of work you do?"

Melanie asked.

"I'm the dean of arts and sciences at a local community college. It's actually a promotion that I just started at the beginning of the school year."

"Oh, that's impressive. Your parents must be really proud."

"I can't speak for my father," said Max. "He left my mother when I was seven years old, but my mother was proud of me and Brian. She passed away last summer after a stroke." A strange confluence of emotions arose in Max as he thought about Betty Strong, Brian's precarious state, and now his mother-in-law's rudimentary line of questioning. *If she and Harold hadn't been so judgmental toward their own son and the matters close to his heart*, Max thought, *we would be well beyond this conversation.* Instead of fixating on this thought, though, he accepted that she was in Cleveland and showing some interest. *I guess her being here should count for something.*

"I'm sorry to hear about your mother. I can see that you and my son have quite a history," Melanie said in a warm tone.

"We certainly do, but that boy you're holding in your arms, Ms. Webber, is our proudest accomplishment yet. For Donté's sake, I'm happy that he's gotten this opportunity to meet you. He was living with his maternal grandmother before being placed in the system. After she stopped feeding Donté and herself for two whole days out of paranoia that their food was poisoned, she was admitted into a senior nursing facility. Staff there tried to see if she would improve, but her delusions only intensified, making their separation permanent. I feel bad for Donté and her. Dealing with such a severe case of Alzheimer's at sixty-three years of age must be devastating."

Max could see an expression of sympathy upon Melanie's sparsely freckled face. She gently placed the palm of her hand on the back of Donté's head and began rocking him back and forth. Max wished that Brian would wake up from his coma to behold his mother cradling Donté. He quickly wiped the tears flowing from his eyes, not wanting to appear too vulnerable to this woman whose future actions, he deemed, were just as uncertain as Brian's prognosis. Until Brian's condition was resolved and he understood Melanie and Harold's long-term plans, Max believed it was prudent to be guarded.

"It's a tragic state to be a motherless child, but to lose a grandmother is a calamity of its own," Melanie said.

"I couldn't agree more," Max responded. "So, meeting you has a certain level of significance for Donté." Max was eager to hear her response.

"Listen, Max," she replied. "I really do understand where you're coming from. Can we agree for right now to take it day by day?"

"We can do that, but I do have one question

for you, if that's okay."

"What's that?" asked Melanie as she stopped rocking her grandson.

"Is there any particular reason why Mr. Webber didn't come?"

Melanie slowly stood up in her seat, making a deliberate effort to prevent Donté from waking up. She turned toward the couch behind her and gently laid him down. With a solemn expression on her face, she returned to her seat before answering Max's question.

"I don't expect you to fully understand what I'm about to say," Melanie began, "but it's the truth. Harold and I are from a generation where the life you and Brian have built together was unthinkable. Men and women married each other sometimes out of love and sometimes out of necessity, but that was life back then. Anything and everything outside of this practice was viewed as an abomination.

"Harold grew up in Charleston, South Carolina, in the '60s and '70s with six other brothers. He didn't have any sisters. It was just seven boys and their parents. All of them were raised to believe one man and one woman was God's only intention for humans. The life of any man who was caught in the act with another man was in jeopardy. At the very least, they were beaten up severely or publicly humiliated. Growing up in Hartford, Connecticut, to parents who taught

Sunday School, I understood Harold's outlook on life and family when we met.

"After getting married in Hartford and having Brian, we suspected that he was *different* as he grew up: most of his friends were girls; he didn't like sports; he always dressed and spoke a little too properly; and he never had a girlfriend all throughout high school. In fact, he became very secretive during that phase of his life. He stopped talking to us as he normally would as a youngster.

"While the majority of his friends were females, every now and again, a strange guy would come around that we didn't know. Brian never shared anything about these friends. Harold and I never questioned him about any of these changes because he stayed active at our place of worship and maintained respectable grades in school. He was the perfect son in many ways, never getting into any trouble at school, with the police, or from hanging with troublemakers. And although he never had a girlfriend, we prayed and held out hope that he would find himself a decent wife in college.

"After Brian left, though, he only became more distant. The only things that he wanted to discuss were his grades, professors he disliked, or the cafeteria food he claimed never matched my home-cooked meals. Whenever Harold or I would ask about his social life or if he was dating a nice woman, he would quickly change the subject or make up some excuse about why he needed to get off the phone. It was during this time when my husband and I started preparing ourselves emotionally for what Brian wasn't telling us with his own God-given mouth. And let me tell you, Max, Harold nearly drove himself mad thinking about where he went wrong as a father. Since Brian was our only child, that made the situation worse for my husband.

"Perhaps now you can imagine how Harold felt when Brian introduced you as his boyfriend four years ago. Meeting you was the confirmation we both dreaded and avoided all those years. It took weeks for me to try and convince Harold that he wasn't a failure as a father, but I must admit that I did my own share of self-blaming. I wondered if I had mothered him too much or was too soft on him. Knowing how the Bible addressed homosexuality and dealing with the blame we put on ourselves placed us in a difficult situation, Max. We kept our distance because we didn't know what to do or say. We didn't want to ignore the Bible's perspective on the matter, confront what we felt was our own failure, or lose our one and only child. To make matters worse, we never told a single soul about what we were going through out of shame. We only had each other.

"I told Harold that your call yesterday was the final straw for me. Even though I didn't know how to sort through all my feelings and beliefs, I would've never forgiven myself if something happened to Brian. Harold is much more stubborn than I am. He would rather die of starvation if he thought that he was being overcharged for a loaf of bread. I truly believe that a part of him wanted to be here, but his mind gets so fixated on trying to make sense of conflicts that are stuck in his own head. The truth of the matter is that he may never find any peace regarding Brian.

"As for myself, I still don't know how I can ever reconcile your marriage with God's word, but I'm glad to be here at Brian's side as his mother." Melanie stopped talking and caressed Brian's free hand as if the act of rubbing his fingers would bring recognizable life into his body. Max sat quietly across from his mother-in-law, as Brian lay peacefully in between them, reflecting on her earnest discourse and how similar Harold's outlook was to Kevin's.

"That makes two of us," said Max, referring to her final comment. "I know Brian will be thrilled that you're here when he sees you."

Melanie and Max continued talking until about 8:00 p.m. when Max offered to drive her to the hotel where she was staying. He had already invited her to stay at their condo shortly after she first arrived, but she insisted on keeping her hotel reservation. Much like during their initial exchange, Melanie declined and informed Max that she planned on staying at the hospital a little while longer. *It's been two years since she has seen*

Brian in person, Max thought. *I'd do the same. In fact, I wouldn't be surprised if she stays at the hospital all night.* It comforted him to know, at least, that someone would be next to Brian if he woke up or, God forbid, things turned for the worse. He would've stayed himself, but Donté had school the following morning and he needed the boy to be prepared and well-rested. And while he was thankful that Donté didn't have any nightmares last night at the hospital, he recognized they could certainly return tonight.

Max woke his son to get him ready for the bitter air outside and their trip home. Donté appeared drowsy and irritated after being awakened but managed to follow his papa's directions of getting into his winter gear without complaining. Melanie rose from her seat to give them hugs before they left, letting them know that it was a pleasure to meet them both, granted the circumstances. She confirmed with Max that she planned on taking a cab to her hotel when she was ready to leave. Max urged her to call him if she needed anything tonight, although he sensed that she would more than likely be too prideful to make such a call. He therefore warned her that she would receive a call from him this evening around 10:00 to ensure that she was okay. Melanie reluctantly agreed to these terms of her persistent son-in-law. Walking out into the hallway toward the waiting area with Donté in his arms, Max said goodnight and thank you to the nurses stationed at the entrance doors.

On the drive home, with Donté sleeping in the back seat, Max called Peter. A part of him strongly resented the fact that Peter had undermined his request, but he still felt entitled to his double-crosser's updates. After answering Max's call, Peter immediately apologized for overstepping his boundaries. Nevertheless, he insisted that the cumulative impact of going to the media and having a vigil was successfully putting public pressure on the investigation. More than one hundred people – not including news reporters – showed up to the vigil to express their support through prayers and chants of 'Justice for Brian.'

Additionally, he shared that after the vigil, a police contact informed him that two cameras were found capturing three guys who matched the physical description of suspects around the time of the assault. There was no footage, though, that captured the attack itself. As of this evening, those images still hadn't been revealed to the public. Peter hoped that their vigil would change that. Listening to Peter, Max understood the rationale behind Peter's approach, even though it wasn't his preference. He also told Max that he planned to call an emergency board of directors meeting the next day at The Center as a result of Brian's situation. As their conversation ended, Max thought about what Melanie had said earlier and realized that at least there were people fighting on behalf of his husband and collectively showing their concern. *Such a response is suitable for Brian, who deserves justice, and whose life is surrounded by love.*

****

The next morning Max arose early to shower and groom before waking up his son. Showing initial reluctance when his father called out "Rise and shine," Donté tossed and turned in bed as if his movements would render him invisible. Eventually, Donté managed to ease out of bed and begin his routine with Max's assistance. Missing Brian's help, Max channeled his energy to focus on one task at a time. Once Donté was fully clothed, Max gave him small jobs to aid in preparing breakfast, such as retrieving eggs from the refrigerator and placing their silverware on the kitchen table.

Donté demonstrated reasonable care in following his dad's instructions, taking his time to avoid dropping or spilling anything. As they prepped their meal for the morning, Max updated him on Sandra picking him up from school and bringing him to the hospital this week, starting this afternoon. This plan was agreeable to Donté, who was eager to spend time with Junior again.

Max's phone started ringing once breakfast was cooked and the table was set. It was Melanie. Concerned that she would be calling him at all, and especially so early, Max answered the phone.

"Hello," he said cautiously.

"Hi, Max," she said. "This is Brian's mom, Mrs. Webber. You need to get to the hospital right away. Brian is up! He's been asking about you and Donté. Dr. Wu is in the room with him right now, going over what happened and testing his memory."

"Thanks be to God! You just made my day, Mrs. Webber," Max exclaimed. He looked at Donté and smiled. "We'll be right there."

"This is definitely a miracle," said Melanie. "Come quickly, Max. He'll be glad to see you and that boy of yours."

"See you soon, Mrs. Webber. I really appreciate the call." Max hung up and swiftly turned to Donté, lifting him freely in the air. "Guess what, son?"

"What?" Donté asked, full of curiosity.

"Your dad is awake from his coma. He's going to be all right," he expressed with elation. Donté made the widest grin that Max ever saw him make.

"Can I go and see him?"

"I wouldn't have it any other way," Max responded, realizing the significance of Donté being next to his dad. "I just need to call your school to let them know that you'll be absent today, but you should definitely plan on returning tomorrow," he warned.

"Okay," said Donté, apparently unphased.

"As for all this food, we can take it with us. Your dad is probably starving anyway." Max found a few plastic containers and began filling them.

"He's been asleep for almost two whole days. That's a long time, Papa."

"It is, son, but we are really fortunate that he woke up. Some people stay unconscious for weeks or even months."

"I think God heard our prayer," Donté said in a confident tone.

"It certainly looks like he did. Now let's get ready to go and see your dad," Max said after packing the food in the assorted containers.

On the way to the hospital, Max remembered that he had planned on picking Pickles up to take her to a proper pet boarding home. None of their friends or family members were too keen on taking in a puppy that wasn't house trained. With Brian being conscious, however, Pickles no longer needed to be kept at a boarding home indefinitely. Max figured that she could withstand one more day at the current facility. *Until Brian returns from the hospital, she can just be kept at home in a spacious crate. I'll pick her up tonight.*

"Is Dad coming home today?" Donté asked from behind the driver's seat.

"I wish that was the case, but it's not that simple. Your dad was seriously hurt, so they'll keep him at the hospital a little longer until his body is ready."

"How much longer?"

"The doctors who have been taking care of him will make that decision. Hopefully, we'll get a better sense of that timeline today."

"Do you know how long Grandma Webber will be here?" Donté asked next.

"She hasn't mentioned how long she planned on staying yet, but she can certainly stick around as long as she wants if she gets tired of her hotel. I'm guessing she'll want to stay a few days to spend time with your dad now that he's awake."

"I like Grandma Webber. Maybe she and Grandpa Webber can move here. I can't wait to meet him, too."

"I think that they're happy in Connecticut, Donté. They've lived in their home with each other for a long time now, but Grandma Webber does seem to really like you, too. At the very least, they can visit us here, or maybe we can make a trip to see them, but there's no need to focus on that now. Your dad is what's most important."

"You know what, Papa?"

"What?"

"I love you a whole lot," Donté expressed from his backseat, as he playfully clicked the soles of his shoes together.

"And I love you more," said Max, touched by his son's unexpected remark.

Driving toward the hospital, he felt a

profound sense of fortune, knowing that he and Brian had Donté in their lives now. Donté's words and the outcome of his husband's brief coma made him emotional, but he kept his tears in check as he had done the previous two days whenever his son was around. The relief he felt knowing that Brian's passing was no longer a likely option nourished his soul. He had a brief flashback of the moment he had first seen Brian at the restaurant across from him, wearing a pair of light blue shorts and a white slim fit polo shirt. Brian's charming smile and commanding personality were obvious then, but less than one hour ago, Max wasn't too sure that he would ever see his husband grin or laugh ever again.

After pulling up in the hospital's east parking garage, Max called the student absence phone line at Donté's school and left a thorough message explaining why his son wouldn't be in this morning. He was sure that many of the staff were likely aware of Brian's attack by this point, as the story had made news headlines. Not wanting to leave any room for the perception that he was being neglectful – fully aware that even an ongoing news story may not afford him the benefit of the doubt – Max provided details of his husband's Saturday afternoon attack that resulted in his being unconscious until this morning. Before hanging up, he promised that Donté would return to school the next day and requested a call back to update him on this afternoon's homework assignments. Donté frowned in the backseat upon hearing his father's closing words.

"Well, you're all settled as far as school goes," Max said after completing his call. "Now, let's go and see your dad."

Upon entering the hospital room, where Melanie sat at her son's side in the same seat as the day before, Brian slowly turned his head toward his immediate family and started sobbing uncontrollably. In excitement, Donté almost ran toward his dad until Max positioned his hand on the boy's left shoulder to remind him of Brian's physical vulnerability. After heeding the hint, he moved carefully toward his dad until Max picked him up so that he could give Brian a hug. When Donté finished embracing him, he walked over to Grandma Melanie who appeared to be moved at seeing them as a family. Max leaned over and held Brian's face between both of his hands and kissed him, oblivious to the tears falling down his husband's caramel-toned face. Max placed his forehead upon Brian's after they stopped kissing and told him how much he missed him, and that he had never been so scared in his life.

"There's nothing to fear, babe. I'm not going anywhere anytime soon," Brian said, giving him another kiss.

"You better not. We have far too much to live for," said Max before looking at Donté, who was sitting in his grandma's lap, closely observing his parents.

"Hey, Dad," Donté interjected.

"What is it, buddy?" Brian responded.

"Did you see the truck I gave you?" Donté asked, pointing toward the toy vehicle that sat on a nearby rolling hospital tray that resembled a short ironing board with an asymmetrical leg.

"You bet I saw it! It was the first thing I noticed in the room after seeing my mother beside me. And more importantly than that, I knew who left it here." Max noted that Brian's speech was slower than his normal rate and that some of his words slurred.

"I want you to have it," Donté replied.

"That's sweet of you, son, but that's a special gift from your grandmother. How about we keep it here until it's time for me to leave and then we return it to your room?"

"I guess that's fair."

"Then we have a deal, son."

"How are you feeling, Brian?" asked Max.

"Physically, it feels like a car struck me, but my spirit is still intact. I'm alive, and I have all of you." Brian paused to catch his breath. "And to top everything off, my mom flew all the way from Connecticut to be here. To answer your question Max, I'm blessed and grateful to be here." Melanie's eyes watered while she held Donté in her arms, who was now saddling her right leg.

"You're so amazing, babe. At least whoever did this to you will never have the satisfaction of crushing the loving and charismatic soul you have always been."

"Amen to that," Melanie agreed. "Don't ever give them that satisfaction, Brian. You're far too strong."

Max thought about the irony of Melanie's words. From his point of view, she and her husband's rigid belief system had crushed Brian's spirit in many ways. His hiding from them and retreating into a community of marginalized peers was rooted in the shame he battled, fearful that his own parents would likely never fully accept him. Melanie and Harold's actions may not have caused any physical bruises or broken bones, but the emotional consequences on Brian's life have certainly been omnipresent. Max wondered if she was aware of how incongruent her words were in relation to their actions. At the same time, though, he had to give her credit for the effort she was making at the present time.

Dr. Wu entered the room as Max sat next to Brian, kissing his partner's hand and shedding his own tears. He cheerfully greeted Max and Donté before giving his morning update. Being a straight shooter, he informed them all that Brian was fortunate to wake from his unconscious state in such a short window of time. Now, he reinforced, their primary goals were to monitor for any cognitive defects that could develop. From a physical standpoint, Dr. Wu assured them that Brian's physical injuries would mostly be healed within the next three months. Furthermore, if no severe cognitive concerns presented themselves, he expected that Brian would be able to return home sometime within the week. Another benefit to Brian's awaking, Dr. Wu instructed them, was that he would be moved to a less acute floor where he could have more visitors. Since Brian was scheduled for an MRI later in the day, he promised everyone that this move would likely take place the following day.

Grateful for the news that Dr. Wu had shared, Max hoped that his husband's short-term memory loss was temporary. "Will physical therapy be necessary at some point?" Max inquired.

"Honestly, that's a decision that he can discuss with his primary care physician in a couple of weeks. In many cases, physical therapy is helpful for those who have fractured clavicles, but it also depends on his healing process and insurance, of course."

"Was there any other interior damage other than his ribs?" Melanie inquired.

"That's a good question," said Dr. Wu. "We've screened for damage to his organs several times and have found nothing other than his broken ribs. Overall, I can't say how lucky you are, Brian," he stated looking his patient directly in the eyes. "It seems that fate was in your corner on Saturday."

"Thanks, Dr. Wu," Brian expressed. "That really means a lot. And being here with my husband, son, and mother, I really feel like the luckiest man on earth."

"You're welcome, young man. Rest up and enjoy this time with your family."

When Dr. Wu left the room, Brian requested that Max let him know everything about the accident. "Are you sure?" Max asked, not wanting to stir up any flashbacks that would traumatize him or retraumatize Donté, for that matter. Sensing Max's hesitation with Donté in the room, Melanie offered to take the boy to the cafeteria to heat the food Max had cooked. Donté wasted no time in getting off his grandmother's lap to finally eat. Once she and Donté walked out of the room, Max recounted everything he knew since being called by the hospital staff on Saturday afternoon. As of last night, the police had finally released images of the three masked suspects to the public. He informed Brian that they were African American males, likely in their early- to mid-twenties.

Brian listened intently to his husband and expressed that he couldn't remember anything that had happened after Max left their condo to meet Darnell. "When I try remembering the details of our walk in the park that afternoon," Brian stated, "it's like my mind is blotted out with a foggy shadow of grey."

"Don't strain yourself trying to recall everything right now. Your memory will return when your body is ready," Max counseled. Despite his request, Max could see Brian attempting to connect the dots of that day in his mind.

After a minute of heavy silence, Brian asked, "So how have things been with Donté?" Max grabbed Brian's left hand and kissed it.

"We couldn't be more fortunate to have Donté as part of our family. He's been remarkably mature these past two days. Your mother and even the hospital staff have taken quite a liking to him. We were all worried about him Saturday night, though, after the attack. He went into a state of shock and refused to talk to anyone until I arrived. He's been a trooper since then, though. The craziest thing is that he hasn't had any nightmares since this all took place. It's a relief, but also quite a surprise."

"I wonder if Donté's own mind prevents him from undergoing a certain amount of duress," Brian replied. "Maybe with the stress of this situation, a nightmare was more than his mind or body, for that matter, was willing to tolerate. Just imagine everything he's been through this past month!"

"You may have a point there, Brian. He has certainly missed you, too. It's amazing how quickly he's bonded with us since moving in."

"I'm proud of you, Max, for taking care of him and yourself. You need to give yourself credit for holding everything down the past two days. I'm just sorry that I wasn't around and that all of this has happened."

"You have *nothing* to apologize for, Brian. What kept me going is the faith that I had in you getting back on your feet and all of us being together."

After Max said these words, Melanie and Donté walked in, carrying the remaining food for him and Brian. Melanie placed a plastic plate in Brian's lap and handed Max his own, while Donté handed each of them small cartons of milk. As Max looked at his family before saying grace, it dawned on him that they were now living out that sustaining hope – they were together after all.

****

The next day, in Brian's more spacious room, Detective Roberts made his first visit to the hospital since Saturday night. Max had given him a call on Monday afternoon because Brian was no longer unconscious, following the policeman's request. Detective Roberts informed everyone present, which included Brian, Max, Melanie, and Peter, that they were working on identifying the three suspects with the public's assistance. He anticipated, though, that the case would be fully transferred to the FBI soon. Several dozen leads had been received so far, he explained, but it would take time to sort through them. Fortunately, the second witness provided a formal statement to the police and agreed to testify if the need ever presented itself.

For Brian's part, when questioned by Detective Roberts about his recollection of the events, his memory was still stumped. Through heavy sighs and complaints, Brian openly expressed frustration at his inability to conjure up any details. Detective Roberts, a seasoned officer in his early forties, cautioned Brian against rebuking himself for the amnesia he was experiencing. Memory lapses, according to the officer, were common in traumatic incidents. Regardless of Brian's memory, he informed them that the bulk of the investigation now rested in the hands of law enforcement and everyday citizens.

"I have an announcement," Peter declared to everyone. "The Center's board had an emergency meeting last night to discuss how we could support Brian and Max during this time. Apart from ensuring that Brian has paid time off while he recovers, we're also collectively putting up a ten-thousand-dollar reward for information leading to the arrest of the perpetrators. A press conference has already been scheduled this afternoon at 4:00 at The Center to make the announcement."

"That's so generous of you guys," said

Brian. “Thank you.”

“It’s the least that we could do to show our support to you during this time. You’ve been such a staple to this community,” said Peter.

“That’s really awesome,” Max stated. “You all have our deepest appreciation.”

“The good news is that a significant monetary reward usually helps with increasing tips, so hopefully that’ll be the case after the press conference today,” said Detective Roberts.

“It’s a shame that money has to be a motivator for something like this,” Melanie expressed, shaking her head with its large buoyant curls that Max could picture her forming with the same large pink rollers his mother used on her own hair and wig collection.

“You’re right, Mrs. Webber,” said Detective Roberts, “but in a case where your son’s sexuality may have been the motivating factor, trust me when I say that this monetary reward will work in your favor. It’s unfair, but the public tends to be less sympathetic to crimes targeting gays, lesbians, and especially those who are transgender.”

“You can say that again,” said Peter. “It’s this same system that I had to try and navigate in the deaths of financially disadvantaged transwomen like Sheryl and Mistie. Their cases still haven’t been solved to this day.”

“Make that reward fifteen-thousand

dollars, Peter," Melanie proudly asserted.

"What do you mean, Ma?" asked Brian, visibly caught off guard by his mother's proclamation.

"I *mean* that your father and I are adding five-thousand dollars to the reward these board folks are putting up."

"Is *Dad* going to be okay with that?"

"Leave that up to me. Don't worry about him," Melanie said. "But Peter, just make sure you announce a fifteen-thousand-dollar reward instead of ten."

"Why, yes, ma'am," Peter said quickly. "That's awfully kind of you, Mrs. Webber."

"This ain't about being nice," said Melanie. "We're talking about my son, and all this talk about discrimination would make any sensible person sick to their stomach."

"That means a lot, Ma. Thank you," Brian stated.

"No need to thank me, son. I'm just sorry that it's taken me so long to see things from your perspective. And being here with you is giving me the chance to do that."

Max, who was sitting in a chair next to Melanie, leaned over and gave her a heartfelt hug. Her firm grasp of his back informed Max of her sincerity, and he briefly thought about his own mother. He pictured Betty Strong's stubby hands pressing into his back as he remembered the subtle sweetness of her favorite perfume. Prior to this moment, Max never imagined that a real relationship with his mother-in-law or grandmother for Donté were possibilities, but now he had a genuine reason to hope.

Seeing an opportune time for his departure, Detective Roberts told everyone that either he or the FBI would be in touch if there were any arrests or significant updates to their case. He also encouraged Brian to call if his memory of that afternoon surfaced. Brian assured the officer that he would notify him as soon as possible if that occurred, vocalizing his desire to see those who attacked him brought to justice. Peter, always diligent and careful in the handoff of important matters, escorted Detective Roberts to the elevators near Brian's new unit, leaving the family to debrief these latest updates.

With Brian's level of alertness being more pronounced than the day before, it was clear to Max that his husband was starting to exhibit signs of anger. These cues had manifested not only in Brian's expressed desire to see his attackers jailed but also through his self-blaming and his lack of patience with his left arm now that his right one was in a sling. Reminders from Max or anyone else that the attack or its consequences were not his fault failed to assuage him. Also, conversations about the assault left Brian in a somber and quiet disposition, much like in the aftermath of Detective

Roberts's departure.

Max knew that if Donté were around, his husband would be more mindful of his attitude, but their child's school attendance was not up for negotiation. He realized that his best course of action was to stay positive and try to help Brian focus on their present situation.

When Peter returned to Brian's room, a woman who appeared to be in her late thirties accompanied him. Peter was surprised, however, to learn that no one in the room recognized her. He had met her on his way back to Brian's room from the elevators when he overheard her telling staff at the nurse's station that she was looking for Brian Webber. Since he was already headed there and assumed that she was a friend of the family, Peter invited her with him. Inside the hospital room, Kim's friendly demeanor toward Peter and the hospital staff quickly changed into a sour grimace, revealing her disgust at seeing Brian and Max together. She smacked her scarlet lips and rolled her light brown eyes before speaking.

"Look what we have here," Kim said as she pointed her finger at Brian. "You must be the punk who's adopting DJ who just got beat up the other day."

"Excuse me?" said Max, as he moved quickly to stand in between Brian and her, knowing that his husband was nearly defenseless.

"I know who *you* are too, Max. The news

has been showing pictures of you two with my nephew, DJ. I just can't believe that they' re letting him be adopted by two fags!"

"Whoever you are, lady, it's time for you to leave. We don't need you in here causing any more stress in our lives. Goodbye!" Max said emphatically.

"I don't have to go anywhere," Kim replied, waving her hands in Max's face and clapping them in the rhythm of her speech.

"Let me go and get security, guys. I'll be back," Peter insisted, looking horrified at the exchange unfolding before him.

"Go and get them," Kim nearly shouted. "I ain't doing *nothing* to these punks but expressing my mind."

"Excuse me, young lady," Melanie said, rising from her seat. "You have no right to come in here and talk to my son and his partner like this. You have been asked to leave, so I think it's best that you go ahead and do that before security arrives."

"Ain't nobody talking to you, old woman! I just wanted to come here and see who was adopting DJ for myself. It's a shame that they wouldn't give me the benefit of the doubt when I expressed an interest in adopting him, but they let two gay men adopt my own flesh and blood." Max could smell alcohol on her breath while she spoke. He assessed that while she wasn't necessarily a physical threat to any of them, she was clearly distressed and, therefore, unpredictable.

"We're sorry that you found out who was adopting your nephew so publicly," Max sympathized. "However, all you need to know is that Donté is in a loving and stable home. Now, do you please mind giving our family some privacy?"

"You think it's *that* simple? DJ is my kin, not yours. He should be with his family, not two gay men."

"I'm sure you know," Brian stated from his bed, "that my husband and I had nothing to do with you being passed over for his custody. That's something that's totally out of our control. What we have done, though, is decided to be the best fathers we can by caring for him unconditionally and doing everything we can for him to be successful. That's all that we want for Donté."

"The problem is that you two think you're better than his real family. Don't nobody care about your money or your fancy jobs. DJ is my nephew, birthed by my sister, Tasha. Blood is thicker than water, *honey*. Don't y'all ever forget that!"

"Blood may be thicker than water, chil', but water came first," said Melanie. "Water is the very source of life. So, if you're going to make that comparison, you've got to understand that water is a basic component of blood. Life boils down to loving and healthy relationships, not just blood. Any two people can make a child, but being decent parents requires more than what you apparently realize or have to offer. Now, I do believe that you've been asked to leave, *chil'*."

After Peter returned to Brian's room with the security guard, a strange silence overwhelmed them all. Speechless, Kim stood staring angrily at Melanie, who likely reminded her, in Max's judgment, of her own mother. At the sight of the security officer, Kim lowered her head in shame and left without any resistance. The young white male dressed in his official uniform watched as she departed in silence. Max believed that Melanie's words must have tugged at the essence of Kim's soul, as even his own mind continued to mull over his mother-in-law's words. Peter stepped back into the room after the security officer escorted Kim out of the unit.

"I don't believe that just happened," said Brian with dismay.

"So that was Donté's aunt?" Peter asked for clarification.

"That's what it looks like," Max replied. "She called him DJ, and his last name is Jones. She must've been really upset when she learned that neither she nor any of her family were deemed suitable to receive custody."

"You can say that again," said Peter, taking a seat on the couch near the doorway. "It's obvious to me that she doesn't need to be raising anyone's children."

"I'm just glad that Donté was at school. That could've been much uglier if he was here," Brian expressed in obvious relief.

"You're right. That could've been a lot worse," said Max. "I must give it to you, though, Mrs. Webber. You definitely set her straight."

"Talking a person down from a rooftop isn't all that difficult when you've been ready to jump yourself," said Mrs. Webber. "More than anything, she's just disappointed with herself for not being in a position to do what you two are now doing."

Max was starting to appreciate his mother-in-law being around. While he could never forget her and her husband's initial rejection of their marriage, she was now showing them a new possibility at the hospital, one that he hoped was permanent. At Brian's suggestion, Max called Theresa to give her a heads up regarding their unexpected visitor. Theresa didn't seem too surprised to learn that Kim had taken it upon herself to confront them in such a hostile manner, citing that family members who were passed over for temporary foster custody occasionally went to such lengths to express their frustrations. She informed Max that she would notify her counterpart in Akron, for the sake of due diligence. Max and Brian's only other recourse, she suggested, was requesting a restraining order against Kim. But given the investigation surrounding his husband's assault, Max doubted they would pursue that option, knowing that their hands were already full.

After wrapping up the discussion about Kim, Theresa expressed her condolences to Max about Brian and informed him that she had learned of the news on Sunday. It was ultimately their privacy, she stated, that prevented her from coming to the hospital to pay her respects. Max thanked her for her words and assured her that there had been no shortage of visitors that afternoon. Theresa also insisted that they postpone their upcoming monthly visit for another week or two to give them time to adjust to Brian's return home. Max expressed his gratitude for her sympathy and thoughtfulness while also ensuring her that Donté had been incredibly resilient throughout this entire ordeal. She reinforced that he and Brian ultimately had themselves to thank since children, by in large, mirror the actions of their role models during crises.

****

Two weeks after Brian had returned home from the hospital, a few guests joined them for dinner at their condo. Max finished the last touches of his meal while Salt and Pepper talked with Brian in the living room on their sectional. Lamont sat at the dining room table coloring unicorns and dragons with Donté. Pickles lay in between the two of them on the kitchen floor, resting and licking her front paws. As Max smelled the aroma of his baked chicken and cornbread and listened to the chatter of his family behind him, he relished this moment. He wished that Todd, Tim, Sandra, Peter, and even Mrs. Webber, could've made it, but he was aware of their own obligations. *In any case, each of them had shown up for us when we needed them most.* Max hoped that Todd and Tim were enjoying their first weekend of cohabitation. He looked forward to traveling to Detroit to visit their friends sometime in the future.

As for Mrs. Webber, he didn't know what the future held other than the opportunity to have a relationship with her. Before leaving the hospital a day before Brian's discharge, she apologized to her son for failing to accept him for who he was. She expressed that despite the distance that had grown between them over the years, she planned to become actively involved in their lives as a mother and grandmother. Her words unleashed an emotional storm in Brian that Max had never observed. Joyfully, he cried in Melanie's arms as the weight that had been carried on his shoulders most of his life started to lift. Max was honored to witness this transaction between them before leaving the hospital room to provide some privacy.

Lamont and Donté cleared the table when Max announced that dinner was ready. Donté took his fantasy coloring books, with his crayons stacked on top, back to his room, while Lamont cleaned the glass table. Salt and Pepper helped Brian up from his seat and slowly escorted him to the table. Once the food was placed in the center and everyone was seated, Brian took it upon himself to say grace over their dinner. Afterward, Max helped Brian, whose right arm was still in a sling, assemble food on his plate. Donté was aided by Lamont, who cut his chicken into small pieces next to his cornbread and mixed vegetables. Patient with the assistance that both Donté and Brian required, Salt and Pepper prepared their own plates, remarking how inviting the meal looked and how hungry they were. Once everyone was eating, Brian prepared everyone for an announcement by tapping his spoon on his wine glass, catching everyone except for Max off guard.

"On behalf of Max and I, thank you for coming out tonight. The three of you, along with Todd and Peter, who couldn't be here tonight, are more than friends. You're our family. I personally appreciate everything that you've done for us over the past few weeks. Your presence during that time was priceless. And we want you to know just how much we appreciate you."

"As for you two ladies," Brian continued, looking at Salt and Pepper, "Max and I would like for you both to accept the honor of being Donté's godmothers. Why have only one when our son could have two?" Brian joked. "Seriously, though, our friendship with you has meant so much, and it would mean a whole lot to us if you each accepted this role in Donté's life."

"I'm so touched," said Salt. "How could we say no to such an honor?" she continued, reaching out to hold Pepper's hand.

"Of course, you can count us in," said Pepper. "Donté is the best godson anyone could ask for," she said, smiling at the boy who looked at them all with curious intrigue, apparently not quite sure what was happening.

"And Lamont," continued Brian, "that just leaves the role of godfather. Would you please do us the honor of accepting that role?"

"You know I would've been fine with being a third godmother," said Lamont, arousing everyone's laughter. "But if that's what you're offering, then I graciously accept."

"Honestly, we can't thank you enough for being in our lives and for choosing to be part of our family," said Max, looking around the table.

Dinner and conversation continued for another hour before their guests prepared to depart into the crisp February evening. Lamont told Brian and Max that he would be happy to drive them to Detroit to visit Todd whenever they were ready. His offer, Brian insisted, was one that they would take up once he fully recovered. The soon-to-be godmothers offered to take Donté out to a musical or play in the next couple of weeks, promising Brian and Max a free evening to themselves. As

Max retrieved their coats from the closet across from Donté's room, their merry voices and laughter filled to the tall ceilings of the condo. Even though Brian's attackers hadn't been caught, Max was thankful for his husband being alive and filled with life, it now seemed, more than ever. Hugs and kisses were exchanged between everyone by the front door prior to their friends' departure.

"What a great dinner!" Max blurted out after their door closed. He walked toward their couch, followed by his husband and their son.

"Yes, it was," agreed Brian, taking his seat next to Max. "We're blessed to have friends like them. What did you think, Donté?"

"They're nice people," the boy replied, who stood in front of them with Pickles at his right foot. "I enjoyed coloring with Uncle Lamont. He's funny."

"That he is," replied Brian. "He's been that way since we've known him."

"Brian is right, Donté. Lamont has been a great friend, and he'll make an even better godfather. The same goes for Salt and Pepper. You have a lot of people who care about you, son." Donté nodded his head before bending down to pick up Pickles. Sensing that he and Brian would have to make room for their son and his companion, Max moved away from his partner to create space between them. Donté placed Pickles delicately on the couch and awkwardly followed behind her.

"I guess this means it's movie night," said Max, looking at his family for their response.

"Yay!" declared Donté. "Can I please choose the movie?"

"Of course!" said Brian, picking up the remote.

As Brian searched, Donté attentively watched him scroll through the extensive options of family movies and cartoons on their television screen. Max reclined back in his seat and felt at ease. He recalled standing in the doorway of Donté's room after the furniture was set up and thinking of the life he envisioned. *The only difference now*, he thought, *is that our family unit is complete*. Smiling to himself, he got up from his seat and told Brian and Donté that he would make some popcorn for the occasion. The aroma from the microwave and the image of his family seated on the couch, including Pickles, nearly moved Max to tears as he stood in the kitchen. *Life is good*, he thought.

Later that night as Max slept, long after he and Brian had read Donté's favorite book to him, Max dreamed of taking a trip to a fire station. He and Brian took their son, who appeared ten years of age, to the fire station in East Cleveland where Darnell worked. Dressed in full uniform, the former delivery man, now in his mid-twenties, provided the family with a tour of the newly renovated fire station and introduced them to his coworkers, including Reggie, Max's former student at Greater Cleveland Community College. Donté followed Darnell around in admiration of the future leader, shaking everyone's hand he met with great enthusiasm. The fire chief, a black male in his fifties, placed a plastic firefighter's hat on Donté before posing for a photo with him. Brian took the picture with pride, while Max stood alongside Darnell and encouraged Donté to smile.

Darnell then took them all to three firetrucks parked in the station, which is when Donté requested to take a seat in the middle vehicle. Before Donté could sit in the driver's seat, though, Darnell insisted that the boy listen to his speech. Theatrically, almost as if he was enacting a one-man stage play, Darnell spoke about the courageous and lifesaving work of firefighters. Seated on the ground with Pickles in his hand, Donté looked up to Darnell in awe as he addressed him and his fathers, appearing larger-than-life in physical stature. Max and Brian stood by one another, impressed with the young man's growth and articulation.

During his speech, Darnell discussed the crucial role that water played when it came to battling fires. As Darnell talked about the powerful force of water, familiar figures mysteriously appeared, forming an audience in the shape of a semi-circle behind the young man. Max couldn't make out everyone, but he was able to recognize his own mother, Peter, Lamont, Todd, Sandra, Mrs. Webber, Jane Budges, Salt and Pepper, and Theresa. The hologram figures, acting like prisms, emanated rays of light in all directions. Their glowing bodies reflected greater intensity the more Darnell spoke, leaving only the echoes of his voice to be heard amidst the blinding and pervasive light that filled the entire station.

Made in the USA
Columbia, SC
19 February 2020

88122478R00170